Praise for *The Reluctant Reckoner*

"J. Lee has created the perfect everyman — think Chris Pratt or a young Jimmy Stewart — sincere in every respect, yet rendered useless by forces he cannot even begin to understand. *The Reluctant Reckoner* simmers throughout as the three-dimensional chess match between the terrorists, the FBI and Mark reaches new levels of intensity. Fans of thrillers will relish the numerous schemes that come to light along the way, and Lee demonstrates his gift for action scenes. Another white-knuckled gem from J. Lee. Move *The Reluctant Reckoner* to the top of your list." – **BestThrillers.com**

"A cryptic e-mail leads accountant Mark Richter on a journey of discovery when his abilities are called into question and a mystery arises that seems to point to him as incompetent at best, or an embezzler at worst. Readers will become thoroughly engrossed in a plot that shimmers with tension, revelation, unexpected twists and turns, and a foray into questions, dubious answers, and tests of trust." - *Midwest Books Review*

**Praise for *The Deadly Deal*
"Medical Thriller of The Year" by BestThrillers.com
And Chanticleer Int'l Book Awards (CIBAs) Finalist**

"The Bottom Line: A perfectly crafted conspiracy thriller with a truly noble hero at its core, *The Deadly Deal* is the twisty tale we've been waiting for. Highly Recommended." — ***BestThrillers***

"*The Deadly Deal* is a fast-moving, page-turning thriller propelled by rapid scene changes, frequent plot twists, and an enemy that grows more powerful and menacing as the full extent of the conspiracy. Fans of plot-driven thrillers will find plenty to like…"
— ***Windy City Book Review***

"*The Deadly Deal* evolves superb characterization, satisfying twists of plot, and a focus that will keep even seasoned thriller readers guessing about its outcome." — ***Midwest Books Review***

"J. Lee does it again with *The Deadly Deal*. Fans of mysteries and thrillers will love this new cliffhanger. I was immediately hooked as the story began to unfold and this fast-paced and intriguing mystery kept me guessing until the very last page. Impossible to put down, I finished the book in days and loved every minute of this captivating read!" — ***Nicky Steinberg, Publisher of Downers Grove Living Magazine***

"J. Lee is a must-read new talent." — ***Mike Lawson, Edgar Award Nominated author of the Joe DeMarco series.***

"Action packed and sharply written. Grabbed me from the start and wouldn't let go. I've already made room on my nightstand for the next J. Lee thriller." — ***Davin Goodwin, author of PARADISE COVE and the Roscoe Conklin Mystery Series***.

"*The Deadly Deal* is my kind of thriller. Clever premise, complex characters, a pulsating plot and a satisfying, but in no way predictable, ending. Easily J. Lee's best work, and that alone is saying something." — ***Drew Yanno, author of In the Matter of Michael Vogel and The Smart One***.

"A terrific follow-up to *The Hubley Case* and *The Silent Cardinal*. J. Lee lays out an explosive tale of political intrigue, government conspiracy, and murder. If you haven't yet read Lee's thrillers, it's time to jump aboard the bandwagon." — ***Alfred C. Martino, author of Pinned, Over The End Line, and Perfected By Girls***

"Regardless of how you feel about the pharmaceutical industry, this book is a must read. J. Lee pulls you into a fast-paced thriller of good vs. evil that never ever lets up. Extremely tight writing, intricate plot, very believable characters, and a sharp, fast-moving dialogue that gels it all together. Put this one on your reading list!" — ***Jesus Leal, author of True Diversity***

"Set yourself some time to read *The Deadly Deal*, because once you start, you will NOT want to stop turning the pages. J. Lee's third book is not only as good as his first two suspense novels, it's the best one yet! The twists and turns are unexpected to the very end." — ***Pamela S. Wight, author of Twin Desires, The Right***

Wrong Man, Flashes of Life, Birds of Paradise, Molly Finds Her Purr

Praise for *The Silent Cardinal*

"A twisty, fast-paced novel-intrigue of the highest order. Highly recommended!" — **Ward Larsen, USA Today bestselling author of *Assassin's Strike***

"THE SILENT CARDINAL is a taut, complex thriller that grabs the reader on the opening page and refuses to let go until the last." — **James L. Thane, Author of *A Shot to the Hear, Fatal Blow, South of the Deuce, Crossroads, Tyndall,* and *Picture Me Gone***

"*The Silent Cardinal* packs a powerful punch with a looming terrorist threat, multiple kidnappings, unexpected killings and some high level political infighting. Lee keeps the reader guessing right along with the hero, struggling to determine who to trust, the payoff coming at the very end with a twist I never saw coming. You won't be disappointed." — **Drew Yanno, bestselling author of *In the Matter of Michael Vogel* and *The Smart One*.**

"Millions of lives hang in the balance in this fast-paced nail-biter. J. Lee delivers a thriller with constant twists and turns, taking readers on a thrill ride that is hard to put down." — **Steve Brigman, bestselling author of *The Orphan Train***

"*The Silent Cardinal* is a standout. A crew of people need Ben to solve this race-against-time case: the FBI, CIA, military, and terrorists all stake a claim on the skills of Siebert. But his family, friends, and ultimately, his country are at risk as Seibert fights a lethal enemy to unravel a deadly mystery." — **Pamela Wight, author of *The Right Wrong Man* and *Twin Desires***

"Fans will not be disappointed with his follow up thriller, *The Silent Cardinal*. Readers will surely cheer the return of former marine Ben Seibert, while enjoying the wild ride of espionage and murder in this taunt page-tuner. — **Alfred C. Martino, author of *Pinned, Over The End Line,* and *Perfected By Girls***

**Praise for *The Hubley Case*
Winner of the New York City Big Book Award
And "Best Book" Award for thrillers**

"A terrific debut. I look forward watching Lee continue to develop as a writer." — ***Kyle Mills, #1 New York Times Bestselling Author***

"*The Hubley Case* is intricately plotted and the action never lets up! A great read that fans of Kyle Mills and Michael Connelly won't want to miss. — **Ward Larsen, USA Today bestselling author of** *Assassin's Run*

"*The Hubley Case* will blow you away and J. Lee is a must-read new talent." — **Mike Lawson, author of the Award Winning DeMarco Series**

"J. Lee has spun a yarn of intrigue that captures readers and brings them on a wild ride involving the FBI, Interpol, a shadowy millionaire, and the PCC, a ruthless Brazilian drug cartel. A very smart, fast-paced thriller." — ***Alfred C. Martino, author of*** *Pinned, Over The End Line,* **and** *Perfected By Girls*

"Move on over Lee Child and Jack Reacher ... J. Lee takes the reader on a page-turning ride that keep you guessing to the end. Five huge thumbs up." — ***Pamela S. Wight, author of Twin Desires*** **and** *The Right Wrong Man*

"Has everything you want in a thriller. Killer opening, breakneck pace, smartly-drawn characters, startling reversals and, best of all, a truly satisfying ending. You'll be left hoping J. Lee is busy working on the follow-up. I know I am." — ***Drew Yanno, bestselling author of*** *In the Matter of Michael Vogel* **and** *The Smart One*

"Has the pace and the stakes of a Brad Thor or David Baldacci novel. Dynamic characters, vivid settings and intrigue that keeps you guessing until the end make this one a must read. J. Lee has burst onto the scene with brand of storytelling that is hard to put down. I look forward to more like *The Hubley Case."* — **Steve Brigman, bestselling author of** *The Orphan Train* **and** *The Old Wire Road*

THE RELUCTANT RECKONER

J. Lee

Moonshine Cove Publishing, LLC

Abbeville, South Carolina U.S.A.

First Moonshine Cove Edition October 2024

ISBN: 9781952439797

Library of Congress LCCN: 2023921964

© Copyright 2024 by J. Lee

This book is a work of fiction. Names, characters, businesses, places, events, conversations, opinions, and incidents are either products of the author's imagination or are used fictitiously. Any resemblance to actual events, locales, conversations, opinions, business establishments, or persons, living or dead, is entirely coincidental and unintended.

All rights reserved. No part of this book may be reproduced in whole or in part without written permission from the publisher except by reviewers who may quote brief excerpts in connection with a review in a newspaper, magazine or electronic publication; nor may any part of this book be reproduced, stored in a retrieval system or transmitted in any form or by any means electronic, mechanical, photocopying, recording or any other means, without written permission from the publisher.

Cover provided by the author; interior design by Moonshine Cove staff.

This is for my Mom, who has always supported me and encouraged me to write—from elementary school journals talking about my life to persuasive essays pleading for a sleepover to the novels I write today. Thanks so much, Mom. I love you.

Acknowledgments

Writing is a solitary act...right up to the point where it isn't. And there are a few people very special to me who have consistently gone out of their way to help my writing endeavor. You know who you are, and I appreciate you all so very much. Six years and four books later, I'm humbled and grateful to no end for all you've done.

The Reluctant Reckoner

1

It was 4:07 on a sunny Friday afternoon in Chicago when the e-mail appeared in his inbox. The cloudless May blue skies and 75-degree temperature begged for an early escape, but Mark Richter knew then it wouldn't happen.

> Mark:
> Don't be alarmed. The discrepancy will be cleared up soon.
> Tom

He ignored the flashing Outlook meeting reminder telling him it was time for his daily reorganization and stared harder at the memo. The OCD that compelled him to align all his desktop items at right angles to the furniture surface would have to wait.

The FROM field was empty and the subject line was blank. None of the 26 employees at Lafferty & Sons Accounting Firm was named Tom, and despite the somewhat common name, he couldn't think of anyone he knew personally with it either.

He leaned back in his chair and sipped lukewarm coffee from the same white porcelain cup he used every day, repeatedly clicking his blue-ink Bic pen, the only type he'd trusted since college. A quick reply e-mail was promptly returned as an undeliverable message by the system administrator. Right-clicking on the memo led to a dead end of un-highlighted menu options.

He briefly glanced at the only personal item on his nearly empty desk: a picture of Katherine in her mother's arms, three weeks after she was born, two years before Mary Ann died. His deceased wife's beautiful blue eyes stared right back. That picture was eight years old, yet those eyes always made him smile and tear up simultaneously, his constant reminder of how bittersweet life is.

Focus, Mark. Get back to the e-mail.

Maybe it was a prank. While this example would be a bit extreme, it'd be just like Bruce, his coworker two offices down, to toy with him right before the weekend. Bruce was always testing the limits of his "excessive planning and scheduling," trying to inject variety and surprise, often at Mark's expense, whenever possible. Mark hated it, which only encouraged Bruce. The problem with the Bruce-Prank-Theory, though, was that Bruce took off early to beat the traffic. It seemed a stretch to think that he'd set up a delayed message.

Just then his phone began to ring.

"Mark, Larry needs to see you."

"Okay, give me a minute to—"

"Right now, Mark. He told me you need to drop what you're doing and meet him in his office. Immediately."

His boss's secretary didn't even try to hide her uneasiness.

"I'll be right there, Jean."

Very odd, he thought. Jean seldom sounded tense. And Larry was never in a hurry.

2

The short walk to Larry McDougal's office felt interminable.

Larry, the firm's Principal Accountant, was the kind of boss you hoped your children work for someday: he was respectful, didn't micromanage, and always had an open door policy. But unplanned meetings like this were exceptionally rare. In the nine years Mark had worked for Larry since the boss was hired to run the day-to-day operations, he could count on one hand the number of times Larry had called a meeting not previously scheduled in Outlook.

Jean's uneasiness had not dwindled. A delightful 61-year-old woman who still dyed her hair blonde and brought cookies every Friday, she carried the not-so-unofficial title of "Etiquette Czar." She looked 40 and always wore a conservative skirt and blouse. A woman of proper, traditional etiquette, business casual attire would never suffice. Her face was wrinkle-free, her body toned, her smile still fully capable of turning a frat boy's head.

But she was biting her lower lip with wide eyes when he nodded hello.

"Do you remember the Trepidid file?" Larry shouted as soon as he entered. The boss rubbed the top of his bald, sweat-coated head, and then smoothed his thick brown mustache.

"Yeah, I submitted it a few weeks ago."

Trepidid was a small but growing business out of Northbrook, IL that manufactured medical devices sold directly to hospitals and private practices. It built the units in Mexico and stationed a handful of regional offices and distribution centers around the country but hadn't gone international yet, which made its tax returns relatively straightforward.

With roughly $60M in revenue the year before, and Uncle Sam taking a healthier bite out of it than they'd anticipated, management had come to Lafferty & Sons to help save some cash. It wasn't a complicated case. He recalled breezing through it with significant success.

"Well, there's a problem with it," Larry announced in a voice just a little too loud.

"What's wrong?"

"Their CFO called and said there's a $320,000 difference between what you told them they'd get back from the feds and what was deposited into their account this morning."

"What? That can't be right. I'll call Chuck."

"No need. They already wrote the IRS directly."

"And?"

"The IRS told them it processed the returns precisely as you filed them."

"If that's true, why don't the returns match?"

"Hell if I know, Mark," Larry said, slamming his right hand on the desk. "You're their accountant. You tell me."

"What I do know is this is the wrong time for a screw up. I told them when they signed I'd put my best man on their file, that we'd take care of them. This is a first-time client with greater potential, Mark. They're trying us out to see if we can save them some cash. We can't have this kind of discrepancy."

The word "discrepancy" brought Mark's thoughts to an abrupt halt. He recalled the e-mail he'd read only five minutes earlier.

The notion that he was even connected to such a discrepancy, much less Larry's not-so-subtle implication that he was responsible for it, left his stomach feeling queasy. He furrowed his brow while stroking his clean-shaven face, looking straight at the boss with an awkwardness he never wanted to experience again.

Does he think I took the money? That I stole it?

Suddenly he felt restless and itchy all over. He wanted to bolt out of the office. To shout at the top of his lungs *what the hell is going on!*

"I don't know what the issue is Larry, but I'll find out. I reviewed the numbers three times and they always came out the same. I'll check the file right away get to the bottom of it."

"You'd better. We've got a client that can bring us big bucks in years to come, and they want to know what the hell happened to the 320 grand you told them they'd get."

***

He rushed from Larry's office to his file cabinet, ignoring Jean and the others he passed, fumbling for the key. This was a fluke, and he was determined to prove it. He processed all corporate tax returns with the same methodical system. Filled with numerous verifications to make sure every number and comma was in place, his system was foolproof, battle tested for all 23 years he'd been doing the job.

It had never failed. It *couldn't* fail.

Every CPA at the firm had private keys to his or her own filing cabinets, which housed client records. He grabbed the Trepidid file and plopped it down on the first table he could find, sifting through each page from the beginning, adding the numbers in his head and with a calculator, perusing every line with eagle-like precision.

Thirty minutes later, he still couldn't find anything out of place and was more than halfway through the file. He thought he heard his name called, but didn't bother to look up.

"Mark!" Larry's shout now came from only a few feet away, just inside the doorway. His 6′2″ frame had always towered over Mark's, but at that moment he seemed even taller. "Man, you sure do get in the zone," the boss observed.

"I haven't found—"

"Relax, Mark," Larry cut him off.

"What?"

"Chuck just called me back. Three hundred twenty grand was just deposited into their account. Must've been some sort of delay in the IRS system. There's no mistake, they got exactly what you said they would get. I had no doubt you did your job right."

Funny, that's not how it felt earlier.

He collapsed backwards into the chair, letting out a huge sigh of relief while gripping the back of his neck with deep-tissue-massage-like force. But the brief euphoria was quickly replaced with more confusion.

"How can that happen, Larry? It doesn't make any sense."

"It's got to be a direct deposit glitch. They keep going digital with everything, and soon enough the computer's going to screw us all. You mark my words. Pen and paper might take longer, but we never had crap like this happen in my day."

My day. Larry said it as though he was from the Stone Age, when the man was only ten years older than he.

"But it's never happened before." He pushed his sleeves up well past his elbows in an effort to cool down.

"First time for everything, I guess. The point is, stop worrying about it. Everything's fine now. Sorry I jumped on you back there. I was just overanxious. Good work as always, Mark," Larry said while walking away. "Get out of here, I'll see you Monday."

Flooded with relief more than anything, he closed his eyes and inhaled deeply. It was a fluke error, nothing more. He didn't know how it happened, but that's all it was. And it wouldn't happen again. A few more deep breaths and a couple long stretches later, he got up to return the file and head home for the weekend.

But then he abruptly reenergized, and his calmness shattered.

"Wait a second..." he shouted, dropping the file and darting to his computer to. He fell into the seat, unlocked the screen and went into Outlook. Then he stared, mesmerized.

He read every e-mail, some before 4:07, some after. He checked the Deleted Items and Junk folders, reviewed each archive, restarted the program and then checked again, seeing the same thing each and every time.

The e-mail was gone.

3

It always started with the background.

And after perusing Mark Richter's criminal history, or lack thereof, birth and family records, hospitalization and medical charts, tax documents, bank statements, work personnel file, and personal police record and FBI files for the third time, Edward Doran still couldn't find anything wrong.

Richter was a Caucasian, brown-haired, blue-eyed, middle-class male with no distinguishing characteristics, physical or otherwise; they needed someone who could blend. He'd worked at the same accounting firm for 23 years and despite their best efforts over the last two to get him to do so, he had not once stolen or lied; they needed someone people would never suspect. He had an eight-year-old daughter without a mom and a sister and young nephew in Wisconsin he talked to weekly; they needed someone who had a lot to lose.

Mark Richter was perfect.

Best of all, he was *predictable.* Surveillance had revealed that his refrigerator was organized by food group, and his linen closet by length and color of bath towel. The man couldn't sleep until all dirty clothes were in the hamper and all ties hung at an equal length from the floor. He made lists the way newlyweds made love: frequently, and with great satisfaction. And he didn't have the ability to leave any item on those lists unchecked.

They'd know his every move before he made it.

On Friday nights, he played racquetball with his best friend, one of the very few people he saw on a regular basis. Brad Tarnow's ex-con status was surprising and at first a touch concerning, a wrinkle in Richter's otherwise pristine character. But follow-up investigation had proven it to be a potential asset that could help unclothe parts of

Richter's past that he'd certainly prefer to remain buried, should that become necessary. Edward doubted that it would, but a hip-pocket insurance card was a valuable asset.

Richter's daughter, Katherine, was at a sleepover. The apple not far from the tree, every week without failure she stayed at the same friend's house, watched *Princess Diaries II*, and ate a Peanut Buster Parfait for dessert, a true creature of habit.

Like father, like daughter.

Edward checked his watch: 9:50. Richter was sitting at the club bar, having the second of what would be exactly three Coors Light beers, always draft. At 10:20, he'd head home. The timing was perfect.

The hidden camera he had planted between the bar's flat screen and the Guinness sign showed Richter droopy and even less talkative than normal, no doubt trying to figure out what happened with the Trepidid file.

He'd find out soon enough.

Edward texted his associate and told him to make the call, then turned up the volume and focused on the screen in front of him, watching and listening to Richter's every move.

* * *

"Mark, you've got a phone call."

The unexpected announcement stirred him from his daydream. It had been that kind of day. The more he tried to understand what'd happened earlier, the more confused he became. On his way out, he stopped by IT. They performed a full application scan and virus check on his computer, searched all backup server files and archived disks, thoroughly tested the hard drive and Outlook connections, and still found no evidence of an e-mail received at 4:07.

So, still in a funk from that mystery and not thinking about the oddness of getting a phone call at the club, he picked up the receiver inattentively, slouching into the leather barstool.

"Hello?"

"How are you, Mark?"

The voice sounded casual and nonchalant, spoken as though the person had known him for years. He didn't recognize it.

"Um...I'm fine. Who's this?"

"I'm your new best friend. You can call me Tom."

Instantly, he sat upright. He felt his heart flutter and his shoulders tense up, then lowered his voice and turned away from the other four patrons at the bar.

"Tom...from the e-mail?"

"That's right."

"Who...who are you? Why'd you e-mail me? What do you want?"

"Easy, Mark. Easy. Slow a bit. I can only answer one question at a time. But let me start with the two irrelevant ones. My name is Tom, and I e-mailed you so you wouldn't worry about the situation with Trepidid. But I'm guessing you still had a panic attack, didn't you?"

"What do—"

"Relax, Mark," Tom cut him off. "I'm getting to your third question. But first, I trust all is well with that little problem? Or should I say, 'discrepancy?'"

He didn't respond. His mind was racing and he felt unable to speak.

"Mark! Pay attention. This is where *you* answer *my* question. The Trepidid situation...it's all okay now? Fully resolved, just like I said it would be?"

"Yeah, it's fine. But how—"

"Okay, it's time for your third question, the one that means something. What I want, Mark, is very simple: to meet you."

"Why? Who are you?"

"I thought we covered that. My name's Tom."

Tom was toying with him, and he didn't like it. He considered himself a patient man, but after what happened earlier that afternoon, he was in no mood for games.

"Mark, I'm not a huge fan of the phone. Plus, I can feel you getting upset, so I'll be brief. I'm not telling you any more about who I am or why I contacted you now. But I promise you that when we meet, you'll get your answers. That's a fair deal, right?"

"No, it's not. I don't want to meet you. Leave me alone," he replied in a harsh whisper, even though the other three people at the large U-shaped bar were engrossed in their own, much louder conversation.

"We don't always get what we want. And I really think you should meet me."

"Leave me alone, *Tom*."

He almost got the courage to emphatically slam down the receiver, but he didn't. Partly because he was curious about where this was all going, but mostly because he was afraid of what would happen if he did.

He should have.

"You're not going to hang up. You're too smart to do something that stupid."

"What do you—"

"Listen, Mark. If you don't want to be arrested on Monday for extorting money from another one of your clients, or for committing computer fraud, or for any other number of possible reasons you now know I can arrange, I strongly suggest that you and I meet. You won't be harmed, I promise. In fact, you'll find it well worth your while. But do understand: today was only a glimpse of the kind of misery we can put you through, so it'd be in your best interest to indulge me."

The "we" told him that Tom was not alone. The rest of what Tom said proved that his earlier paranoia was justified.

"I'm guessing your IT department didn't find a thing, did they? No copy of that e-mail anywhere, I'll bet. Next time, the discrepancy might not just go away."

Responding was pointless.

"So what do you say, Mark? Want to get together this evening?"

"Okay," he choked out.

"Excellent. Head on home and get ready. I'll pick you up in front of your house. Eleven-thirty sharp. Oh, do me a favor and keep this conversation between us."

"My *house*?" Mark blurted out.

But it was too late. He heard a click, and the connection was dead.

4

A late May breeze carried just enough chill to consider a coat. But as he stood outside his Arlington Heights home, Mark shivered more from fear than wind. After a few minutes, he walked to the curb.

Maybe, he teased himself, if he wasn't standing by the door, Tom wouldn't know which house was his. Or that maybe he really was dreaming and any minute he'd wake up.

Always the pragmatist, however, he then recounted yesterday's revelations: the same people who created a $320,000 mistake in his client's tax refund and made an e-mail disappear from his account also knew which gym he belonged to and where he lived.

And all he knew of them was their ability to handle the IRS.

A vibration in his pocket interrupted the horrifying thought, and he checked his cell phone. There was a new text message:

> I LOVE YOU, DADDY. GOOD NIGHT!
> KATHERINE XOXO

He sighed and thought of his beautiful angel, staring at the dark houses on the tree-laden street in the northwest suburb of Chicago that he'd lived on for a dozen years. It was the house he and Mary Ann had planned to raise their family in, and he couldn't find it in him to move after she passed and their world turned upside down... It was the kind of subdivision where neighbors still watched each other's kids without fear of perverts, where people still had picnics on the backyard patio and didn't lock the front door, where couples still walked the streets hand-in-hand on a sunny day. It was a tight-knit, safe, blue-star community, highlighting shared commitment between police and residents to prevent crime.

And now, *Tom* was driving into it.

That didn't sit well. And it didn't sit well that Mary Ann wasn't here anymore.

Precisely at 11:30, a white stretch limousine turned on his block and slowly drove down the street. When it arrived at his house, it came to a gentle halt before the driver, in full black-suit uniform, exited the car and opened the rear door.

He took a final breath of fresh, safe-neighborhood oxygen, and climbed inside.

* * *

With one exception, it was like any other limo. Plush leather seats formed a half-moon around a mini-bar, small fridge and television. There were tinted windows and no seat belts. It seemed normal enough, save the man sitting opposite Mark.

"Tom" wore olive green dress pants and a white collared button-down shirt. His face looked young, perhaps 35 or so. Large dimples appeared as he smiled at Mark. Thin, pointy eyebrows flexed above dark brown eyes.

"Mark, it's great to finally meet you."

"Tom, I'm guessing?"

"That's right. Nice ride, huh?"

"Been in one limo, been in them all."

"That doesn't mean they're not nice rides."

"Look," he said, "can't you just tell me why I'm here? Have I done something to you?"

Tom chuckled. "Mark, Mark, Mark you've done nothing but impress us."

"But what do you—"

"You're here because we need your help. Everything will be explained. But first—"

"Can't you just tell me now?" he snapped.

"Mark, don't interrupt again. And have a look in the paper bag on the seat next to you."

The limo hadn't budged, and he had a strong feeling from how this conversation was going, that it wouldn't until he obliged. He picked up the bag, the kind that had held so many of Katherine's innocuous school lunches, and peaked inside.

His eyes widened.

Five thick stacks of crisp $50 bills rested neatly on the bottom, each bound by a rubber band.

"Ten thousand dollars for your time this evening."

"I don't want it," he said after a slight hesitation.

"It's impolite to refuse a nice gesture."

"I said I don't want it!"

"It's not an optional gift."

"Just tell me what you want already."

"Relax, Mark. You can always give it to Susan G. Komen."

He froze. Tom smiled.

"How do you know so much about me?"

"So much? You have *no idea* how much we know about you."

If that comment was intended to frighten him, it worked. All he could do was look at the man who'd turned his life upside down in eight short hours and still wouldn't tell him why.

"My apologies, Mark. That came out wrong," Tom murmured. "It's just that we take this very seriously. We do a lot of homework, a lot of grueling research. And the things I've said about you aren't very hard to come by. Your company posts professional biographies on its webpage, your address is in the white pages online, your large gift to the Susan G. Komen Foundation after your wife died from breast cancer four years ago was listed in its brochure as a testimonial. We haven't exactly needed a private investigator on you 24/7 to obtain that information. An eight-year-old could've gotten it with a few clicks of the mouse."

He told himself it was a coincidence that Katherine was eight, and then thought back to Larry's earlier comment: "They go digital with everything and soon enough the computer's going to screw us all."

"What about the $320,000?"

"That required a bit of expertise, but not as much as you think. You'll see when we get there."

"Get where?"

"That's what I was trying to tell you, but you kept interrupting. I'm not your biggest fan...I'm his associate. The person who *really* wants to meet you is waiting for us."

Since 4:07, his emotions had progressed from confused to upset to afraid, and now they were circling back to confused. He shrugged his shoulders in a way that said: "Whenever you want, just get on with it..."

"I'm sorry, but I've got to do this," Tom said, holding a roll of duct tape and small black cloth. "As I said, we take this very seriously. And my associate is just as thorough as you."

He wiped the unrelenting sweat off his forehead. Just what had he gotten into here? Duct tape and blindfolds? Were these guys in the mafia? Or worse? Was he going to wake up in some third-world jail cell in his underwear and a T-shirt? This felt like a horror movie, but worse. Why him? And why this? People who impress thugs don't get duct taped and blindfolded. And accountants who impress sure as hell aren't supposed to get duct taped and blindfolded.

Once unable to speak and in total darkness, he heard Tom lower the glass window and tell the driver to get going. He couldn't control his panting.

"Remember, Mark, we don't view you as a threat. If we did, you'd already be dead."

5

He'd once read that when a person loses one sense, those remaining got stronger. That didn't seem to happen. Without his eyes or speech, he tried to use his other senses get any indication of where he was. Could he ascertain how they exited his subdivision? Were the tires making high-pitched or low-pitched vibrations on the road surface? Were there any bumps that might be railroad tracks? Did he smell smoke from the old factories along Highway 83? Did he hear airplanes landing or taking off from O'Hare airport?

It added up to a lot of effort with no return. It seemed to him they drove in circles for ten minutes before catching an interstate or high-speed highway with no lights. Maybe they backtracked, anticipating his attempt to figure the route out. For all he knew, they were right next door.

When the car finally stopped, he was led blindfolded into a building that felt warm. Before he went inside, a large diesel-engine truck zoomed past him. He then rode in an elevator but didn't hear voices. It must not have been a public building. Surely people would have said something if they saw a man being escorted blindfolded. Wouldn't they? But then he remembered, it was pretty late; perhaps no one was around to see him at all.

When the odorless black cloth was finally removed and the duct tape ripped off, despite being able to see he still felt in the dark.

The room was about 1,000 square feet. Bookshelves lined the walls. Hardwood floors lay beneath a vaulted ceiling and expensive-looking chandelier, and there were no windows in sight. A large mahogany desk was in front of him. The light was dim, the temperature cool.

The door opened and a man standing 6′6″ strolled into the room. He quickly shut it, eliminating the chance for Mark to look through, and walked towards him.

"Mark Richter. At last we meet."

It felt bizarre shaking hands with the man responsible for his captivity. His grip was gentle, yet firm. Neither of them said a word as Mark studied the man's face, planning to describe it to the cops the very next day.

He had very short, light brown hair, almost a buzz cut. He sported a well-cut charcoal gray suit, was clean-shaven, and thin as a beanpole. He looked young, even younger than Tom. No tattoos, scars, birthmarks or any other distinguishing features that he could see. Yet 30 seconds later, Mark knew he'd never forget the man's face.

And that he wouldn't be describing it to anyone.

* * *

"My name is Edward Doran. I didn't mean to cause a ruckus this afternoon. It was simply the only way I could get your undivided attention."

"I've already been apologized to. I just want to know why I'm here."

"I'm not apologizing. And you want more than that."

"You're right. I want to leave."

"You're going to. But don't you also want to know how we made $320,000 disappear from your client's account? Especially given the fact you've been informed it might happen again, aren't you the least bit curious to understand how that's possible?"

"Tempting, but I'd rather go home and never see you again."

He wasn't sure where his courage or, more likely, his stupidity, was coming from. But it just didn't seem like the time to back down.

"Let's face it, that's not going to happen."

Despite sensing that reality beforehand, hearing the words uttered aloud made his chest feel like it was squeezing carbon atoms to make a diamond and prevented any oral response.

"Hopefully, you feel $10,000 is fair compensation for your time this evening. But regardless, let me get to the point. If you'd like to see how we created that discrepancy, come over here and have a look at my computer screen."

He glanced at Tom, who sat behind him at a small table, nodding at the obvious: it wasn't a question.

There was an HP monitor with a Dell mouse. A large gray box with three search prompts filled the screen.

```
SOURCE:> —
DESTINATION:> —
AMOUNT:> —
```

He didn't recognize the application. No menus, folders or icons were in sight. It didn't look like an ERP or CRM system he'd seen used by clients for supply chain management or sales lead tracking, respectively. It clearly wasn't a bank app or any other kind of website application he'd ever seen.

"Obviously, online banking usage has taken over the country's spending, both professionally and personally, wouldn't you agree?" Edward asked, sipping a Coke.

"Sure."

"People do everything through their phones or computers. E-commerce purchases, paying bills, managing their money, checking account levels, investing. Don't even get me started on crypto. The fact is, people in this country, and most first-world countries, walk around with their entire financial lives in their pockets. Am I right?"

"Uh, yes..." he replied, exaggerating his pause.

"More than anything, digitization of our money and how we manage it has changed the way we bank. You can do everything you used to have to do through the mail with the click of a button.

People set up automatic payments and recurring deductions for all their bills and never *see* an actual dime from any transaction. Tellers are a dying breed and even ATMs are being slowly replaced by mobile applications. Why do you suppose it's gotten that way?"

He shrugged his shoulders. Where the hell was this going?

"It's because money, as we know it, has changed. Nobody carries cash anymore, let alone visits the bank or tucks $100 bills under the mattress. Many companies don't even use paychecks. Your firm, for example, files every client's return digitally with direct deposit reimbursement. It's all about digits on a screen, not paper in hand."

"Sure," he nodded, feeling pressure to engage from Edward's piercing stare. "Money has changed because of online banking. So what? Credit cards replaced cash before online banking arrived. Cash replaced bartering before credit cards. Currency evolves. What's your point?"

The day's events had already curtailed his patience, and he certainly didn't like being held captive, but he couldn't deny to himself that Edward had an odd effect on him. The accountant in him wanted to know more about where this conversation was headed. It felt almost inevitable that Edward's mundane observations were leading to an important and uncomfortable revelation, but he had no idea what that revelation would be.

Or why.

"As currency needs have changed, a door has been opened for people like me."

"People like you?"

"As an accountant, I assume you are familiar with the security precautions in place to prevent fraud with electronic currency?"

He merely looked back at Edward, whose question was rhetorical.

"There are passwords, of course, with varying and ever-growing requirements and security questions, but CAPTCHA also tests to ensure we're not robots, there's two-step verification, confirmation codes, ever-changing system requirements, virus protection programs, and computer hardware support tools. And that's more or less just the tip of the iceberg, right?"

"I guess."

"So, what's the problem with all those things?"

"They can be copied or stolen."

"That's incidental. The problem, or opportunity, depending on your vantage point, is that they're all based on the threat of identity theft."

"Not sure I follow, Edward."

"You will call me Mr. Doran."

Edward's single comment terrified him more than all of Tom's dialogue, duct tape and blindfold put together. He sat up straight and tried to hold his ground.

"Obviously," Edward continued, "identity theft is not a novel concept. Every time you turn on the news, there's a story of the little old lady who got ripped off by a computer hacker, or the guy who found that thousands of dollars had been charged to his credit card without his knowledge. And every time it happens, the banking folks come out with some new technology or process to prevent it. The computer folks develop new software to stop the hacking, and a self-proclaimed expert writes a book about how consumers should protect themselves.

"Then the hackers come out with a new virus or malware that gets around the latest precaution, and identity thieves look in different places to get your private information. And the wheels on the bus go round and round."

"I still don't see your point."

Edward chuckled quietly, as if he were one of those pull-back toys ready to be released with a forward whoosh.

"Each of those precautions is designed to validate your identity. They aim to ensure that someone can't transfer money until he proves it's *his* account he's transferring from. But once he proves that, he's free to make as many transactions as he likes. In fact, banks encourage it. Do they not? Take your personal Bank of America account for instance, Mark. Once you're inside, you can click a button to transfer money from multiple accounts to multiple places simultaneously. Snap, just like *that*. They even offer incentives to encourage you."

"There are transaction limits, though."

"Sure, anywhere from a few grand up to unlimited for most consumer banking accounts, but they also reset every day and in some cases you can tie different accounts together to increase the limit. But think about Current Accounts; by definition they don't have transaction or dollar limits and even brag about that to draw more high-dollar customers."

He nodded in silent response, still not sure where Edward was taking this.

"Well, what if you could skip the identity verification steps altogether?"

"How would you do that?"

"Take a look at the screen. Type in account numbers to the SOURCE and DESITNATION prompts and indicate an amount. Then press ENTER. It's as simple as that. It doesn't ask what bank or type of accounts. Just plug the numbers in and instantly transfer wealth."

He stared with conspicuous skepticism. The software Edward was describing would somehow have to find, in the maze of some 50,000 banks or credit unions, billions of users, and hundreds of billions of accounts, the two very specific accounts noted in the prompt. Then it would have to magically perform a transfer that somehow wouldn't trip any one of the numerous security measures that each account's companies had in place.

This wasn't possible. Banking systems were too protected, and the safeguards were far too strong. They weren't perfect, but they were well beyond this.

"I know what you're thinking, Mark. But believe me, it's very possible. And I'll bet you $320,000 I can prove it."

6

"Now you see why the discrepancy this afternoon was absolutely necessary. If it hadn't happened, not only would you not want to meet, but you also wouldn't believe me now."

Mark was certain there was another way to create the $320,000 mistake, but he sure couldn't think of it. And then there was the question of why Edward would lie. If he was lying, all he was doing was pretending to have something that could win him a small cell in a maximum-security prison for the rest of his natural life.

Sure, it was light years ahead of today's technology, and sure, there were some geeky types who might be tempted to concoct a story to appear super-intelligent. But Edward didn't strike him as one of those types.

Whether or not the software tool was real wasn't the frightening question, however. The frightening question was: assuming it was real, why was Edward telling him about it?

"I'm sure you still have your doubts," Edward continued, "but that doesn't matter. What does matter is that you understand the level of discretion your job requires."

"My job?"

"I told you I needed your help."

"How can I possibly help you?"

"I'm glad you asked. Do the names InfoHelp, Techbot, Larry's Consulting, LPK Incorporated, and The McDougal Firm mean anything to you?"

Lafferty & Sons wasn't a Big 4 or large accounting firm by any means. But it wasn't tiny either. In fact, with 26 employees and roughly 120 clients, by industry standards it was considered mid-tier. And it certainly wasn't big enough to prevent him from recognizing five of their clients.

"They've retained your firm's services for anywhere from four to twelve years, each has a different principal accountant, and their revenues range from about ten to eighty million. None are local to Chicago. They're scattered across the country and strictly domestic," Edward said.

"Sounds like you know them pretty well yourself."

"What I need from you is their corporate account numbers and information, with verification. I know Lafferty & Sons stores all its clients' files in-house, and I'm sure you can find a way to obtain those files if properly motivated."

"You want to steal from these companies?"

"I don't see it as stealing. More like re-distributing funds for a special purpose."

"What special purpose is that?" he dared to ask.

"That's none of your concern. You know why you're here, which is what you've been asking since we contacted you."

* * *

"If this software really does what you say it does," he said, "what you're doing now is like inventing the bulldozer and asking me to steal a shovel. Why can't you just get the numbers yourself?"

Edward smiled. Mark realized that he was playing right into the man's hand.

"The main reason is because we don't have to. That's why you're here. We strongly prefer to stay under the radar. As I said, most of the security measures out there are designed to prevent identity theft on the front-end. Meaning that if we procured this information, we'd have to go through security to get it. Since you work at the firm, it seems logical that we let you handle that part."

Keep it together. There is an answer to every problem.

"Why me? Lots of people work at Lafferty & Sons."

"You're the most qualified."

"What's that supposed to mean?"

"Think about it from our perspective, Mark. We don't want to use the accountants who handle these files. This way, when the cops come knocking, it'll be easy for them to say they had no idea what happened with a very straight face. Honest innocence is the best deception."

"They'll talk to everyone in the firm, including me. They're going to *know* someone is involved if all the companies you steal from use Lafferty & Sons."

"Of course they will. But you'll just be one of many people who just happen to work there. The primary suspects will be the five accountants who directly manage the files. And they'll be proven innocent because they didn't do anything wrong, and no facts will show that they did. Meanwhile, you'll blend in with everyone else."

Mark stroked his chin and then rested his index and middle fingers on his lips. This didn't add up. The feds wouldn't just leave it at that. The accountants working the files would be the fall guys. He would be setting them up.

"Why not steal from companies that don't use Lafferty & Sons to spread out the risk?" he asked.

"We're not going to add risk to the operation to protect Lafferty accountants, Mark."

It was as much confirmation as he'd get.

"What am I supposed to tell the police?" In came out in the town of a petulant child mixed with that of someone being robbed. Whiny, high-pitched and full of fear.

"You'll have to work on your story."

The process by which accountants were assigned to clients at Lafferty & Sons was more or less based on rotation. Although Larry always approved the final match, at the senior accountant level it was basically luck of the draw. Mark could've just as easily been assigned one of those five clients, and now wished more than ever that he had been.

"I still don't understand—"

"No matter what I say, you're not going to like my answer. The fact is: we chose you, Mark. You're our reckoner."

Just as quickly as he opened the subject, Edward slammed it shut. Something still didn't add up; getting account numbers couldn't be that difficult for these guys. But there would be no more answers.

"Why can't you just pick random numbers and wait for one to match? You said yourself it doesn't require a company name."

Edward took a long swig of Coke and stood up, shaking his head.

"Mark, Mark, Mark. You disappoint me. Your first question was great. This one…not so much. Remember: we prefer to stay *under* the radar. If we tried that, we'd undoubtedly strike out a few times. And the government does have a way of catching on if you're stupid enough to leave things to chance."

"But if you—"

"But let's say we did randomly match an account on the first try. Chances are we'd get some sap's personal checking account with 20 bucks in it. The transfer won't go through if there's not enough currency to cover the transaction, and we're right back on the radar. We're planning to transfer a considerable amount of money by most people's standards. And I can't just hope that we'd get Bill Gates or a major corporation on the first shot."

The logic was bitter, but made sense. Dishonest as it was, Mark could see why they were doing it the way they were. He could think of only one more question to delay the inevitable.

"Why not pick a big company? There's more money to steal, and they won't miss it as much. Why not go after Google or Wal-Mart or Apple?"

"The more money you take, the more it's missed. The bigger the company you steal from, the louder it yells and the more people listen. It's like cheating in Vegas: you get greedy, you get caught."

He sat twisted in knots by straight logic. Before he could speak again Edward continued.

"Listen, Mark, I appreciate your questions, I really do. But believe me, we've thought this through and it makes sense to us. We've chosen you. You don't have to like it, but you do have to accept it. Tom?"

Tom abruptly reappeared in his line-of-sight, this time carrying a black duffle bag. He dropped it on the desk and quickly opened the zipper, withdrawing a few more stacks of money and handing them to him.

They looked similar to the stacks in his pocket, but instead of $50 bills, they were $100 bills. And the stacks were thicker.

"Mark," Edward said, "this may seem a little bizarre, my paying you to help me steal, but I believe people should be compensated for services rendered. You already have $10,000 from the limo, and I want you to keep it. You're holding another $20,000 right now, so you've made out just fine for tonight.

"But once you get me all five companies' account numbers and files, I'll give you a hundred times more. Literally. Just keep your mouth shut and memory short."

Some quick math said Edward was promising him three million dollars.

Three million bucks.

"Mark," Tom almost whispered, "we know these aren't ideal circumstances for you, but think of this opportunity. You've been at Lafferty & Sons since you were 18 years old. One day you're a college intern, and the next it's been 23 years. We know you had what it took to move up the ladder but couldn't afford to leave. We know you would've been an international banking star in Europe but had obligations here you couldn't ignore. You missed out on a very lucrative opportunity so you could sit at the same desk in the same office in the same building all these years. Here's your second chance."

He couldn't help the dollar signs that danced uncontrollably in his mind. The fear was still there too, but even it had taken a backseat for the moment.

Three million dollars...

"I need the account numbers exactly three weeks from today," Edward said. "You'll be contacted with an exchange point and time. I don't care how you get them, but I suggest you think it through. If you get caught, you'll go to prison. Then we'll have to kill you to protect our interests, and I'll have to start this process all over again with someone else. Someone far less capable.

"I don't want that, and I know you don't want that. So take your time and do it right. Be careful; develop a solid plan. You'll find a way. When you do, the money is yours and we'll never see each other again."

He stared at the duffle bag, thinking equal parts wealth and personal safety. It seemed there was only one way to get both.

Without any indication whatsoever, Tom reached around from behind him and applied a fresh strip of duct tape across his mouth, then quickly jerked the black mask over his head. The image of Edward's stoic, icy face was replaced with darkness, but he still heard his voice.

"Mark, just to prevent you from asking another dumb question, don't say no. That's a lot of money to turn down, and you've got too much to lose. I'm sure you know what I mean."

7

"What's wrong, Daddy?"

He couldn't help his inattentiveness. He arrived home around 2:30 in the morning and spent five sleepless hours staring out the window of a house that was almost certainly being watched. The butter hadn't yet softened and the juice wasn't poured when Katherine got home from her sleepover.

"Nothing's wrong, sweetheart. Just a little tired. That's all."

With that, he became the liar he'd always instructed Katherine not to be.

"Do you like my picture?"

"I love it, sweetheart," he replied, thankful she had changed the subject. He smiled at the scribbly rendition of Daniel Tiger, Katherine's latest artistic masterpiece from the beloved kids' show. To him, she would always be the next Monet. He put an arm around her and pulled her close, giving her a kiss on the top of her head.

"Ready for your pancakes?"

"Yup! Want me to set the table?"

"Sure thing. You can be my special helper today, like old times."

"Oh, Daddy," she laughed. "I like being your special helper every day. Can we put some strawberries in the pancake mix this time?"

"We sure can," he said, thinking of her favorite *Daniel Tiger's Neighborhood* episode from when she was much younger, and the two of them only had each other and Daniel Tiger to comfort them. That enchanted garden, where the show's characters picked strawberries, would always have a special place in his heart.

Her ravenous appetite for Saturday morning pancakes, and her unrestrained enthusiasm for it, brought a warmth that only she could provide. But today, he couldn't even enjoy it.

"Did you have fun last night with Uncle Brad?" she asked.

Despite his best friend's ex-con status, Katherine still called him Uncle Brad, and he was still welcome in their home.

"Yes sweetheart, lots of fun."

She didn't say it, but he could see in Katherine's face that she didn't believe him.

***

Was the gentleman at the corner table, who was nibbling a breakfast sandwich and reading a newspaper, watching him? Did the lady feeding her baby follow him inside? Were the teenagers standing in line secretly taking notes for Tom and Edward?

Sip and Shop was a small family restaurant in Elmhurst, an upscale town about 20 miles west of Chicago laden with quaint shops and Mom-and-Pop businesses. Downtown's uneven red brick roads and original buildings created a historic feel, but it was very hip with plenty of modern restaurants, shops and watering holes. The people who lived there were affluent, well-educated and cultured. And although they appeared to be minding their own business, Mark couldn't help but wonder if that business was somehow connected to him.

The fear Edward had created was bad enough, the paranoia it led to felt insurmountable.

He sipped his black coffee acting like he knew how to spot a spy. Trying not to think about Katherine's safety, or the multiple lies he told her, or Edward's horrifying stare, or the three million reasons to consider becoming a professional racketeer, he stared aimlessly at a KenKen puzzle in the newspaper he was pretending to read.

Finally, the man he'd been waiting for walked through the door.

Sam Fisher was always late. Not once in the 24 years Mark had known him could he recall punctuality. He also never dressed up, shaved only when he felt like it, and didn't care what anyone thought or said about him. He was the definition of marching to the beat of his own drum and had no boss, family, or obligations that Mark was aware of.

"How's it going, buddy?" Sam flipped Mark the bird and collapsed into the booth across him in the same motion. Sam's black hair was thicker and longer than Mark remembered, and was unsurprisingly uncombed. He also looked heavier, north of 300 pounds, but made it perfectly clear how much he cared about that with his order:

"Double cheeseburger, extra cheese, fries, loaded, Pepsi, and a piece of chocolate cake. Hold the frosting, I'm watching my weight," he told the waitress in a thick Kentucky accent. She didn't even try to keep a straight face.

That was Sam. If there was such a thing as an opposite of Mark, Sam Fisher was it. The man hated planning of any kind, including schedules and appointments, and fiercely rebelled against them with surprising efficiency. He drank Pepsi at 9:30 in the morning and coffee in the evening just to be nonconforming. He broke laws for fun: parking in red zones, smoking in restaurants, driving the wrong way on a one-way street. If he got a ticket here and there, it was a fair price to pay for the joy of nonconformance.

The list went on.

It surprised most people who knew them both that Sam and he were even friends at all. But the college freshman roommate bond is stronger than most people give it credit for. Even after Sam was kicked out after that first year for trying to manufacture his own marijuana in his dorm room, the two had remained in touch and relatively close friends ever since.

"So this smokin' hot blonde walks into a bar and—"

"Sam, I'm not in the mood."

"Shut your mouth, boy! How dare you interrupt my finest blonde joke?"

"Sam ..."

"And she says to the bartender—"

"Sam!"

"Whoa. What the hell's wrong with you?"

"I'm...I'm into something. And I don't know what to do." It sounded pathetic to him and had to sound even worse to Sam, but that's how he felt. He fought back the tears, forcing but a shred of his dignity to remain.

Sam stared, speechless, and within seconds, everything about his body language changed. His smile evaporated, he cleared his throat, and he moved from slouched to a fully upright position. The Pepsi arrived and Sam took one long swig, then pushed the glass aside and rested folded hands on the table, giving Mark his full attention.

"Tell me everything, bud. Don't leave out a single detail."

And he did. He told Sam *everything*. And Sam listened intently, displaying focus that he didn't know his old friend had. Sam remained silent and, with the exception of an occasional wipe of his forehead perspiration with a paper napkin, he didn't move.

Sam didn't ask why he was sharing all of this, but both already knew the underlying reason: Sam was very trustworthy. Despite his oddities, the man was one of those guys who would always be there when it counted, when almost no one else would.

And despite not having the slightest clue what Sam did for a living and his strict adherence to "Don't Ask, Don't Tell" when it came to the subject, Mark knew Sam would be able to help. In his tiny arsenal of friends, Sam Fisher was his first and only resource.

When Sam finally did speak, he didn't say much.

"You got *any* idea why they'd come after you?"

"Not for the life of me. You don't think it was just—"

"Nah. If they're legit, it don't seem like no random choice to me. They picked you for a reason."

"Do you—"

"Hold on there, buddy. I said *if* they're legit, which ain't proved yet. They talk a good game, but talk's cheap and whiskey costs money. That's where my money is, but I gotta find out."

"But the thirty grand and the three million dollar promise is—"

"Don't blow your wad just yet, Sputnik. Hold your horses and let me look into it. Could be a smooth-talker just tryin' to scare you."

"Well he's doing a good job."

"Gimme some time. I'll call you."

Sam yanked himself out of the booth and dropped a $50 bill on the table. His food arrived steaming as he stormed out of Sip and Shop. Mark remained behind in a fog.

8

Mills Community Health Center on the South Side of Chicago was a part of the Illinois Association of Free and Charitable Clinics. It was open seven days a week and treated an average of 1,500 patients per month. The primary clientele were either unemployed people or those whose work didn't come with health insurance, and couldn't afford private health care. Roughly 42% were children and about half were undocumented immigrants. Its patients were in the abyss between making too much money or not qualifying for Medicaid but also not able to afford private coverage. The number of patients treated had grown over 47% the past three years.

Poor lighting and filthy floors were tolerated by the hard-working doctors, dentists, nurses and technicians – essentially volunteers – who performed basic medical services for people who would otherwise not receive them. Almost 20,000 people were treated last year. Due to a federal stimulus program, that number was projected to grow another 20% in the next six months.

Edward cringed as he looked through the binoculars.

Over 95% of the clientele were black, usually single mothers who emptied a truckload of children into the waiting room. They crawled around on the floor like animals because their mothers didn't stop them. No surprise, however. Typically those mothers were strung out on one drug or another and couldn't take care of themselves, much less their children. But it sure didn't stop them from having more babies.

That's right, he thought, *keep having those soiled little creatures. The world needs more drug dealers, pimps and prostitutes.*

The building itself was over 50 years old and in serious need of renovations. Its conditions and overcrowding made it look like a zoo.

But that was about to change.

The brittle structure would crumble like a cookie when the device exploded. Its foundation would shatter, walls implode and roof cave in. In a mere matter of seconds it'd be nothing but a pile of ash and carcasses.

It was almost noon. The Sunday Baptist service three blocks away was about to conclude. The church was close to 100% black and might as well have put up a sign excluding everyone else. He'd suggested to The General that the church be the next target. It was under consideration, but first they needed to address the clinic.

One step at a time.

They'd stroll in like a band of gorillas, straight from the church, moving from one free service to another. When the waiting room exceeded capacity and the line stretched to the sidewalk, all he had to do was push a button.

Sunday was the center's busiest day and noon its busiest hour. Worst case: they'd only get fifty. Best case: as many as one hundred. The medical professionals would be casualties. Every war had them, unfortunately; they should've known better anyway. He didn't feel guilty. He felt giddy, waiting for the herds to arrive.

And thinking about how much more they'd accomplish once Mark Richter delivered the information.

9

The name Edward Doran was heard in very few circles by very few people. No one knew much about him, which told Sam volumes. Not many people weren't an open book to his sources.

Those sources included drug dealers, dirty cops, pimps, crooked politicians, former inmates and convicted felons. To protect their anonymity, he always carried a small, white pill that would kill him within twenty seconds if he ever found himself in a situation where revealing it was inevitable.

And he didn't kid his sources or himself: such situations do exist.

For example, getting interrogated by a seasoned gang leader seeking intelligence on the competition. The human body can take only so much pain; everyone has a breaking point. And in reality, any of his clients' enemies could reach it.

Rather than deny those situations exist, he avoided them by using extreme caution, always having the latest and greatest technology, and being very selective about what jobs he accepted.

Hence, he carried the little white pill.

Sources were paid quite handsomely for the information they provided. Not with money, but with favors. In an unorganized version of organized crime, favors and "I Owe Yous" were the hard currency. It was a small industry with few players, but favors traded between them made the market engine run.

He was the facilitator of those exchanges.

His occupation could most aptly be described as "freelance private investigator and justice-rendering service provider," but that only scratched the surface.

Most of his clients were being tailed by the police. But there were any number of folks who solicited his help for any number of reasons, ranging from protection to information to revenge. Trust was the key in his business, and he had earned a reputation for discretion and reliability. People came to him for that reason.

And because he was the best at what he did.

Sure, most of his clients were labeled "bad guys." But those labels were generated by a system that operates under alarming levels of corruption and hypocrisy every day. Who was he to judge right and wrong? The world was very gray, and Sam never knowingly helped a true fiend.

Had he killed people? Several. But only when their actions had forfeited their right to live. The guy whose DNA proved conclusively that he raped a six-year-old girl before getting off on a technicality because the police didn't follow proper procedure? He didn't have any problem whatsoever putting a bullet between his eyes after administering two hours of torture. The guy who landed his wife in the hospital three times in one month, once by nearly beating her to death with a garden rake, and always got off clean because he had connections in the police department? It actually felt great to hold the plastic bag over his head.

Most people judge others without seeing all the facts. And that's because they've never been accused of something they didn't do, or had to face family members with an undeserved label attached to their name. They've never been screwed by the public or stabbed in the back by people they thought were friends because it's easier to believe the papers than it is to get off your butt and find the truth.

He had. He'd gone through those realities. He knew the price of the phrase "presumed innocent until proven guilty," and he was a strict practitioner of it. In his opinion, he knew it better than the cops and courts.

Sunday night, the sunset starting, he paced west on Division Street towards his final appointment. Previous conversations were less than fruitful, but he already knew Mark was in way over his head. If what he'd heard was correct, which he still needed to verify, he'd need to meet with Mark immediately. He found it hard to believe, but his meeting with JP would give him confirmation.

And if he got it, he'd find and kill Edward Doran. The man was simply too evil to be left alive in the world.

* * *

Katherine sleeping peacefully upstairs, Mark stared at the wedding photo in his lap. Her gorgeous smile on display, Mary Ann watched him from behind the glass. He still vividly remembered the day she was diagnosed; that bright, sunny June 29th that had since brought so much gloom. Katherine was barely two, and all he could do then was take care of her and comfort Mary Ann as much as possible. All he could do now was stare back at the photo, tears blurring his vision.

The ringing house phone he'd refused to get rid of despite almost always being robocalls theses days didn't remove the remorse, it only snapped him out of his self-loathing funk.

"Mark. Sam."

"Hey Sam."

"Can you sneak out for a few?" Sam's voice was upbeat, even jovial, which he took as a good sign.

"Now?"

"No time like the present."

"What did you—"

"Aww sheet, buddy. We'll catch up in person. I need a beer."

"But—"

"I *said* I need me a beer! Meet me at that joint where I got kicked out for smokin'."

"You mean—"

"Yeah. That one."

It took him a few seconds of silence to realize Sam had already hung up.

10

His car was still in the Applebee's parking lot, but Mark was miles from it. Without explanation, before he'd even gotten out, Sam had pulled up next to him and told him to climb in his truck.

Fifteen minutes later, around eleven-thirty, he was in a smelly, sticky-floored gas station bathroom off Highway 83, watching Sam operate a contraption that looked like it belonged in a James Bond movie. It was long and black and had three buttons at the end, opposite a small plastic handle. It made strange sounds and looked more advanced than what TSA used at the airport.

"Sam, what are you doing?"

"Shh. Spread your legs," Sam implored, scanning him for what he presumed were bugs. He did as asked, still very much in shock. Sam combed his body thoroughly, slow around the shoulders and chest, even slower around the feet and legs. Then he scanned his jacket, shoes and the $30,000 Mark had brought just as assiduously.

No smiles, laughs, or blonde jokes. Sam didn't even look at him. His focus was solely on the task at hand.

This was the same guy who got arrested for smoking pot outside the police headquarters when he was 19 and then called the judge a pompous douchebag at the arraignment; the same guy who, during his ephemeral college career, told a professor to shove a textbook up his ass; the same guy who cracked a cold beer in the front-row pew at a wedding.

Sam was always honest and dependable, but Mark wasn't aware of a serious bone in his body before now.

"Okay, you're clean," Sam announced after over 20 minutes of silent inspection.

"Okay?"

"I scanned you for bugs and wires, even though those ain't hard to miss. Few other things too. Let's just say that as far as the best anti-bugging technology out there is concerned, your person is clean."

"Sam, why are we in a gas station bathroom?" he asked. The combined stench of the unclean toilet and stagnant air was starting to nauseate him.

"I was wrong, bud. This Edward Doran guy...these guys are the real deal."

Despite anticipating the blow beforehand, it still hit him like a hard gut punch.

"What'd you find out?"

"Not much, which is a lot."

"English, Sam!"

"I don't have specifics right now, but I've got enough to know he's one bad-ass dude. High-tech surveillance guru, technology expert, mercenary background, the whole deal. He's the nastiest guy I've ever looked into, and I've looked into a lot of nasty guys. That computer tool with the money transfer's probably legit. *That's* why we're in a gas station bathroom."

He failed to make the connection.

"It's a place I know they ain't got bugged. Can't be too careful with these guys, bud. Gas station bathrooms are the best places. I already gambled too much, callin' your house, but didn't see any other way. Let's go, we'll talk in my truck."

Sam turned back before opening the door.

"When we leave, don't say nothin.' Got it? They could be watching. Probably have them a parabolic microphone."

"A what?"

"Works like a satellite dish, but the reflector transmits sound waves 'stead of radio waves."

Perfectly clear now, he thought.

On the outside, he tried to keep his composure. On the inside, he was an absolute mess. Parabolic microphones and bugs and reflectors and wires weren't for people like him. Apparently, they were for people like Sam, but not him. He shook his head and stared into the bathroom mirror for a moment, wondering how this was all going to play out.

"Take a deep breath man. You *gotta* relax, you *gotta* act chill. I know it ain't easy, but they might be watching. And if they are, you gotta act normal. Don't give them any hint you know something."

He still didn't quite understand what Sam was saying. It seemed to him acting a bit paranoid would be par for the course after his little chat with Edward, but he was a fish out of water here and Sam was a Bass. After what he felt was an insufficient amount of time to "relax," they exited the bathroom, hopped back into Sam's black Ford Maverick pickup, and started driving. He could tell by the way Sam checked all the mirrors when pulling out of the parking lot that he too was terrified.

He'd never known Sam to be scared of anything.

* * *

"We're safe in here. My ride ain't bugged."

Mark took quick inventory of the safe setting. Multiple soda cans and empty fast-food bags on the floor, AC/DC humming in the background, windows covered with multiple layers of crud, seats sporting numerous cigarette burns.

"What do you think I shou—"

"Like I said, first thing is you *gotta* be more careful. It ain't overkill and you need to be safe, not sorry. They made them 320 G's disappear, and from what I gather that's child play for this Edward guy. You have to assume everything is bugged at home and at work: voice-activated transponders, audio recorders, hidden cameras, car tails, the whole shebang. Hell, we're probably being followed right now."

Sam then took an extremely abrupt, hard left turn across three lanes of traffic. There were only a few cars on the road at the late hour, but the resulting horn honks and one finger waves expressed the drivers' feelings on the maneuver.

He wasn't surprised. "Erratic" didn't do Sam's driving justice. Out-of-nowhere U-turns, regular speeds 40 miles per hour over the limit and sporadic lane changes were common maneuvers, used with regularity.

"Just makin' sure," Sam explained.

He finally made the connection that Sam was referring back to the possibility of being tailed and felt even worse. He would've much preferred just good old-fashioned reckless driving.

"Sam, I don't have the first clue how to spot a bug."

"I've got some stuff to help you with that. Microphone detectors, bug sensors, RF detectors, and so on."

"RF?"

"Radio frequency."

"Is that supposed to mean something to me?"

"Don't matter. Like I said, I got some stuff for you. That's why we had to meet. Some cool Spy Hawk Pro and Spy Zone kind of stuff. Take some of that thirty grand, it's clean, and buy a bunch of prepaid cell phones. Get some new clothes you know ain't bugged; shoes, socks, the whole shebang. Get stuff for Katherine, too. Start renting cars."

"Renting cars?"

"I know it's a pain, but you gotta do it. You gotta assume they bugged your house, car, desk, everything. Don't use your computer for anything you don't want them to know about. Go to wireless cafés and Internet lounges and libraries. Set up a couple e-mail addresses with fake names. And don't do anything in your house you wouldn't want 'em to see."

"Sam, how do I—"

"Hold on, sport," Sam cut him off before veering right towards the I-290 eastbound ramp towards Chicago.

"Never thought I'd say this, but you actually need to plan *more*. You want 'em believing you're playin' right into their hand. Only tell 'em what you want 'em to hear. You give 'em a whiff of anything else, and they'll take a smell. Tell 'em you'll get what they want. Three weeks ain't much time, but you definitely gotta act like you're game. Don't tell Katherine nothing neither. I know that ain't gonna be easy, but leave her out of this. Doesn't do any good to bring her in."

He thought of his angel's Daniel Tiger drawing, and the sorrow he felt for how her childhood had unfolded without a mother. And now, he'd endangered her life.

Some father.

"What should I *really* do? Should I get the account numbers?"

"You should do what I tell you to do. Buy some new gear, keep things on the DL for a while. Normal as you can be. I'm gonna do some more checking before you make your next move with this Edward Doran."

"Might not even be his real name."

"Let me worry 'bout that. You just get yourself together so when you do have to do somethin,' you ain't pissin' in the wind. You gotta be ready when it's time to make your move; now's the time to plan. Here, take this."

Sam pulled a cell phone from the glove compartment and handed it to Mark.

"I'm speed dial number one. Call me whenever but not from your house. Go somewhere you've never been before to make calls. The thing about bugs is they can't put 'em everywhere. And the stuff I'm gonna give you ain't exactly on the market, so you're way ahead of where they think you are."

"Should I still go on my business trip to San Antonio on Tuesday?"

"Yeah, it'd be good for you to get outta here and not raise any flags by cancelling. Go on the trip and lay low. Let me do some work and by the time you get back, I'll have us a game plan."

He tried to use that to feel better. It didn't work.

"Alright. We'd better get back. Remember, play it safe. Use your head, assume the worst. Be the boss of what they see and hear. Got it?"

He gently nodded.

"You need anythin' at all, you just give me a buzz."

As they approached Applebee's, he couldn't help it. He was putting his trust in Sam and Sam in harm's way at the same time, and now he needed to know.

"Sam, I've never asked you before, but what do you do exactly? How do you know all this stuff?"

"Let's just say I got some experience with it."

"What's that mean?"

"You know how it's better that Katherine just doesn't know about Edward Doran?"

The implication needed no explanation. Sam parked the truck and Mark turned towards his friend.

"Sam?"

"Yeah, bud?"

"Thanks man. I really appreciate it."

"Anything, anytime." They quickly embraced and Mark opened the door.

"Be careful, Sam."

"Don't worry 'bout me. Been doing this for a long time, my friend. *Too* long. You just focus on layin' low and keepin' quiet."

11

"Going somewhere, buddy?"

Frazzled, Mark looked up from the itinerary and saw Jason Albers smiling behind him. With short salt-and-pepper hair combed to the side, more salt than pepper, he wore traditional, black-rimmed glasses that looked almost wedged against his puffy, bloated cheeks. Usually clean-shaven, today he sported a little stubble that was all salt. The security guard was always in a good mood and very friendly. His wide smile and jovial disposition were two things that everyone in the office expected whenever they saw him.

"Yeah, headed to San Antonio. I leave tomorrow morning for a conference."

"Oh, that's nice. The River Walk is beautiful."

"Yeah, it is."

"You've been there before?" Jason asked.

"I go every year for a tax conference after Memorial Day."

"Oh, that's right, so you already know. Fantastic. Be sure to check out Saveurs 209 if you get a chance. It's the best French restaurant I've ever been to," Jason said cheerfully in his slight southern accent.

Mark nodded and forced out a tiny smile. As much as he liked Jason, he was in no mood to talk. Even on normal days, he felt a bit uncomfortable with Jason's incessant positivity. It sometimes felt like a slap in the face to his way of life, which tended to be more reclusive and pensive.

Unfortunately, Jason prolonged the conversation. "Girls had a lot of fun on Friday. *Princess Diaries II* was the winner again."

"Surprise, surprise."

It was great that Katherine got along so well with Jason's daughter, Kristina. It didn't take much spark to light that fire. They first met at a company picnic five years ago, about a week after Jason started as a security guard at the building and was assigned to Mark's floor. And ever since Kristina's fourth birthday party at Pottery World later that summer, the girls had been inseparable. Mark and Jason, both single dads, had become friends as well.

At first, Mark did have his doubts. The friendship's potential felt limited because of their many differences. Kristina was a proper young lady who liked sundresses and played House; Katherine's preferred attire was gym shorts and a T-shirt and she had the goal of getting as dirty as possible every time she went outside. And he'd also had some initial apprehension about Katherine sleeping over with no woman in the Albers house. But after the first couple times, with the girls talking all night and Katherine telling him the next day just how much fun she had and how much she liked Kristina, that concern subsided relatively quickly. With both of them both still adjusting to life without Mary Ann, who'd passed eighteen months earlier, he was delighted Katherine had such a good friend.

"Yeah I think—" Jason was interrupted by Mark's ringing phone.

"Sorry Jason. Have to take this."

"No problem! Catch you later." Jason turned around to stride down the hallway toward his next positive interaction.

It was the "other" phone, the one Sam gave him just eight hours earlier. Not expecting it to ring, he didn't know quite how to react. Caller ID was still blank and it was already on the third ring.

He headed for the stairwell exit and flipped opened the phone.

***

"Hello?"

"Mark. It's Sam. Where you at?"

It was nine o'clock on a Monday morning. Where did Sam think he was?

"I'm in the office."

"Good. Keep up the routine. But we gotta talk."

"Now? I leave for San Antonio tomorrow morning."

"Tonight. We gotta talk tonight. It's important."

"We just talked…what'd you find out since one o'clock last night?"

"Can't say right now."

"Can't say? I thought you said this was a secure phone?" he whispered with a harsh tone.

"Just don't tell *anyone* 'bout any of this. You hear me? Keep it to yourself and don't do nothin' outta the ordinary." His voice was even more charged and nervous than the night before.

"You already told me that."

"Just do what I say, okay dude?"

"Okay, okay. Where do you want to meet? Back at Apple—"

"No. From now on we don't meet in the same place twice. Got it? And don't name specific places neither. Meet me where I got into that fight with that guy for tellin' him to shut up or I'd make him. We'll go somewhere from there."

Gino's East in Arlington Heights.

"There ain't no chance in hell they won't be following you. I told you before you gotta be more cautious. But it's worse than I thought. A lot worse. Meet me at eleven and keep your mouth shut. This is some serious, serious stuff, dude."

12

The target was alone, driving east on Grand Avenue in a green Ford Mustang convertible. When it reached Lake Shore Drive, it would head north for a half-mile to Skyline Condominiums. It was a premier location with pristine views of Lake Michigan to the east and easy access to Lincoln Park and Lakeview neighborhoods to the west.

Dan Kevil tailed the target from the black van three vehicles back, though he already knew exactly where Sam Fisher was going and how he'd get there. He'd been warned that Fisher was more experienced with surveillance than most targets, so he took the extra precaution. Fisher's file was thick enough to merit the warning, but thin enough to show he'd gotten away with much more than anyone knew.

It was 9:43 on a Monday night. The air was crisp but not cold; the sun had long set and the moon was in full effect. The streets were empty and traffic moved fast. Perfect. No need to worry about unexpected gridlock or construction delays. He placed the revolver back in the glove compartment, the safety precaution unnecessary.

The first time he held a gun, it didn't feel right. The cold steel met his warm hand with uneasy hardness, and the heavy .357 caliber felt awkward and uncomfortable. But that was 20 years ago. Now he felt naked without it. And in that time, he'd grown quite proficient at using it. There were, of course, far more sophisticated guns available now, but the .357 never jammed up like automatics tended to, and the reassurance it offered could not be matched.

His proficiency had earned The General's upmost respect, and his responsibility had grown exponentially as a result. Every time he got an assignment, the exchange was the same. The General said who and when, Kevil complied completely and without question, provided impeccable and reliable results, and was tremendously well compensated. He didn't want to know why. That question was for The General, for the strategists and the planners. All he wanted to know was the target's name, and when The General wanted the target gone.

He'd take care of the rest.

This time, however, The General had asked him to obtain some information first, and he relished the opportunity. It had been a while since he'd practiced that particular skill set, and it made things more interesting. The pliers and screwdrivers sat in waiting on the passenger seat, necessary tools for such a task.

When the target arrived at the condominium complex, Fisher parked his car in the same spot, used the same elevator, and went to the same residence. So far, the so-called expert had played right into his hand, doing precisely as expected and offering little challenge. Unimpressed, he began to wonder if Fisher was really that good.

He pulled the van into a McDonald's parking lot a few blocks away on Clark, concealed from Fisher's view, and popped open the portable TV monitor. The screens turned on instantly, revealing multiple views of all six rooms in the luxurious abode.

The search through Fisher's personal effects earlier that afternoon provided no answers as to why Fisher was asking questions about Edward Doran. Kevil was neither surprised nor disappointed. If he could've obtained what he needed simply by looking through a folder or tracing a call, then Fisher certainly wasn't the challenge he'd been promised.

He was indeed looking forward to meeting Sam Fisher in person.

The motion-sensitive cameras were tied together through a toggled satellite signal that beamed directly into the portable monitor, offering a complete panoramic view of Fisher's activity. His entrance, visit to the bathroom, kitchen, and finally the living room. Once done with all that, the target had his feet on the coffee table and turned on the 75-inch flat screen, a beer in hand from the kitchen fridge.

That was his cue.

He grabbed the revolver from the glove compartment, reviewed the impressive assortment of various information extraction devices, and prepared to exit the van.

But when he checked the monitor again, he saw a blank screen. The signal must have faded, and he tapped the monitor twice to get the picture back. When he did, static lines filled the screen. He smacked it harder, waiting for reception. Moments later, he heard the voice of the only man to ever catch him off guard.

"Drop the gun before I drop you."

* * *

Sam studied the man's hands, waiting for him to make the wrong move.

Sweat dripped from his forehead, but he let it be. This guy broke into his condo and had access to the most advanced hidden camera technology on the market, which meant he wasn't to be taken lightly.

Good thing for Sam that he had stuff that hadn't yet reached the market.

The interrupter had generated a one-way interference signal that disrupted the transmission and gave him the privacy he needed. He spotted the tail following him on the drive and used his cell phone's satellite imaging to tell him precisely where the van was parked.

Even with the beer and ballgame as decoys, he knew he had only had a few precious minutes. It wouldn't take long for the man to figure out he'd jammed the signal, and he needed to be at the scene before that happened. So as soon as he pressed the button on the remote control, creating the disturbance, he bolted from the couch to the fire escape, gun in hand.

A long slide down the metal railing and a three-block sprint later, he was at the van. Though overweight, he could still move better than most folks. And far better than you'd think to look at him, a deception he'd used to his advantage many times before.

"Very impressive," said the bald man with the graying goatee. His long-sleeved black T-shirt and dark pants certainly suggested intentions of entering Sam's condo.

"Drop the gun," Sam instructed.

The man tossed the revolver onto the passenger seat floor, still staring at Sam.

"Why are you following me?"

"If you're half as good as I think you are, you probably already know. And you know I'll never confirm it. I'm Dan, by the way."

There wasn't an ounce of trepidation in his voice; smooth and fearless. It clearly wasn't the first time the man had stared down the barrel of a gun.

Sam would, however, make sure it was the last.

He checked the empty seat next to him, surveying the unzipped duffle bag.

"Nice tools you got there, Dan. Maybe I'll give 'em a go-round on your sorry ass."

Almost as soon as he said it, he felt a sharp pain tear through his lower back. Stunned, he instinctively hunched over, dropping the gun and watched it bounce off the window before hitting the ground. In the same instant, hunched down, he felt another sharp pain, this time in his chest.

The bullet went straight through him and into the van's black paint finish. He immediately felt cold and numb and didn't try to fight it. He didn't howl or scream or attempt to escape. He'd been outsmarted for the first time in his life, but once was all it took.

He watched the bald man give a thumbs up, telling his sniper partner it was finished. The man looked at him and said nothing. No words were necessary. They both knew the business of killing, and they both knew that every match had a loser.

He was thinking of Mark when he finally dropped to the ground and took his final breath.

13

Thirty seconds into the conversation, Mark pressed the phone against his ear and got lost in thought for the umpteenth time that day. And Caroline wasn't shy about how it made her feel.

"Mark? *Hello?* Are you there? What's going on with you today?" His only sibling, Caroline sounded more and more like Mom used to every day. Mark didn't try to explain. He'd been down that path before and knew it would only lead to another impasse.

"Sometimes, I wonder what it would be like if Mary Ann was still here," he said. "She'd take Katherine shopping, they'd do their nails, brush each other's long hair. She's...she's missing out by not having a woman's touch."

"Remind me again: what does Katherine always tell you?"

He didn't reply, his mind still imagining Mary Ann and Katherine in formal dresses headed to Pinecone Cottage in Downers Grove for high tea. Mary Ann had always said she wanted them to do that when Katherine was eight. Now that Katherine actually was eight, it only made him wish the year could go faster.

"Mark! What does my niece say to you?"

"That Mommy is in Heaven watching over us, I'm doing a great job, and she just wants us to be happy."

"You need to listen to her more."

"Remind me again: what does my nephew always tell you?"

"I'm not having this discussion. Good-bye Mark."

He closed the phone and dropped it on the table, remembering things he wanted nothing more than to forget. The annual tax law seminar couldn't possibly have had less of his attention. Not exactly the most enthralling event to begin with, the past few days had given him all the more reason to block out the eight different speakers, twelve unique subjects, and mounds of new tax law information it had to offer.

It was held in a San Antonio Convention Center on Market Street connected to the River Walk and opposite the Marriott. Despite the beautiful venue outside, the conference itself was held in a large open room with no windows, poor ventilation and a thermostat that had to have read close to 80 degrees. He'd tried to think the situation through, telling himself he was away from Edward Doran and Tom, and that Katherine was safe at Jason's house with her best friend having fun.

That didn't work too well.

Scribbling notes, replaying what he knew, mapping out different strategies and revisiting his options numerous times only led to two conclusions: he didn't like the options, and he didn't know which to take.

Sam was a no-show at Gino's and had told Mark once, years ago, to never go to his condo unless he was expected. Mark had always tried to stay away from the kinds of things he was now neck-deep in, like surveillance, illegalities, etc., so he didn't ask questions then. He simply didn't go to Sam's place without calling. Multiple phone calls had yet to be returned, so he would have to wait to find out what Sam had learned about Edward Doran.

Of all the things San Antonio had to offer, including The Alamo, the original Fuddruckers, and the glorious tax seminars, the River Walk was his favorite. The water spanned 15 miles with a peaceful 3.5-mile walking path on either side. With gondolas in the river and trees and local restaurants up and down the sidewalk, it was ideal for a calm stroll. Five miles from downtown, it wasn't as crowded you'd think, and the adjacent San Fernando Cathedral area was pristinely kept. Every time he visited, he was reminded why the River Walk was the most popular tourist attraction in Texas.

He ate at the same two places every year. Since he'd visited the Saltgrass Steak House the prior evening, tonight he sat at a small table outside Casa Rio, his favorite of the many delicious Mexican restaurants on the River Walk, Spanish guitar music behind him and a slight breeze on his face. The weather was an unseasonably cool 78 degrees with no wind. Perfect for a night out.

Nibbling on pulled chicken nachos, he scanned a *USA Today* article about the Mills Community Health Center bombing, gasping in horror at what had happened. Close to 90 people dead, and the cops had no leads. Such depressing news made it easy to put the paper down when his main course, the combo dinner, finally arrived.

He'd just taken his first bite of the soft taco when a man appeared from behind him and sat down. It was a two-person table, and the man promptly moved Mark's backpack to the ground without so much as a hello.

There were plenty of empty tables in every direction.

He looked to be about 60 and reminded Mark of a younger Tom Selleck without the mustache. He wore circular, black-rimmed glasses and had curly grey hair. A noticeable scar ran under his right eye, which he softly rubbed as he leaned back in the seat.

"Excuse me, but—"

"Mark, we need to talk. My name is Ron Mitchell, and I work for the Federal Bureau of Investigation."

"The FBI?" Mark responded, partially chewed taco still in his mouth.

"That's right. Something's come to my attention that can't wait."

Mitchell then withdrew a small black leather ID case and opened it. On top were Mitchell's name and his picture, along with "FBI" in large blue letters and the organization's seal. On the bottom, a gold badge and a few lines of text above Milton Montgomery's signature, the FBI's National Director.

Mark looked at the man closer. His face was expressionless. No smiles, no frowns. Very matter-of-fact.

"Did I do something wrong?" he said after finally swallowing what was left of the taco bite.

"No. But I have a feeling you might. And we need to talk before that happens."

"What's that supposed to mean?"

"Finish your dinner. Then meet me at Boudro's. It's north of here about 100 feet down the River Walk, still on the west side."

Ron Mitchell then got up from the table with Mark's newspaper, folded it under his arm, and began to walk away like any other older man going for a walk in the park.

"Wait a second!" he shouted. "I'm not going anywhere until you tell me what this is about!"

"I'll explain when we talk. Finish your dinner."

"But—"

"Your friend Sam Fisher is dead."

14

The appeal of the River Walk disappeared forever that night.

He'd no longer hear the lively music or flowing water, smell the delicious spices, or notice the beautiful scenery surrounding him. It was all dead. Gone for good.

And so was Sam.

Instead, it would forever remind him of Ron Mitchell, who leaned against the metal fence wearing a black jacket and tan pants outside Boudro's. The combo dinner went to waste, and Mitchell motioned him for a walk. The River Walk was nearly desolate at ten o'clock on a Wednesday night, so there was little concern, or hope, of others overhearing their conversation.

"You head back to Chicago tomorrow afternoon, correct?"

"Um, yeah. Two-thirty."

Mitchell nodded, as if offering approval of his schedule. They passed a few workers sweeping the ground who clearly didn't want to be there and a young couple making out at a nearby table, neither of which appeared to be coming up for air anytime soon.

"How do you know Sam's dead? Did you find his body?"

"No body. But his car's still parked at his condo and no one has seen him since Monday night."

"That doesn't prove anything. Sam disappears for weeks on end."

"We found a signal-jamming device in his apartment and several hidden cameras that didn't match the only brand Fisher ever used. Forensics determined that someone slid down the fire escape, and Fisher's fingerprints were all over the railing. The window was still open yesterday, despite the rain that soaked the carpet."

"None of that proves he's dead," he said, denial winning the first round.

"Okay, Mark. You tell me: why would someone jam his own satellite signal, slide down the fire escape, and leave the window open for days? According to the cable company, the TV had been on since around ten o'clock Monday night. Same channel the whole time. Lest we forget, not only did he abandon his condo in an obvious rush, but he blew you off at eleven even though he set the time. And I'm pretty sure you haven't heard from him since."

"How'd you know about our meeting?"

"Then he decided to fall off the face of the earth. His cell phone rings and rings; he hasn't made contact with any of his sources. He's gone, Mark. If you need a body for closure, be prepared for it to stay open. The people who killed him don't leave bodies."

They reached the end of the River Walk and promptly turned around, headed south. The restaurants were now completely empty, except for the kids making out as though their plane was going down. The gusts picked up, and Mark zipped his windbreaker.

"How do you know so much about Sam?"

"It's our job to know things."

That answer didn't help him validate Mitchell's identity. Mark's expression told Mitchell as much, who then elaborated with palpable agitation, raising his voice and turning sterner.

"Sam was private, and he was very good with surveillance. But in his business, it's impossible to stay hidden. A few months ago he gave some confidential information about a police investigation to one of our undercover agents posing as a drug dealer. We wanted to know how he got the intel, so we started tailing him. Our hope was he'd lead us to the source."

"If you were tailing him, then why don't you know for sure what happened on Monday?"

"Not that it's any of your business, but he wasn't under constant surveillance. He was too sharp for that. And we couldn't afford to jeopardize our inside guy's position. We had a few theories about who the informant was, so we watched those individuals like a hawk and hoped Sam would come to them. It just so happened that Monday night we weren't watching him."

"There's the FBI for you. Citizen tax dollars hard at work."

Mitchell's response to the witty remark revealed a very short fuse. The agent stopped walking and pointed his finger into Mark's chest, nostrils flailing.

"Just keep the smart-aleck comments to yourself, Richter! I know you're not the FBI's biggest fan right now, but one-liners don't help."

"What's that supposed to mean?"

"We didn't want to lose Fisher any more than you did. Yeah, he was a criminal. Yeah, he'd killed people, and he probably got what he deserved. But he was also a key part of our investigation. Things don't always go as planned in the world of protecting people like they do when you're a boring-ass bookworm accountant."

"Screw you." He started to walk away.

"You know why we weren't watching him on Monday? Because we were busy watching *you*. I'm here to help you, and you're making wisecracks."

Mark stopped walking and faced Mitchell, the notion of Sam's death ripping through his mind like an electric saw through cheap plywood. He recalled his friend's jovial personality and dirty humor, now both gone because of him. He hoped Mitchell was wrong, but the forwardness of the FBI agent's words made that difficult to believe.

Egging Mitchell on even further wouldn't do any good at this point, he told himself. He needed to see where this conversation was going.

He took a steady breath and blew out, "I'm just a little overwhelmed by all of this."

"Look, we know you're a decent guy, Mark. You play by the rules. You're a good parent, you don't break the law, you do yard work for your neighbor. I know this talk isn't your cup of tea, but we don't have much choice here."

It seemed that everyone knew everything about him. His life was suddenly in a fishbowl, and the privacy he thought he valued before had been ripped from his grasp, making him realize just how much he'd taken it for granted. All he wanted now was to get it back. To get his life back.

Mitchell's next words told him he never would.

15

"Edward Doran, and that's just one of his many, many aliases, has been connected to terrorist organizations for over 25 years. We suspect he's planned and executed upwards of 50 bombings and is responsible for thousands of deaths across the country. We know he contacted you, and that he wants you to do something illegal for him."

Mark stopped walking and froze, silent. Mitchell continued providing details he'd demanded earlier but now no longer wanted to hear.

"He started small, bouncing between terrorist networks, radical groups and criminal orgs, freelancing his computer technology and high-tech surveillance expertise. For most of his career, it was all about the money, and he went to the highest bidder. About five years ago, he settled down and joined one organization full-time, the PEACHES. We think he's found a cause he truly believes in, which isn't good news."

"The PEACHES? I've never heard of them."

"Most people haven't. It's an underground terrorist network out of only a handful of locations. They don't advertise or have websites or put up signs announcing to the world who they are or what they believe. They're too smart for that. They don't try to grow too fast or convert the world all at once. What they *do* do is execute perfectly. Take a look."

Mitchell unfolded the newspaper and flipped to the article on the Mills Community Health Center bombing. Mark prayed the words might change. When he saw that they didn't, he took a seat along the water.

"They did this?"

"We think so, but as usual we don't have any proof. They cover their tracks better than any group we've seen. Common explosive material that can't be traced, perfectly disabled security systems and countermeasures, remote detonation from unknown locations. They put the device where they did to maximize its proximity to load-bearing members, so it will cause as much structural damage as possible. It adds up to a technically proficient group that invests a lot to understand its targets. They don't do many hits, but when they do, they're executed flawlessly. And it's only a matter of time before they start thinking bigger."

"Why would they bomb a health center?"

"They're a lot like the Neo-Nazis. Anti-Muslim, anti-black, anti-Catholic, anti-homosexual; they hate anything they aren't. And it's a passionate hate, the strongest I've ever seen. Best we can tell, they're based in Chicago, but nobody really knows. Their hits range from grocery stores to abortion clinics to cultural centers. They never hit the same type of place twice. They don't protest and march, they don't yell and scream. They just pick their targets and eliminate them."

"If you know they're doing these things, arrest them. You're the FBI. Lord knows you don't need evidence to arrest someone."

"Just because we suspect them doesn't mean we can just start arresting them. We don't have anything concrete, Mark."

"What do you mean you don't have anything? What have you been telling me?"

"It's all hearsay and none of it would hold up in court. The FBI can't start putting people behind bars without concrete evidence. The media and social rights groups would rip us apart and let the PEACHES off scot-free all at the same time."

"But you know Doran is involved."

"We don't even have definitive proof of that. And we know he isn't the leader. Even if we arrested him now, the group would carry on."

He was amazed at how little power Mitchell claimed the FBI had. His impression from the movies was that they could do whatever they wanted, whenever they wanted. The limits Mitchell was implying didn't seem right.

"But you—"

"So we give up our biggest advantage, the element of surprise, to arrest someone who's not essential to the organization's success, and then release him back to the world because we don't have any proof. Then we start watching all over again. Only this time, they're watching us too. Doesn't sound like a good plan to me."

"As opposed to waiting for the next bomb?"

"Right now, they don't know how close we are. We can't give that advantage up until we know we've got them."

"Why are you telling me this? What do you want from me?" He pleaded, nearly shouting. Whatever patience he once had was now gone. He was a CPA with a daughter and a house and a Kia. He didn't deal with terrorists and shouldn't be hearing about how the FBI couldn't stop them.

"I'm telling you because they're recruiting you to join their team."

16

"Terrorism has evolved. It's not local anymore. Technology has changed everything. Now it's multi-layered, with computers, global communication, and detailed planning. The best shot at bringing down a terrorist organization is to find their source of cash. But the Internet connects people from across the globe, which has made financing these groups relatively straightforward. In the old days, if a small group needed funding they robbed a convenience store. There was a clerk's description and video camera to review, patterns to trace, and an actual person to pursue. You know what the main sources of terrorist funding are today?"

"I'm sure you're going to tell me."

"Front companies and charities. Try tracing money that's been laundered through any one of a thousand seemingly legit businesses, or sifting through all the charitable donations made on any given day, with a guy like Edward Doran on the other side trying to stop you. The deck's stacked too much in their favor, and the PEACHES are too smart. It'd be blind luck if we ever nailed them that way."

He recalled some of Doran's words: *honest innocence, under the radar, small enough to go unnoticed, doing homework, eliminating guesswork.* It all fit into place. They needed him to help fund their next massacre.

"Most terrorist attacks don't cost as much as you think, either. Everyone thinks of 9/11, about the half-million it took to fund it, and they assume that's the norm. London's subway bombing a few years after that cost about two grand. A group like the PEACHES can do a lot of damage with little money."

"Can you trace the money back from hits you think they did?"

"Don't think we're not trying. Problem is they run their money through so many filters it comes out cleaner than a virgin's honey pot.

We suspect their biggest charitable contributors are the KKK and the American Nazi Party. Of course, we can't prove a thing. They're not political, like Proud Boys or MAGA groups. And only a small portion of their cash is from charities anyway. Candidly, we don't have the slightest idea how or where they get the rest."

He did. He remembered Edward's computer, the screen's large gray background.

The software was real.

"I don't see what any of this has to do with me."

Mitchell scratched an imaginary goatee and studied him with a hint of pride. Despite Mark's questions, Mitchell knew he was convincing him. Clouds covered the moon, casting an eerie shadow across the glistening water. A storm was coming.

"We know you met with Doran. What did he want?"

"What do *you* want?"

"Answer the question. What do they want from you?"

* * *

He would've loved to just tell the truth and be free of it all. But his lack of faith in the FBI and what happened to Sam, an expert in espionage and surveillance, encouraged caution as opposed to mere wishful thinking.

What if they were watching him? What if they followed him to San Antonio and were staring at and listening to him right that very moment? This guy seemed far less careful than Sam, despite being in the FBI. And all it took was a parabolic thing-a-ma-jig or a transmitter or a laser beam or something from the future, and he was dead.

"Given what I just told you about the importance of terrorist funding, and that it's the most plausible way we can bring them down, I'm surprised that you, an accountant, don't see the connection to yourself."

He remained silent.

"Chances are," Mitchell paused, "they asked you to do something involving money. Something you know is wrong. Maybe they even dangled a carrot, which would make you a contracted employee of the PEACHES. Why you? What's so special about you?"

He wished he knew. Instead of trying to figure it out again, he swayed his head from side-to-side, looking for spies, delaying his answer. He started to sweat despite the brisk evening chill when he thought of the $3M offer and the cash in his hotel room.

"We're alone. Trust me. I wouldn't be talking to you if we weren't."

"That's not very reassuring," he replied.

"Once you do whatever it is they want you to do, they've got you. You're theirs as soon as you help them, especially if you accept payment of any sort."

"What are you talking about?"

"Think of it as recruiting. Instead of having public sessions on the Capitol Building steps with megaphone like the KKK, they coerce people like you one-at-a-time into their little family. You think you can just do the job, take the money and never see them again. You've got another thing coming."

"There's no reason for them to want me."

"Don't give me that, Mark. You fit the bill perfectly. You're a WASP. You've got a lot to lose, including a daughter who can carry the torch in years to come. They probably view you as a prized asset."

Katherine.

He recalled his doubts during the meeting with Edward, how it felt like there was a reason they chose him, that it was more than just chance. But he never thought of his angel. He ran to the pier and couldn't stop the vomit that went into the water. A few minutes later, Mitchell joined him with a napkin.

"*What do you want from me?*" he whispered, his hands on his knees.

"Help us get Doran. Get us enough hard evidence so we can bust him once and for all. Then we can get him to roll on the leader and bring the PEACHES down."

He sighed, still refusing to believe this was real.

"We just want you to help us stop criminals from killing innocent people. Work with us, Mark. Once you tell us what they want and when they want it, we'll develop a plan that'll minimize the risk on your end."

Minimize the risk?

The precautions that Tom and Edward took last Friday, and the fact that he appeared to be the FBI's only lead, didn't make him feel warm and fuzzy after hearing Mitchell's promise. He stood upright and faced the agent.

"Let me get this straight. You want me to help you bring down a terrorist organization that has killed thousands of people, including Sam Fisher, even though you've been watching them for years but can't touch them because they've always outsmarted you? Do you really think I'm that stupid?"

"We don't know what they want, but we'll find out. We'll watch every company Lafferty & Sons deals with and study every employee. Something will happen, and we'll trace it straight to you. And when we do, we'll consider you an official member of their team."

Mitchell's nostrils flared in anger as he spoke. For sure, the good cop routine was finished. The pitch had been made, and now it was onto threats. It was probably standard operating procedure, but it was working.

"They're going down, Mark. You can be sure of it. Yeah, they've eluded us so far. But we'll get them eventually. It's a matter of when, not if."

Mitchell then took a step towards him leaned in even closer, his face now only an inch from Mark's, gritting his teeth as he lowered his voice and strengthened its tone.

"They have to be on their toes all day, every day, with no mistakes. We're closer than we've ever been, and we're *going* to get them. All we need is one lucky break, and we're due. And if you refuse to help us, you're going down too. All the way down, with the rest of them. You think about that on your flight tomorrow. I'll be in touch."

Mitchell turned away and headed up the stairs, leaving him alone on the River Walk for a round of dry heaves.

17

"Mills was excellent."

Beaming, Edward Doran thanked him for the compliment. The General gave out very few and almost never said "excellent." The health center operation had in fact gone quite well, strictly according to plan. There was reason to be proud, but he restrained himself. The General valued humility.

The General also valued hard work, and a lot of it had gone into that operation. It was the standard, the expectation. Agonizing details and painful research were the keys to flawless execution. The sun wouldn't rise for another two hours, yet he, The General and Tom had already been meeting for over 90 minutes. The office was chilly. Condensation clouded the windows, and a dim light on the large desk was the room's only illumination.

The General preferred darkness. Shadows.

"The next operation is coming along?" The General asked. It was phrased as a question, but both he and Tom knew it was not. The General's voice was soft, and he uttered few words, but those words had a commanding presence. When he spoke, people listened.

"Yes sir," he answered. "We're in the intermediate planning stages right now. So far, there haven't been any surprises."

"Keep me informed of your progress. I want those people gone."

"Yes sir."

"What about Operation VIXEN?"

"Development is moving along more quickly than expected. The extra funding will come at just the right time."

"What about the reckoner?"

The General switched gears rapidly when he got the answers he expected, which was always Edward's goal and almost always what happened. Tom, who'd been assigned surveillance, cleared his throat and stood upright, trying to appear confident and poised.

The General no doubt saw right through it. And straight into his nervousness.

"So far Richter has responded just the way you said he would. He got back from San Antonio yesterday at about six o' clock after the delay we caused at the airport. Took a cab straight home and called his boss's secretary to tell her he'd be out tomorrow."

"Vacation day?"

"Yes sir. Said he needed a day at home after the trip."

"What did he do then?"

"Picked up his daughter around eight o'clock."

"What'd they do?"

Edward carefully studied The General's unbroken concentration and recalled two certainties about his boss: 1) he was always thinking, hardly ever revealing what about and 2) he wanted to know the nitty-gritty details of the surveillance, particularly the personal and sexual details. He was secretly convinced that it aroused The General. If they were watching a couple, he'd want to know about their sex life and routines. Teenagers, whom they talked dirty to over the phone, if they did anything risqué, and so on.

The General wanted to know everything.

"Nothing out of the ordinary," Tom answered. "They ate dinner together and watched a movie, then went to bed a half-hour earlier than usual. He's driving Katherine to school in a few hours."

"What's he going to do after that?"

That was the other thing: The General always asked about the future. Educated guesses based on surveillance and intelligence were expected. Never stop predicting, The General had told him once. Always be on the horizon, and always look ahead. Play through the scenarios. Expect the unexpected.

"He's a creature of habit. He'll probably go to the gym. Play some racquetball to burn off some steam. Then he'll stay home the rest of the day."

"But he's cancelled his weekly match with Brad Tarnow?"

"Yes."

"Why do you think he canceled it?"

Edward watched carefully. Tom had potential, The General had told him once, but the lad still needed to learn. The General was always teaching and advising Tom, and at times that pissed him off. He didn't particularly like the jealousy he felt, but he reminded himself that he brought The General value Tom could never bring.

"He needs time to be alone. He thinks better when he's alone," Tom answered.

It wasn't a half-bad guess. Larry McDougal's secretary had commented that Richter called the office fewer times on this trip than any other. They knew from the wiretaps that Richter didn't send catch-up e-mails in the evenings or place calls between sessions. Not even to his daughter. The man was trying to think, to focus on his dilemma.

"Any reason to suspect Brad Tarnow knows something?"

"Not right now. When Richter called to cancel the match, he responded appropriately. Asked a lot of questions and wanted to make sure Richter was okay because Richter almost never cancels anything. But when he said he was, Tarnow let it go and offered to listen if he wanted to talk. He knows his friend is off somehow, but he doesn't know why."

"Good. What about the Sam Fisher investigation?"

Just like that, The General had shifted back to him, satisfied with Tom's answers. Edward noticed Tom sigh in relief and felt like punching him in the face, the competitive juices rising to the top.

"So far the police don't have any suspects."

"Will they ever?"

"They'll need a body first, and they won't find that."

"Does Richter know Fisher is dead?"

"Not yet. It's not out of character for Fisher to blow off a meeting. So Richter likely assumes that's what happened and will try again to contact him soon."

"Keep a close eye on him. I'm okay that he contacted Fisher, I told you he would. What you need to find out is if Fisher told him anything before we got to him. It's a shame we couldn't interrogate him first."

He knew The General made that comment specifically to remind him that such a mistake could not occur again. His anger bubbled at the underestimation of Sam Fisher, and internally he directed it back towards Tom, who was no doubt smiling on the inside because of his embarrassment.

"What about Fisher's source?" The General continued.

"The gang member was eliminated on Wednesday morning. The police haven't connected his murder to Fisher's and never will."

A search of Fisher's apartment had revealed that JR, a relatively new member of the Gangster Disciples on the south side, had given Fisher some important information. But Edward still didn't know what information exactly: The General had said he wanted to look into it personally.

"Do you think the three million will hook Richter?" Tom asked.

The General would know, no doubt. The General knew things about people that they didn't even know about themselves. The man possessed clairvoyance. It was as if he could see into the future.

"It'll tempt him, but it won't hook him. You'll need to execute the plan," The General replied, looking at him, not Tom.

He slowly nodded. It was precisely what The General had said before they contacted Mark in the first place. The money would tempt, not convince.

"And the plan is still on track?"

Again, not a question.

"Yes sir."

"We can't lose him."

"I'll make sure he understands."

18

Friday morning. Eleven o' clock. Mark sat alone in the kitchen at the small wooden table staring at Katherine's breakfast dishes. The cereal long eaten, her short glass was stained with dried orange juice rings. She had been at school for over three hours while he sat alone. The kitchen hadn't been cleaned up, and neither had he.

Even his routines were being ignored.

With a half-cup of cold coffee next to him, he found that taking deep breaths didn't relax him like it did the yoga masters. He fidgeted with his wedding ring, a ring he'd never stopped wearing, and listened to the sump pump in the basement kick on and off as the birds chirped outside. Spring was putting on her show, revealing flowering shrubs and leafy trees in beautiful blooms of color and fragrance. The temperature was pleasant, and a light breeze circulated the house through the open window.

He contemplated his options, crappy as they were:

Tell Edward no. *Be polite, but respectfully decline*, he'd thought, before facing the obvious stupidity of such an idea.

Run. Grab Katherine and drive fast and far. Until the tank was empty, far away from the FBI and even further from the PEACHES. Then reality set in again: that was just as unrealistic as saying no. Just as stupid, too.

Say no and help the cops? He'd end up like Sam.

Say yes and stay alive? Then he's a criminal, feeding the next atrocity, waiting for Ron Mitchell and the feds to toss him into solitary confinement.

Ask someone for help. Not a bad thought, but who? Plus, that didn't exactly turn out well for Sam, something he already had trouble living with. Not looking to repeat.

None of those options considered the enormity of what Edward wanted. It wouldn't be easy to get that information. Not by any stretch. When he factored that in, he felt even more trapped. He was stuck in a no-win situation with time quickly disappearing. It was a horrible nightmare from which he wasn't going to wake up.

"Time to get the mail," he said aloud.

It was simple and small, but it was a part of the routine he could maintain. And the routine comforted him. He didn't need to understand why it made him feel better. He just needed to feel better.

No neighbors were out. Kids were in school and parents were at work. An old, retired couple lived three doors down, but they rarely ventured outside of their split-level. He walked to-and-from the mailbox, begging for an interruption. One of those long, arbitrary conversations with a blabbering neighbor he used to dread and avoid. Any distraction was welcome.

He didn't get one.

The contents of the mail were like that of any other day, an impressive collection of credit card applications and coupons he'd never use surrounding one worthwhile piece of mail. Today, that one piece was a Hallmark card in a blue envelope.

There was no return address, and only "MARK" was written on the front of the envelope. No address or stamp or anything else. He studied it momentarily, thinking through the possibilities. A belated birthday wish from Brad? A long overdue thank you note from his neighbor? An invitation to the next civic association meeting?

He ripped it open and found a large white cross in the center of the card. In the upper-right corner was a handwritten date: exactly two weeks into the future. Large, printed gold-colored cursive writing lined the top, sparkling with glitter, uttering tragic words:

"Our Deepest Sympathies."

Beneath the cross was a King James Bible verse, 1 Thessalonians 4:13-14. It mentioned grieving and Jesus and falling asleep, but he didn't fully read it. Bemused and terrified, he quickly flipped the card open and read Hallmark's note.

Our Deepest Condolences On The Loss of Your Daughter
We're Praying for You

His heart thumped as though it were a drum being played by a six-year-old. Erratic, hard, and painful. Paralysis overcame his legs as his rapidly-shaking right hand dropped the card and his left covered his mouth. He felt warm and dizzy all over. Katherine flashed into his mind.

It was the handwritten sentence beneath the print that caused his knees to buckle.

You've got two weeks, Dad.

19

Three hours and 170 miles later, they were almost there.

He thought exclusively of the Hallmark card, pressing his foot even harder onto the accelerator.

"Why did we rent a car, Daddy?" Katherine asked.

"I don't want to put too many miles on our car."

"And why do I get to miss afternoon class? I never get to miss school for *anything*."

"It's a special trip to Aunt Caroline's, honey. Every once in a while it's okay to miss school. This is just one of those times."

The tension between him and Katherine was even more apparent than at last Saturday's breakfast. She knew he was lying and didn't try to hide it. She rolled her eyes and flung back her long, blonde hair. At her age, she certainly wouldn't complain about missing school, but he could tell Katherine knew her dad was lying.

Right to her face. But there's no other way. Is there?

"Does this have to do with Mommy or Uncle Brad?" she asked after a few moments of silence.

"What? No, honey. What gave you that idea?"

"Nothing, Daddy. Forget it."

The consequence of dishonesty was unrelenting. Always a straight shooter with his daughter, Katherine never had reason to doubt or question him. And her maturity and understanding made him feel like he never had to hide the truth either. But now, all bets were off.

* * *

Caroline watched Katherine sprint up the steep, muddy grass hill to embrace her. Katherine, with her bright smile, that precious piece of pure innocence and her brother's greatest joy, was on center display.

"How are you, Mark?" she asked while being mauled by a bear hug.

"I'm good. You?"

She flashed a look of disapproval right back at him. He wasn't getting off that easy.

"Is that my cookie monster? Will!" She could tell Mark said with as much energy as a man could fake, diverting her stare.

Her blond-haired, blue-eyed six-year-old boy hid behind her leg. Bashful to no end, he nibbled on his fingers until finally a smile appeared when Katherine said hello. The kids had always gotten along, something for which both she and Mark were immensely grateful. It didn't take long for them to run off together to inspect Will's newly built log-cabin fort.

Time for some answers, she thought.

She had known right away something was wrong. Mark's voice on the phone was unnatural and forced. It sounded from the start like he was hiding something. His body language didn't contradict.

"Nice car," she said, pointing to the Jeep Grand Cherokee. She hated SUVs and wasn't shy about her aversion. On their last family vacation, Mark had deliberately rented one just to piss her off.

"Thanks. I thought you'd like it."

"Sure you did. Did you catch traffic coming up?"

"Nah. Piece of cake."

Platteville was a tiny town in southern Wisconsin, no more than five square miles and just over 10,000 residents. Home to the University of Wisconsin-Platteville Pioneers, it was a reformed mining town from the 1800s that proudly celebrated its agricultural roots with events such as the Dairy Days Festival and "A Day On The Farm" family day held at the university. In an area known as the Driftless Region, rolling hills lined the roads and Highways 80 and 81 ran through, serving as the main arteries into and out of town. Small-town living at its best, there was plenty of space for those who chose to brave the fierce winters and vast wilderness.

Their family of four had moved there five years ago at Richard's request for country living, just before he died. He loved the privacy and seclusion of country living, and wanted Will to grow up in it. Despite her initial doubts, it grew on her pretty quickly, and now she couldn't imagine living any other way. Peaceful sunrises and sunsets every day, free of the traffic congestion that plagued Chicago's streets.

She looked directly into her brother's eyes without flinching. She knew Mark got the message that as his sibling who'd been through just as much as he had, including losing her spouse, she was done getting the runaround from him.

"What's going on, Mark? And don't lie to me."

* * *

Caroline was a bright lady.

You don't own a thriving graphic design business for twelve years without something working upstairs. She was always ahead of the curve, smarter than him in a lot of ways. But noticing that something was wrong wasn't rocket science.

"Nothing," he tried on for size.

She brushed her long, chestnut hair out of her eyes. Blue jeans and a dark-green Packers sweatshirt complemented muddy brown boots, evidencing recent outdoor work. He could see her studying his tentativeness and poor cover-up expressionisms.

"Don't say 'nothing,' *Marcus*. If you don't want me to know, I can live with that. *For now*. But don't you dare lie to me again."

"Okay. I don't want you to know."

She was noticeably disappointed and remained silent, clearly not expecting him to take the Fifth but confronted with her promise to accept it.

Sadly, he wanted to tell her everything. Caroline had a way, partly because of her maternal role in his life, of making him feel better. She was upfront and painfully candid, yet she possessed a delicate balance of warmth and compassion. Underneath her rough, get-stuff-done exterior, there was empathy and there was tact. Caroline could size a situation, and person, up in seconds and then deliver bad news precisely in the way it needed to be delivered.

He didn't want to get her involved, but after the Hallmark note realized he had no choice. He had no place else to go, no one else to turn to. When he considered that he was putting his sister and her son in danger, reality hit: they already *were* in danger. These people, and the FBI, already knew about them. There was nothing he could do about that. At least this way he could keep the attention on him for a while instead of Caroline and the kids, though deep down he knew she'd need to execute the contingency plan regardless.

"Fine."

"Thank you, Caroline. How long can you keep Katherine?"

"As long as you need me to. But after a while, Marcus, I'll need to know why I'm watching her."

He was off the hook for now but answers were expected soon.

"Thanks."

Caroline waved her arm, motioning him to accompany her to the backyard to marvel at Will's fort. He stayed back, waiting for her to turn around. After she did, she inched closer.

"There's something else," he whispered. "Here," he said, handing her one of the untraceable, prepaid cell phones.

"I'm on speed dial one. Don't dial any other numbers, and don't use any other phone to contact me. And take this too," he said while dropping a healthy portion of the $30,000 from his pocket into her hands.

Caroline was starting to object when he cut her off with a raised finger. Time was wasting. She would have to understand.

"I know this doesn't make sense. I'm not telling you everything, and that kills me. But I need you to trust me right now, and to do what I ask. The money is for emergencies, for the contingency plan. Hotels, food, whatever. I don't know. You may not need it, but I want you to have it. I'll call you later on this phone. Please, don't ask questions."

20

"The General," his honorary title, was tribute to the early pioneers of the Ku Klux Klan, particularly General Nathan Bedford Forrest, the group's first Grand Wizard. A courageous man with incredible vision and relentless drive, Forrest's leadership took the organization to new heights. He'd been to Forrest's grave in Memphis and his monument in Georgia several times. People still celebrated his work and respected his results.

Thus, it was indeed an honorary title. But he had a job to do and there wasn't any room for vanity.

His office was plain, much plainer than Edward's. No pictures, no expensive furniture. Half the size and none of the frills. On his desk sat a stack of white paper, an old-fashioned fountain pen, and a small candle lantern. He didn't like computers and wouldn't have one. There was no radio or television. He had a cell phone but only out of necessity, and he used it very sparingly.

His extracurriculars were just as mundane. A voracious reader, he perused the Constitution from cover to cover three times a year and knew it better than any lawyer or judge. He devoured history books and read four newspapers every day to stay up on current events. He knew more about the Tanakh, Koran, and Bible than most of the rabbis, Imams and pastors in the United States. He never drank and he didn't use tobacco. Drugs couldn't be further from his house or office. Pornographic material was nowhere to be found. His mind remained clear. No distractions could interfere with his work.

When his cell phone began to ring, he reluctantly answered.

"Yes," he said, adjusting his position in the stiff wooden chair.

The luxury of comfort served only to distract.

"General, I have the information you requested," the voice replied. His FBI contact moved more quickly than he'd expected. He grabbed the fountain pen and a fresh sheet of paper.

"I'm listening."

He took meticulous notes and wrote down every single word. The information was powerful but not unexpected.

"You're absolutely certain about this?"

"One hundred percent."

"Well done. I'll be in touch."

He ended the call and folded his hands, elbows resting on the desk. Then he reviewed the notes twice more. The information certainly posed a significant risk that needed to be remedied. He sipped his water while dialing the number.

It took less than two rings.

"Yes, General?"

"It's time to execute the plan."

"Yes sir. When would you prefer?"

It was getting late, but there was still enough time. This was a professional and would be able to accommodate.

"My preference would be as soon as possible, but I don't want to rush you. If a day to make final preparations would help, take it."

"That won't be necessary."

"So you can handle this tonight?"

"Yes sir."

"Excellent. This problem needs to be removed."

"Consider it done."

21

Brad Tarnow, who knew from Mark the world was watching him, drove slowly towards Dunkin Donuts, a half-mile trek.

He carefully obeyed the speed limit and used his turn signal when appropriate, both hands on the wheel the whole time. A light drizzle coming down, the car's lights were on, and the wipers cleared the windshield every few seconds. The right one had a broken rubber strip, causing its metal arm blade to make a scraping sound across he glass.

He didn't care. There were far bigger fish to fry.

At the one yellow traffic light he encountered, Brad jerked the black Hyundai Sonata to an uncharacteristic halt. He avoided lane changes and tailgating to blend in with other drivers. He hoped it was all an unnecessary precaution.

But he'd been told not to count on it.

Once parked, he was careful to keep his head down and walk at an average pace, as instructed. He wore a Cubs hat, blue jeans and a light, zipped up red jacket. It wasn't cold outside, but the late spring chill combined with the light rain made him happy to have the North Face.

Dunkin' Donuts was on almost every corner in the Chicago area, and each branch is pretty similar upon entering: sticky tile floors, poor lighting, often Indian-operated, and full of excellent aromas. He ordered a dozen double-chocolate doughnuts and paid with cash.

Then he walked around the corner, towards the unisex bathroom located on the far end of a short hallway, passing a drinking fountain and small mop bucket that had seen much better days. Again, he told himself not to walk too fast.

He entered the bathroom, locked the door, and got to work.

* * *

First he stuffed the Cubs hat and jacket into the trashcan next to the sink. Next came the jeans, which when removed exposed a pair of black sweatpants underneath. Then he unbuttoned the long-sleeved IZOD dress shirt and withdrew a blond wig. After placing it snugly on his head and re-buttoning the shirt, he checked the rusted mirror above the permanently stained manila sink.

Given his supplies, he looked as different as he could. Cognizant of the time he'd been in there, he exited the bathroom quickly. But instead of turning left to go back to his fresh doughnuts, he took a hard right towards the EMPLOYEES ONLY sign. The metal door was unlocked, just as he'd been told it would be.

Inside the small rooms there were cleaning supplies, cardboard boxes, crates of raw ingredients, packaging materials, and dirt. A lot of dirt. Cobwebs hung freely and water dripped from the ceiling, causing a recurring plip-plip sound. The lighting was much worse than in the front-end of the store and flickered as if in a horror film. The odor was pungent, a far cry from the trademark doughnut scent people associated with the franchise.

But there was also a rear service door.

It too was unlocked, also as he was told it would be. He pushed through it and outside into the small employee parking lot with gusto. Immediately he saw the white Dodge Ram Dakota pickup truck, parked in between two cars that needed a scrubbing as bad as the service room. The drizzle had grown to a gentle rain.

He didn't run, but he felt the urge, his nervousness beseeching him to sprint to the truck and peel out as fast as possible. The door was open and the key was precisely where he was told it'd be: under the passenger side floor mat.

He turned left out of the parking lot and headed north, away from the main entrance, again minding his speed. Checking the rear-view mirror every few seconds, he was certain that any second he'd see cars speeding up from behind to catch him.

22

Saturday night at precisely 9:07, Mark's cell phone began to ring.

He'd drifted off in his La-Z-Boy, exhausted from fruitless thinking. The TV still rambled on in the background, meant to drown out any mumblings of intelligence the surveillance bugs might pick up. That turned out to be unnecessary, he hadn't said anything intelligent the entire evening. Stuttering over to the table while adjusting his green golf shirt around the shoulders, he noticed it was his original cell phone, not the one Sam had given him. Caller ID said "PRIVATE."

What good was caller ID if the callers he cared about remained anonymous?

"This is Mark," he said.

"Mark. Tom. How you been?"

The residual drowsiness disappeared immediately. He stared at Katherine's picture, resting on the entertainment center. Their good-bye at Caroline's was the toughest he'd ever given. And the notion of saying goodbye to her the way he did to Mary Ann was well beyond his tolerance for horror.

"Mark? Are you still there?"

"Yes."

"Good, thought I lost you," Tom replied, chuckling.

This is funny to him. It's a game.

"What do you want?"

"I wanted to make sure you got the card."

Fully aware that Tom was trying to get a rise out of him, he recalled Sam's "three pillars" of advice:

> *Composure*: don't fight a battle you know you can't win or let emotions give away your edge.

Illusion: make them think they're in control. Don't tell more than they ask and give short answers; reveal nothing.

Clarity: don't let fear or anger make you lose sight of your goal. Most people will make mistakes. You've got to be focused to notice.

Using those three pillars makes the difference between a happy ending and a sad one, Sam had told him.

"Yes, I got your card."

"Good. I'd hate for you to need it, but that's in your hands."

Don't say anything. There's nothing to say.

"A bit quiet tonight, eh? Ah, no matter. Listen, Mark, we've decided two weeks is a bit too long. We're getting edgy, so let's say one week from today. We'll call you with the specifics, but plan on next Saturday."

"That's not enough time!" he cried. It didn't take long for him to abandon Sam's first pillar of advice, he thought to himself.

A whole week...*gone*. Between Mitchell and the FBI and Tom and Edward, he needed the extra planning time.

"Sure it is," Tom replied.

Don't fight a battle you know you can't win.

He breathed heavily into the speaker, giving Tom an impression of enhanced panic. It wasn't that difficult...

"Okay."

"One other thing: if I were you, I'd keep this situation to yourself from now on. Bad things happen when people don't follow the rules. The first time around, we were pretty forgiving. We left your family alone. We let Fisher pay the price for your mistakes. But next time...I don't know, man."

Keep it together. Don't let emotion control you.

Tom had just confirmed they knew he spoke to Sam, yet he was still alive. That meant two things: they did see value in him, and Ron Mitchell's theory might be correct. Trying to figure out what else they knew would be daunting, but there was a bigger battle to fight. It seemed they did *not* know he was already aware of Sam's death. If they found that out, they'd connect him to the FBI. He had to support Tom's ignorance.

Immediately.

"You...you killed Sam?" he said as genuinely and heartfelt as he could, certain that Tom would see right through it.

"Remember what's at stake before you open your mouth again. We can get to anyone, Mark. Katherine, Caroline, Will, whoever. Hell, Daniel Tiger could be ours if we wanted. Don't test us again."

He stood there for a few moments on the empty line. Partly for the cameras and whoever might be watching, but mostly because he was terrified.

Mitchell was right. He was being recruited.

And now he only had seven days.

* * *

Eleven-forty on Saturday night, 20 minutes before The General's deadline.

Dan Kevil sat quietly alone in the van, watching the monitor and with a full mouth of stale beef jerky. This was the best part: anticipating the unfolding of a great plan. He'd been doing the job for a long time, but this part would never get old.

Light rain danced off the windshield and gusts of wind shook the black van. The street alley was narrow and grimy, and blue light police cameras at the adjacent intersections indicated this wasn't the safest part of town. Alone and unworried, it was the perfect setting.

The General had hinted some time ago that this mission might come. Thus, he didn't flinch when he heard the target's name. It was his job not to flinch. Of course, in this case the target's occupation made the job a bit more challenging, so he took extra precaution. Still disappointed by his underestimation of Sam Fisher, he insisted to himself that this operation go perfectly.

No more glitches, no more mistakes.

This time, unlike with Fisher, extracting information wasn't requested. While that made the mission less difficult, the target's role more than made up for the lost challenge. Remove the problem, The General had said.

"*Bingo*," he said out loud when he saw it.

The screen revealed the target walking into the office, right on cue. The target hung his umbrella on the coat hanger, dropped his bag on the floor and tossed some folders on the desk. Then he moseyed across the room to the ornate silver tray atop the small, two-person table.

As he did every night, the target pulled a freshly cleaned, genuine-cased, hand-cut glass down from the shelf and poured the Russell's Reserve Single Barrel bourbon halfway up the $100 tumbler. Then he collapsed into the leather chair against the wall and leaned his head back, eyes closed.

Finally, he put the glass to his mouth and sipped its contents. He took one drink, then another, then another. He did it every night, and there was no reason not to tonight. Each time he finished a sip, he rested the glass on the arm of the chair before taking another, soaking in the flavor. But the time between drinks got less and less, and before long he might as well not even put the glass down.

After the target finished his first of what would be three rich drinks, he put his hand to his throat, further loosening the collar. At first it was a subtle motion, but seconds later he grasped it again, with more force.

Here it comes, Kevil thought to himself, tightly gripping the monitor with anticipation.

The target started to panic, gripping his neck tighter and stirring from the seat. Breathing became noticeably difficult. He dropped the $100 glass and it shattered on the glossy hardwood floor. One hand holding his throat and the other flapping in the air, he rose from the chair, gasping for oxygen. His mouth opened and closed frantically, the grip on his throat growing stronger.

After several sways and losses of balance in either direction, the target finally collapsed to the floor with a loud thud. The struggle was over. Movement, and life, had ceased. The problem removed, The General would be pleased.

Edward Doran's corpse lay motionless on the floor. One of his hands was still wrapped around his throat, the other lay outstretched towards the desk, towards Mark Richter's FBI file.

23

Tuesday. Five days away from Tom's deadline.

As Mark exited the 500-car parking garage and took one of the four elevators up to the sixth floor, Edward Doran's offer looked better and better. For Katherine's sake, do the job take the cash, and bolt from Chicago and its cold winters to live the rest of his life on room service with another name in a foreign country.

Remember why you're here.

Lafferty & Sons leased the fifth and six floors of a nine-story office building on West Higgins Road on the outskirts of Chicago. Though technically within city limits, most people associated it with the nearby suburb of Rosemont. In fact it was so close to the city that Rosemont was home to a minor league baseball team, fashion outlet mall and just about any entertainment or high-end restaurant there was, despite having a population of fewer than 4,000 people. It was a coveted location, close to Interstates 90 and 294, O'Hare Airport, and a lot of action. The building itself was very clean, fitted with the latest technology and a fresh, modern look.

The ground floor housed a large, ornate lobby with a waterfall fountain and pristine three-story windows. On south end of the building was a cafeteria and convenience shop called "Necessities" that charged fifteen bucks for a small salad and $3.50 for a candy bar. Before that was a barber shop that started at $40 and a Giordano's Pizza joint.

The high costs and constant buzz of people running to their destinations reminded Mark of the airport. Folks were always in a hurry, and vendors were always willing to rip them off because there were no other options.

"Hi, Jean," he said as he exited the elevator and walked through the keycard-locked, heavy glass double doors.

"Good morning, Mark" she replied, offering a bright smile. On a typical day, he'd smile pleasantly in return, then silently count the steps from her desk to his cubicle, adjusting the length of a few of them to ensure it ended on the same number.

Today, however, just "Hi, Jean" sapped his emotional reserves. He couldn't return the pleasant grin or even care about the step count. He saw Jean raise her eyebrows slightly before he turned away with hunched shoulders and a sense that if the greeting was hard, this was going to be a very long day.

When he got to his cube, he realized how hard it would *really* be.

He, like his coworkers, spent eight or nine hours every day for the past two years at this exact location. Telecommuting didn't work in this business and management had been clear butts were expected in seats five day per week. However, even being there that often, when you're looking for something specific, something out of the ordinary, you see things you otherwise completely miss. You find out how blind you really are.

Each door leading to an office, conference room or hallway was protected by the keycard that tracked every entrance and recorded it in a log. They locked automatically and couldn't be forced open with the Jaws of Life. And if they were propped open, the silent security alarm would be triggered after 30 seconds.

Further observation led to further disappointment. Not only were the windows permanently closed as a safety measure, but beneath them was nothing but six stories, *84 feet*, of air. Any attempt to jump was suicide. There were no ladders, outdoor fire escapes, railings, pipes or bars to grab. Not that he saw himself using any of those things to get to the ground level, but it revealed even more challenges the building's footprint presented.

Windows encompassed the entire floor outside central cubicles and the interior offices. Those offices had only one door each and no windows or ceiling tiles. There were no other entrances or exits, which was why he turned down an office when they moved. They were dungeons. Or, in this case, traps.

The bright fluorescent lights in both the hallways and offices were motion-controlled and couldn't be turned off manually, rendering a sneak entrance impossible. Every cube had the same dimensions, and the largest office was, at best, 20 square feet or so bigger than the smallest. It was mundane and uniform, just like an accounting office should be.

Thus, getting to the files on a normal day was impossible. So he looked into the extremes.

In the event of a fire, SOP called for employees to evacuate the building via the east and west staircases to get to the ground level. Then they were to rendezvous at the large flowerbed inside a circular drive that led to River Road, east of the parking garage.

But in reality, people would go wherever they could to get out of the building. They might exit via the north door. Or run west to leave through the garage. There was no way to know what people would do or where they would go, and that didn't bode well for a plan of any kind.

For a tornado, it was even worse. Everyone was supposed to climb into the stairwell or one of the few windowless offices. But there wasn't enough space to accommodate all the people in the building, so there'd be spillover into several floors. And there was no reason to suspect the sixth wouldn't be one of them.

"Richter, let's go," interrupted his thinking. He looked up to see Fred, fellow CPA and coworker, standing over his desk.

"Huh?"

"It's Jason's birthday. We're singing in the conference room."

Another birthday celebration, another song, another cake. Before 4:07 last Friday, excessive celebration was his favorite fringe benefit of working at Lafferty & Sons. Now it just annoyed him.

"Be right there," he replied.

He also had to prepare to face Jason and his compassion. He'd not yet returned Jason's call from the weekend, checking to make sure he was okay after he cancelled the girls' sleepover on Friday night. It was a sincere message from a sincere man, but Mark grew more annoyed by Jason's thoughtfulness and southern charm as the week wore on.

Jason had said he knew something was wrong, but he failed to see that didn't mean he was entitled to know what it was. Mark was thrilled Jason and Kristina were a part of his and Katherine's lives, but he was in no mood for the man right now. All he wanted to do was stare this daunting, seemingly impossible challenge in the face and find a solution.

But cake time interfered.

***

"No, no, *no*! Don't tell me you *think*. Tell me you *know* or don't tell me!" FBI Special Agent Ron Mitchell was quite aware of his runaway capricious temper, often set off by the tiniest of things, but he was in no mood to address it now. And this junior investigator's total lack of progress didn't help.

"I'm sorry, sir," Scott Flowers answered. "It's just we can't know for sure until we find the body." Flowers swayed back and forth as it almost losing his balance, wide-eyed and breathing deep.

"Then find the body!"

"Sir, with all respect, you know that's not very likely."

"Does that mean you shouldn't try?"

"No sir. Of course not."

"Then why are you here instead of outside with a shovel?"

"Sir, we haven't placed him for almost three days. We tracked him on late Saturday afternoon, but since then he's been a ghost. Not a single spotting with a team of men doing nothing but looking for him. We've visited his last known location three times, combed over all of his known hideouts, checked with the local contacts and establishments, and tailed every confirmed correspondent. And we still haven't found anything. Not one whiff in the past three days. We've never gone more than 24 hours without a spotting, not once in the past five years. He either made us, or he's dead."

Mitchell didn't like either of those options. He loosened his tie and jettisoned out of his seat. This was not the conversation he, or his temper, needed to be having.

"Scott, it's 11:30 on Tuesday morning. We're way too close for this to happen *now*."

"I understand..."

"This could lose us Richter, and we can't lose Richter."

"Sir, I don't know what you want me do."

"You've looked everywhere, and I mean *everywhere,* the man could be? You've listened to every audiotape we've got and traced it back to the source? You've followed every bogus lead, every random intelligence report? You've turned over every single rock this man could possibly be hiding under as we speak?"

"We've—"

"Because if you haven't, if you've so much as ignored some minor childhood acquaintance of his who might still be in contact with him, get the hell out of my office and go do that. And once you've done it, go do it again. And then again. And then *again*! Don't you dare come back to me with anything other than a dead body or his *precise* location. Am I clear?"

"Yes, sir."

Scott Flowers left the room without another word, his tail not as far between his legs as Mitchell had expected. Flowers certainly knew of his legendary temper and had certainly anticipated how deeply disappointing this news would be, and didn't push back on his orders. Besides, everyone knew once he made a decision, there was no changing his mind. Stubbornness and his temper would be his legacy.

But at least he'd have a legacy.

He shook his head, violently cursing in a loud ramble, pacing the empty room. It was a lost cause and he knew it. The body wasn't turning up. Period. They could look until they were blue in the face. They could start digging in Chicago and make it to an ocean and back again with multiple search teams and a nationwide APB and still wouldn't find the body.

Edward Doran was gone.

Fifteen minutes and two cigarettes in the non-smoking building office later, he'd cooled down and confirmed Scott Flowers was right. That didn't mean he was going to take his foot off the gas, no chance in hell of that. But it did mean he had to act on that assumption.

He couldn't lose Richter now.

After the first drag of his third Marlboro, he grabbed one of the three cell phones on his desk and dialed a number committed to memory.

"It's Mitchell. Listen, I need a favor. There's this guy, his name is Brad Tarnow..."

24

Mark's day didn't get better.

Every thought he had resulted in a dead end, and somewhere around ten o'clock he stopped trying to find the mirage loophole. Instead, he submitted to the fact that the building wasn't designed for an average accountant to easily access confidential client files when he wasn't supposed to.

Imagine that.

He also felt guilty throughout the entire morning, working on one client's file while planning to purloin others, watching his coworkers innocuously do their jobs as he sought a way to effectively break the law. He'd never so much as bent the rules before. And now he was taking a sledgehammer to them. But even worse was the notion that they could be blamed and imprisoned for it.

For what reason? To save his daughter's life? Noble enough, he rationalized. Any father would understand that decision. But to help secretly fund a terrorist organization and make three million dollars in the process? Not so noble. Would it be better to take the files but not the money? He told himself no, but...

Frustrated, he snuck out for an early lunch just before eleven, avoiding any possibility of company. He couldn't face his coworkers, and he needed to stay focused. He hopped in the rental and drove a mile east to the Outback Steakhouse, throwing the car in park and grabbing another prepaid cell phone. As if the challenge of accessing Lafferty & Sons offices wasn't hard enough, his phone call to Brad felt overwhelming:

"I'm screwed, man," he whispered. "Actually getting the files will probably be the hardest part, and I haven't even gotten there in my head."

"So get there now," his best friend answered.

"OK, say I somehow find a way to get in the office. It's ridiculous how safeguarded the files are. Every client's dossier is in a private filing cabinet, accessible to only two people: the CPA assigned to it and Larry, the Principal."

"Principal?"

"The boss. My point is, accountants are only supposed to remove a file when they're physically working on it. Otherwise it stays under lock and key at all times to keep it safe and private. We all follow that rule implicitly."

"Look at it this way, you *always* know where the files are. That's a good thing."

He hadn't thought of that, and Brad had a point. But the task still felt insurmountable.

"Okay, buddy," Brad continued. "I know you think to talk, but let's try it my way and talk this out. Start with Larry's key."

He breathed in deeply, resetting. "All right, getting Larry's master key is pretty much impossible. He keeps it in a safe that has its own key and a private combination."

"In his office?"

"Yeah," he replied, checking the rear view mirror yet again.

"Do you know the combination?"

"I don't even know where he keeps the key."

"What about just asking Larry for it? Pretend you lost yours and need to get in. Isn't that what master keys are for?"

"If I did that, I'd call way too much attention to myself. I'd have a huge sign on my back if people found out anything was missing. Plus, I'd have to have a pretty convincing story as to how I lost it."

"Give me a break, dude. Even accountants forget stuff ever now and then. Tell him you left yours at home."

"Larry would only get me files I personally work on. He wouldn't just hand me the key to take whatever I want."

"So you have to break into Larry's office and *then* crack a safe? What's in these things, the truth about JFK?"

"Don't forget it's a locked office, and that I'd have to do all of this and take the files without Larry noticing. Not going to happen, man."

"What about the other accountants' keys? The ones who do work these files you need."

"Five companies, five accountants, five keys. I'd have to steal all of them without anyone finding out. And if one person realizes his key is gone, he's supposed to report it to Larry. When he does..."

"The others will check theirs," Brad finished the sentence.

"Standard protocol. And it's not like these guys leave their keys laying around, either. They all keep a pretty tight watch."

He tried not to think about the fact that he knew all five of those "other accountants." And that they knew him. And trusted him.

"Take a breath, buddy. There's a way to do this. We just have to find it."

Brad didn't broadcast tremendous confidence, but Mark certainly appreciated the calm demeanor and quiet responses, both of which usually came from him as opposed to Brad.

"The bottom line," he continued, "is that the whole point of the system is to keep anyone from gaining access to a file other than the person who actually needs it."

Imagine that.

He ended the call and drove back to the office at one o'clock, an over two-hour break. Most employees were still at lunch, and he went straight to his desk. There, he saw a white envelope sitting on his chair. His name was written on the front in blue ink, and inside was a piece of folded notebook paper with a brief message:

Hancock Building, 5:30 tonight
Don't talk to anyone
RM

25

It was a small, one-story house, not more than 1,100 square feet. There was a tiny yard, mostly covered in mud and weeds. What little grass did exist hadn't been green for some time. Adorned with filthy sky-blue siding and once-brown sun-faded shutters, it was decades behind the times and in desperate need of updating. The roof peeled away like dry skin after a bad sunburn. Rust covered the metal window frames.

The driveway was very long and narrow, covered with cracks and weeds, and led to an unattached two-car garage. Its contents included, among many other things, an old lawn mower engine, a variety of archaic gardening tools crusted in mud, three spare car tires, and an oversized footlocker.

If he didn't know any better, he'd think a family of eight crammed into the small home and simply chose to ignore the mess around them, creating more garbage than they threw out. There were plenty of examples like that in this neighborhood, totally overrun by illegal immigrants or Mexicans or Indians.

But in fact, the house belonged to one man: a bachelor, a former prisoner. His name was Brad Tarnow, and he was Mark Richter's best friend from childhood. He'd purchased the foreclosed home only seven months ago and, hard as it was to believe, had greatly improved its aesthetics and cleanliness in that time. In another ten years, it might even be inhabitable by most people's standards.

Twenty feet from the garage were three white cinder-block steps that led to the back door entrance of the tiny home.

It was there that over 20 police officers focused their attention.

Hidden in the trees next to the garage, standing behind neighbors' houses, waiting in parked cars on adjacent side streets, and looking through binoculars several houses down the block, the policemen waited for him, the captain, to give the signal.

The three o'clock sun and dormant air made the long-sleeved black shirts and full body armor feel like a toaster oven. He'd worn the uniform for many years and could relate to the sweaty heads and wet arms they all had. He personally knew the feeling of the machine gun each man carried growing heavier by the minute, and how their shirts were sticking to their backs like glue while they waited for the go ahead.

But today, he assessed the scene in a T-shirt and jeans from across the house in a parked Honda Civic, pretending to read a newspaper. Everything in place, he picked up the communicator and said only one two-letter word, a short but powerful phrase.

"Go."

On command, they stormed the house from every angle in perfect sequence. The two point teams rushed through the back door and main entrance; the third penetrated the garage service door. The remaining officers encompassed the perimeter of the property while the point men moved through it quickly, their guns in front, armed for use.

Communicating to each other when a space was clear, they dissected the house room by room until the point men met in the middle. Their heads and guns swiveled swiftly to ensure they saw everything but didn't over-focus on anything.

He waited outside, holding his radio, refraining from interruption. This was the toughest part about being Captain. He wanted to be in there, covering one of the rooms. He could smell the adventure but not taste it.

Minutes later, his second-in-command radioed, pulling him from the brief moment of reflection he always had during a raid.

"Captain?"

"Go ahead Lieutenant."

"The suspect is not here, sir."

"You're sure?"

"Yes sir. We've combed the place. He's not here."

He paused to assess the situation. He'd been told ahead of time this may happen. But he'd also been told it was very, very probable that Mr. Tarnow would be home at this exact time. Bad intel for the field was hardly uncommon these days, but that didn't mean he wasn't disappointed, either. But what should he have expected? The operation was unplanned from the start, pulled together haphazardly because he owed an old friend a favor.

He didn't have enough time to plan it right. They needed to track and tail Tarnow, measure his patterns, confirm his presence, etc. Calling the operation three hours beforehand on a whim was *not* the way to do it. And he'd told Ron Mitchell just that, but Mitchell pressed and said they needed to act fast.

This is what happens when you press. This is what happens when you cut corners. And that's exactly what he'd tell Mitchell when he called him to relay the bad news.

* * *

The John Hancock Center was on Michigan Avenue, a few blocks north of Northwestern Memorial Hospital, a half-mile west of Lake Michigan. Very few Chicagoans so much as acknowledge its relatively new official name, 875 N. Michigan, still simply referring to it as The Hancock. Regardless of what you call it, it's a monster: 100 stories and 1,500 feet tall with 360-degree views that span four states. Yet it was still only the fifth largest building in Chicago, behind Aon Center, St. Regis, Trump International and of course the Sears Tower, which will never be "Willis" to the locals, despite that change taking place back in 2009.

Tourists preferred the allure and popularity of the Sears Tower rooftop and its full glass windows, featured prominently in *Ferris Bueller's Day Off*. Chicagoans knew The Hancock was the place to go for a spectacular view, preferably from the 95th floor "Signature Room" bar for years, before it unexpectedly closed. The 95th floor had been somewhat of a secret, and most locals preferred to keep it that way. Let out-of-towners pay the cash for the overcrowded Sears

Tower. They had The Hancock's 95th. But now that was sadly gone too.

At a little after five o'clock on a workday, streets were in gridlock. Chicago Avenue was bumper-to-bumper, horns honking incessantly. Lake Shore Drive traffic crawled to a stop. Pedestrians waited impatiently at all intersections for the white WALK sign. Yet the cab ride down Michigan Avenue to Chestnut Street, past The Drake and Palmolive Building, seemed to go way too fast. For the first time in his life, Mark was reluctant for it to end.

When he reached the final amphitheater-style step, he saw Ron Mitchell sitting at a two-person circular table, reading the SPORTS section of *The Chicago Tribune*. Mitchell wore a brown leather jacket, white polo shirt and tan dress pants. He saw Mark and motioned for him to take a seat.

* * *

"Did you know The Hancock has a swimming pool on the 44th floor, the highest indoor swimming pool in the nation?" Mitchell began, plopping the SPORTS section on the table while finishing a Sprecher Root Beer.

In the shadow of The Hancock, Mark shivered with chills. The table was uncomfortable, made of concrete, permanently affixed to the ground. But he knew it had little to do with his discomfort.

What really made him uneasy was that he sensed he needed to hear what Mitchell had to say more than Mitchell needed to tell him.

"It's amazing, absolutely amazing. People live up there too," Mitchell said, pointing upwards. "Used to be the tallest condos in the world, but that's Central Park Tower now in New York City."

He refrained from a smart-ass comment about giving history lessons. Last time he pissed Mitchell off, he saw a side of the man he didn't want to see. His temper went from zero to 60 in less than a second and he didn't want it to emerge.

Not yet, anyway.

"Did you give any more thought to my offer?" Mitchell asked.

"I'm considering it."

"Well, consider faster. My patience is running thin and your time is running out."

"If I'm not fast enough for you, feel free to leave me alone for the rest of my natural life."

Mitchell's ephemeral smile vanished into stoicism.

"You don't have any other play here, Mark. What? Are you going to join the terrorists? Do what they want so they can bomb another hospital, or a shelter, or an abortion clinic? You're not that kind of person. You know what's right. I don't see a choice."

Mark stared pointedly at Mitchell's rugged face.

"You don't know a anything about what kind of person I am. You don't know everything from your precious files. If you did, you'd know I value my daughter's life a lot more than your missions. They threatened my daughter, Mitchell. *My daughter!*"

"We can protect her. We can protect you."

"How? By sticking us in a witness protection program? Yeah, that sounds great. We could live in fear for the rest of our lives. I could pretend I'm in some mob movie, waiting for a car bomb to explode. Maybe I'll get to sleep with the fishes, like Luca Brasi. We could change our names and cut off all communication with what's left of our family. Great idea, Ron. I'm sure glad the FBI has a plan."

"Once we get the PEACHES' leader, you won't have to do any of that. We can protect you."

"There's the whole 'protection' thing again. You're asking me to take all the risks here. You've been following Edward Doran for what...four, five years? And you *still* haven't gotten him? You claim the PEACHES are responsible for all these terrible acts, yet you can't arrest anyone. Who's to say anything I do will give you what you need to finally make your move. Protect me? Protect my *daughter*? You people couldn't protect a monkey in a zoo."

"Now you listen to me you insolent little *prick*," Mitchell shouted, not nearly as concerned with the people passing them on their way out of The Hancock as he was. "Like I told you before, if you think you can just run away, you're going down with the rest of them. It might take a little while, a year, a few years, maybe...but we're going to get them. And when we do, the first one I'm coming after is you. You understand me? *You don't have any other play here."*

Mitchell's gritting teeth and increased volume exposed the agent's tells tenfold. Even the FBI Agent's breathing grew heavier and his pointy eyes projected pure rage.

There's that temper again. Proof last time wasn't a fluke. Keep it up, my friend. I'm going to need it.

He knew projecting the right image was important, remembering what Sam had told him: surprised, and with obvious false confidence, as if trying to stand his ground but clearly not knowing how. He cleared his throat and raised his own voice.

"I'd rather outlive my daughter from jail than help you and watch her die."

"She'll be protected!"

"I won't do it, Mitchell, not unless I'm sure she'll be okay. I don't care what you say or what leverage you claim to have. You can't stop a terrorist who's willing to die from killing people, and you can't stop a father who would do the same to protect his daughter. No matter how much you plan or how many files you read, you'll never be able to do either."

Mitchell sighed, shaking his head. "Mark, the situation has gotten a lot more complicated."

"You bet it has. You're assuming you have all the answers, and you don't. There's a lot more to this than me just handing over the proverbial smoking gun and disappearing into a witness protection program."

"*Listen*, we know a lot more than you think. We know about the five companies Doran asked you about. InfoHelp, LPK and the rest of them. We know you've got your daughter staying in Wisconsin with your sister and nephew. We know you told Brad Tarnow to get out of Dodge."

He'd figured they'd go after Brad to get to him. Sam had told him that cops were predictable, and it felt good to see it coming beforehand.

But he didn't expect them to know about the five companies Edward Doran asked about. It made him wonder what else they knew. Did they know about the money transfers? The software? Was Mitchell fishing here, or did they really know what Edward wanted?

"What does Brad have to do with any of this?"

"Don't play dumb with me, Richter. You warned him to get away because you figured we'd pay him a visit. Kudos to you for thinking ahead, but you only delayed the inevitable. I can have 30 agents here tomorrow morning doing nothing but searching for him. How long do you think he'll last after that? And remember, he's an ex-con, manslaughter to boot. You know how easy it'd be to send his sorry ass to jail for 20 years? Snap of my finger. So don't even try to play hardball with me, capiche?"

He tried to remain perfunctory and imperturbable.

Nothing bothers you. You expect everything.

"And don't get me started on what I do and do not know about the PEACHES. I'm the one who told you about them in the first place. I'm the one who told you that they killed Sam Fisher. And I'm the one telling you this..."

He waited, the unknown lingering in the air.

"Edward Doran is dead. And Jason Albers ordered the hit."

He slouched, involuntarily and helplessly. His mouth felt more open than it physically could be.

"Jason Albers is the leader."

26

The act was over.

His surprise was as genuine as genuine could be. There was no more pretending. No more masking true feelings. He let them all out, uncontrollably, and stopped trying to fight it.

He concentrated on Mitchell, staring without blinking. Pupils undilated, voice prosaic, demeanor calm. This was not a test. Seconds after Mitchell said it, against every natural reaction and hope he had, Mark knew he was telling the truth.

"What did you say?"

"I hesitated to tell you. You *are* a citizen, and this is confidential, but given your relationship with Albers and everything happening, I decided to take a chance. Like I told you before, we've known for some time that Doran wasn't the mastermind. He did the heavy recruiting and at times gave impressions of leadership, but he never made the big calls. Until late this morning, we didn't know who did. When I found out it was the floor security guard at your building, a guy you've known for almost five years on a personal level, I figured we needed to talk."

"But how—"

"When they contacted you, we first looked into every employee at Lafferty & Sons. It was a longshot, and we didn't expect to get lucky. For a long time, it looked like we wouldn't. Every associate is clean. But when we checked the property owner's staff, Jones Lang LaSalle, and got to Albers, we found some things that I can't get into specifics on right now. But...well, let's just say it's more than a strong theory."

The day he learned of Jason's widower status flashed into Mark's mind. Before then, he remembered thinking how strange it seemed that Kristina was in Jason's full custody. He'd assumed Jason's wife was alive, and chose not to pry into his personal life. Life is tough.

Divorces happen all the time and some mothers are unfit, and Jason seemed like a terrific father. But when he learned that Jason's wife had died tragically in a bicycle accident in Ravenswood, he instantly felt a deeper connection to the man. Misery loves company, and he'd abruptly learned they had more in common than he realized.

Or so he thought until now...

"So you don't know for sure?"

"It was a mistake on his part to contact you, and this guy doesn't make many mistakes. He must really want you to take the chance he did. We suspect that's why he joined the firm in the first place."

"You think he joined Lafferty five years ago because of me?"

"This guy is beyond thorough. It would fit his personality if that's precisely why he joined."

Not exactly hard evidence, and Mitchell left out all the details, but ultimately it didn't matter. He recalled Tom's reference to Daniel Tiger over the phone. How could Tom know about the picture? It was strictly between him and Katherine, except that she drew it at Jason's house. Then he recalled Jason's questions earlier that day at the office party, wanting to know if everything was okay, and about the message after he cancelled Katherine's sleepover.

Jason was probing, seeking information.

"You've got to have it wrong. Jason Albers is a security guard and single father. I've never seen him do anything that would suggest he has a violent bone in his body. He's the most jovial person I know. What could possibly drive him to do these things?"

"I wish I could tell you definitively, Mark. I wish I could tell that being abused as a kid taught Jason how to bottle up his hate and put on a good front when needed. Or that his mother getting gang-raped and murdered by some black thugs who never served time put him over the edge. Or that being a closet KKK member fuels the fire of his violent engine. But while all that's true, I can't explain why a man would do what he has done."

"But what—"

"Or that he's pissed the world doesn't care about reverse racism. That he wants minorities to burn for crimes committed against white people that the media doesn't give the light of day to in the middle of BLM movement. Some of that would at least help the psychiatrists begin to explain who he is."

Mark remained silent, and his mind was like the ball inside a pinball machine, bouncing from one thought to the next.

"But I can't," Mitchell continued. "The truth is we have no idea why he is the animal he is, or how he got that way. I can't pretend to understand what drives his evilness. Sometimes, we in the FBI don't get that comfort. But let me ask you, what does it matter how he got this way or how we got here? All that really matters is that we're here."

Mitchell's eyes were now wide and appeared moist, as if he was afraid. Afraid of an unexplainable yet undeniable devilry.

"Mark, just think about this for a minute. Your daughter goes over to his house every week. You see him at the office every couple days. He has access to room keys and building security tapes.

"Did you ever ask yourself why it was that they chose the five companies they did? Or why they chose you, of all people, to help them? Or how they knew so much about you on personal level? I'm sure you did, and now you have an answer. Jason Albers is the leader, and he's been watching you for a long time."

He felt the same urge to vomit he'd felt on the River Walk.

"You could chalk it up to excellent surveillance on their part and piss-poor luck on yours, but when you tie in all the coincidences, it seems like one hell of a stretch. The fact is, Albers is living a double-life, and he's so good at it that nobody knows."

Katherine's face simply wouldn't leave his mind. Nor would her friendship with Kristina, or the relationship they both had with Jason.

"I told you they might see something in your daughter," Mitchell said, reading his thoughts.

"Doran's dead?" he quickly and desperately changed the subject.

"We haven't spotted him since last Saturday, and that has never happened before."

"Maybe he knows you're watching him."

"Possibly, which is why I've got half the local bureau scrambling like hell to find him. But as you're aware, we often don't find bodies with these people. You know in your heart Sam Fisher is dead, and we never found his body. Know it about Doran, too."

Tom's earlier confirmation of Sam's murder now seemed so immaterial and redundant. He wondered how Tom fit into Doran's death.

"Why would they kill Doran?" he asked as if he cared.

"Our best guess is Albers found out we were getting too close to him and cut the tie. You don't stay under the radar for as long as he has by not playing it safe."

Under the radar.

"If you're so sure, go arrest him now."

"Everything we've got is still hearsay and circumstantial. There's no hard connection or link between him and the PEACHES. He's a sharp man, and he's distanced himself well. We need something concrete."

"This is stupid!" he nearly screamed, checking his surroundings yet again for anyone getting too close. "Here you go again, telling me you know something but can't do anything. What good is it to just know something? All you do is make your little theories? What the hell do you want from me?"

He jumped out of the increasingly uncomfortable cement chair and started pacing south away from The Hancock towards Chestnut Street. The sun was waning, along with his patience and sanity. The breeze had picked up, yet he was burning hot. He unbuttoned the top of his collar and picked up the pace, staring jealously at all the people who weren't him. The elderly man playing chess with his grandson at the small table; the twin brothers munching on snow cones; the middle-aged woman leaning against the wall with a paperback; he wished he was *any* one of them.

Mitchell followed with compassion in his frowning face, or so it seemed. The mercurial agent inched towards him and put his hand on his shoulder. Then he managed to make Mark feel even more trapped than he did before, overmatched and hopeless.

"We need you to plant a bug."

***

"What?" he replied, his raspy voice barely getting the word out.

"Mark, I'm sorry for the position this has put you and your daughter in. And if there was any other way, I wouldn't be here. But you *are* in this situation and there *isn't* any other way. If we pick Albers up now, without any evidence, he'll beat the charges and the PEACHES will carry on. They'll keep doing these terrible things to innocent people, and they'll keep coming after you and your daughter until you're both dead."

"A surveillance bug?"

"I know it's not fair, but talk to the Supreme Court. I don't get to judge the law. I just enforce it. If I had my druthers, we'd kill them all right now. No arrest or trial needed."

"How am I supposed to plant a bug?"

"Start by doing what they ask. Give them the information they want. Don't fight it. Act like you're on their side to protect your daughter. But when you meet with them to hand that information over—"

"I don't know I will."

"You will. They won't do it any other way."

He didn't answer. This was too much.

"That's when we need you to plant the bug."

His face was sure to be the definition of skepticism. He shook his head and stared at the ground, fixated on the crushed plastic Jamba Juice cup and feather that was starting to flip-flop in the wind along the sidewalk towards a hair transplant clinic.

Mitchell reached into his jacket pocket and withdrew a small, ring-sized box. It contained a clear, circular object no bigger than a tiny dress-shirt button. It rested on gray foam and looked like a small piece of transparent and flimsy plastic.

"They might check you for bugs or wires, but this is invisible and untraceable. You can stick it on your finger or hand, and they'll never see it. It's got a natural camouflage feature that blends it into anything that's not foam, including skin pigment. It sinks into your wrinkles and creases and becomes 100% flush. And it transfers just as easily. All you have to do is shake a hand or pat a back, and it'll stick. It's the most advanced surveillance technology we have, Mark. No one knows about it yet, not even field agents."

Both of them still standing, Mitchell took the bug out of the box and gently placed it on his own palm, revealing how invisible it really was. Even knowing it was there, he really couldn't see it. It blended into Mitchell's hand and disappeared. *Disappeared.* He traced Mitchell's palm very slowly but couldn't make out any shape or protrusion.

Not a thing.

Mitchell extended his arm to shake Mark's hand and did so very gently.

"The bug's on you now."

He looked at his own hand, bringing it inches from his eyes. He couldn't see or feel anything. He smelled his palm. Odorless. Then he walked into what was left of the diminishing sunshine and saw no visual regardless of his hand's angle to the sun.

"That's it, Mark. A simple handshake. That's all you have to do. You don't have to press, you don't have to squeeze. Any contact transfers the bug immediately, and it won't fall off in water. You could scrub your hands until they're hard as sandpaper, and it'll still be there. It's equipped with both visual and audio surveillance at an impressive range. We'll hear clear as day and track their location to the square foot."

"What if they transfer it to someone else unknowingly? If it's that easy, it's bound to happen."

"We only need it in place for a few minutes. Once we're on Albers, we won't lose him."

"But what if Albers isn't there? He might send someone else like last time," he asked, already fully aware of the answer. "There's this guy named Tom."

"We know, and that's precisely why we need you to plant it. Plant it on whomever you meet. Whoever that person is, he'll eventually meet Albers, and we'll follow the bug straight to the top of the food chain. Let me get that off of you."

Mitchell supposedly removed the bug from his hand using a pair of tweezers. He didn't feel anything or see it in the tweezers, leading him to question if the agent had actually removed anything.

But when Mitchell placed the tweezers flush against the gray foam, the small dot outline again appeared. His senses had deceived him. He still couldn't believe what his eyes were showing him.

Mitchell handed him the box, along with a blank business card, a phone number written on the back.

"Call me day or night."

He took it silently and reluctantly.

"That's it, Mark. That's all we're asking. The bug is impossible to trace and it's totally unnoticeable. Do what they ask, plant the bug, walk away, and leave the rest to us. Then let us get you and your daughter out of this mess and watch a terrorist organization get what it deserves."

It was a decent sales pitch considering his lack of options, but he'd already made up his mind. He didn't care how close or good the feds appeared to be now. The PEACHES always seemed to be a step ahead of them. And if they were, he'd join Sam and Edward in an unknown resting place.

He wasn't playing. Not their way, not by their rules.

"I don't plant bugs for a living, and I'm not going to start now."

"There's no other way."

"Yes there is."

He handed Mitchell back the tiny box housing the scariest surveillance technology he could imagine, happy to be rid of it.

"I'm only helping you if you help me."

"What's that supposed to mean?"

"I'll call you," he answered, holding up the business card.

He scurried down to Chestnut and took a right before hailing a cab on Michigan, leaving Mitchell alone calling his name to no avail.

27

Brad Tarnow learned a lot of lessons from his one encounter with the law and everything that happened afterwards, the biggest being that the moment you step out of prison and back into the free world, people who knew you before you went in see you differently.

They keep one eye open, they tend to point at you when there's someone to blame. Your credibility is shot, and you can no longer be trusted. Even if what put you in prison is something any one of them would've done, the fact is they didn't do it. You did. And the ex-con label sticks with you in ways beyond your criminal record. Not only the job interviewers doubt you, but also the so-called long-time friends you thought you had.

Trust has to be earned over a lifetime. Doubt can be acquired in seconds.

Brad could still recall that life-changing night to the very last detail. That snowy, blistery February 6th Saturday night thirteen years ago in downtown Chicago. The bar, dark and uninviting, the half-lit neon sign in front, the hardwood floors, the Star Wars pinball machine. He'd remember it all for the rest of his life.

He'd had more than a few drinks, but he wasn't driving. Julie looked great. She was wearing a light-blue shirt that ran beneath her shoulders, exposing smooth skin and awesome breasts. Her jeans were snug, showing off a perfect butt. Six months into dating and she got better looking every day. And boy did she look good that night.

Which was probably why when he came back from the bathroom that nasty-looking filth was hanging all over her. The man was huge, an easy 350 pounds, wearing ripped jeans and a red-checkered flannel shirt with a John Deere hat. His face full of scruffy red stubble, his cheeks rolled with fat.

His hands were on her shoulders despite her protests, his buddies encouraging him from the bar. Julie's eyes revealed a fear Brad had not seen in her before. She looked at him, pleading for help, the man's fingers digging into her petite shoulder and no one else doing anything about it.

He didn't hesitate.

Despite the tremendous size disadvantage, he did precisely what he'd hope any man would've done: he walked right up to the prick and ripped his filthy meat hooks off his girl.

When a man twice your size grabs your throat and squeezes, you don't think about the consequences of smashing a beer bottle over his head. You don't wonder if he has a history of concussions or if the impact will give him another. You don't assume that it could somehow kill him, or that self-defense wouldn't apply if it did.

You just react.

Because he "started" the fight, the judge gave him two-to-four years, involuntary manslaughter. He didn't get the nine years that scumbag district attorney asked for, but what the hell kind of sense did it make to put someone in prison for protecting his girl? With all the criminals out there, with all the murderers and rapists in the city of Chicago, they put *him* in prison.

Not even the circumstances of his imprisonment or his shortened one-and-a-half year sentence kept him from losing old friendships. Prison was prison. An ex-con was an ex-con. Even Julie moved on, ditching the apartment and changing her phone number. Family stared behind his back, enemies snickered, old friends faded away. He was alone.

Except for Mark Richter.

His best friend since grade school never doubted him. Mark supported him during the trial, visited him in prison and invited him over for dinner with Katherine the very night he was released.

They played racquetball every Friday night at the club. Katherine made cookies on his birthday, shared in the Richter home with cold milk. No questions, no shame, no doubt. He was "Uncle Brad." No more, no less.

And because of that, he would do anything for Mark, and that included breaking the law again. He'd meet him anytime, anyplace. Loyalty didn't describe his feelings.

So when Mark called him Saturday afternoon and told him he might be under surveillance, needed his help and didn't have time to explain everything, he didn't panic or rifle questions. He listened to what Mark had to say and asked what he could do.

The answer: ditch the tail he likely had at Dunkin Donuts and check into a hotel for a week. Pay cash. He was surprised, Mark wasn't the kind of guy the police followed, but how could he doubt the man after what he did for him?

The call came early Tuesday evening to the hotel room. Mark asked him to take $5,000 from a locker in Union Station and use some of it to rent a small office for a month. He got the money and went straight there. No questions about the five grand or anything else. Answers would come soon enough. Trust was what mattered now. He knew that.

And so did Mark.

* * *

The small office was on the first floor of a shady building a few blocks from Lafferty & Sons east towards the city. Interstate 90 traffic whizzed by just in front, and Brad saw a Walgreens just west of it on the north side of Higgins. It didn't have a sign, or even a name, best he could tell. The windows were covered with stains, unclean and untreated. A small blinking neon OPEN sign hung above the bars covering the door.

The inside left plenty to be desired as well. The laminate floor in the so-called lobby was caked with rock-hard dirt. Dried yellow water stains covered the walls like cheap paint. The desk had a large chunk missing from its corner. No computers, printers, telephones or fax machines were in sight: this was an establishment run on paper and memory. But luxury was unimportant.

What was important was the no-questions policy it was sure to employ.

The heavyset man showing him the office was a black guy named Ray with tattoos on almost every visible part of his body. His long black hair was pulled back into a slick ponytail and a tongue ring as big as a dime emerged when he spoke. Ray wore gray sweatpants and a gray sweatshirt, both of which had lost their elasticity years ago.

It was precisely the image they needed. After a short walk from the front door, Ray unlocked the corner office on the easternmost side of the building.

"Here it is. Told you it ain't much," Ray choked out over a smoker's hack without attempting to cover his mouth.

The office was 800 square feet if that and looked even more shameful than the lobby. The dark blue carpet looked like it hadn't been cleaned in years. The cracked and stained desk made the one in front look like an executive model. Cobwebs hung from the ceiling and Brad could only guess how many creepy crawlers called this place home.

One window faced north, its blinds coated with visible dirt and bent 90 degrees. The room had been poorly repainted; shades of lime green were plainly visible beneath the white topcoat.

He didn't even walk inside.

"I'll take it," he said, flipping a light switch that didn't work.

Ray opened his mouth and shot him a suspicious glare. The owner had certainly planned on the visit being a bust and didn't try to hide it.

"What's a rich white dude like you want with this place?"

He ignored the comment, focusing instead on the large brown stain in the center of Ray's sweatshirt. Coffee? He could only hope. But filth meant hunger, hunger meant desperation, and desperation meant negotiable.

"That's my business. I want it for a month. You renting or not?"

"It'll cost you," Ray answered, smacking his lips.

"How much?"

"Three thousand. Thousand upfront. Nonrefundable. You break anything, you bought it."

He'd learned a few things in prison. One of them was how to negotiate with guys who were less than straight shooters. Office gurus, big shots like Mark, had their own set of challenges, but street guys were a unique breed with a particular language.

And he knew that language and the people who spoke it.

They had their own rules with their own logic. He had no idea if Ray had ever been to prison, but it sure seemed to Brad that he'd put the lessons he'd learned there to good use.

Lessons he had to learn to survive.

Lesson #1: don't accept the first offer and make your counter quick and firm. No room for debate, no back-and-forth negotiating. Speak strongly and with confidence, even if you don't have any. If you stutter, they own you.

Lesson #2 was perhaps the most important and overlooked lesson in the world today: hard currency is king.

It was amazing how easy it was to avoid questions and how much stronger your position became when you dangled the goods in front of folks. Whether it was baseball cards on the playground, cigarettes in the prison yard or cash in a store, hard currency took negotiations to new levels.

"There ain't much to break, and I ain't paying that. I'll give you $1,500 cash right now. Take it or leave it."

"Sheeet, dude," Ray responded with an exaggerated chuckle. "Can't do it."

"Your call, boss." He'd walked halfway to the front door before the inevitable:

"You got the money with you?"

28

It happened at 3:30 on Wednesday morning.

Most houses on Evergreen Lane were dark. Another normal day of work and school was ahead for people. Just not for him. A minivan was parked at the end of the otherwise empty cul-de-sac. Except for the soft whistling wind, still silence permeated the neighborhood.

At around 3:20, Mark sat at the kitchen table, being watched by everyone and comforted by no one. Katherine was asleep in Wisconsin. Caroline was still being the good sister and not asking questions. Mary Ann was still with the angels looking down, probably shaking her head at this point.

He pushed his fingers into the corners of his eyes, exhausted but unable to sleep, staring at his laptop. He'd been paying the Nicor gas bill online for years. A quick check of the amount, a few clicks of the mouse, and boom, the fee was paid. Free and immediate transactions with instant e-mail verification had replaced years of slow snail mail and uncertain delivery.

But since meeting Tom and Edward, he'd decided the old-fashioned USPS was the way to go. He wrote the check, sealed the envelope, and applied the stamp. As he walked down the sidewalk to drop it in the mailbox, he questioned the futility of paying bills now. But he'd been paying bills the day he got them for a long time, and old habits die hard.

Incredulous about Jason Albers winning him over, he logged onto his Bank of America account to delete all the payee accounts and swore that if he made it out of the week alive, he'd never pay for anything online again.

After removing Nicor and getting ready to do the same to ComEd, he froze and stared into the screen.

Eyes wide as soccer balls, he didn't stir when the teapot whistled. He just looked harder, scanning the screen carefully, imagining the possibilities. Then he pressed his finger into the center his forehead, his trademark position for intense concentration. After minutes of high-pitched screaming from the stove and blink-free staring, he had only one question about the idea that just came to mind.

Could it really work?

Probably not, his conscience answered. There were many ways it could go awry. There were too many catches, too many assumptions. He wasn't that lucky.

29

"Ron Mitchell."

"It's Mark."

Ron jumped out of bed and flipped on the light, much to his retinas' dismay. Richter's voice was raspy. He hadn't slept much.

"Mark, how are you?" he said after clearing his throat.

"How do you think I am?"

"Where are you?"

"I'm in a gas station bathroom. Aren't you watching me?"

"Of course we are." He grabbed his phone and scanned the latest update from the field agent, sent ten minutes earlier. The details matched the live-feed 24/7 report on his laptop sitting on the floor next to the bed. Field agents were great and all, but the bug he'd planted on Richter was the ultimate tracking tool. That remained his little secret, however.

"You left your house at a quarter 'til four and drove to the Shell gas station on Algonquin Road. You car's still there, parked at pump five."

"Then why'd you ask where I was?"

"Brad Tarnow's car is still at Dunkin Donuts, isn't it?"

"Good point."

"We're going to find him too, you know."

"You ready to talk business?"

"Absolutely," he cleared his throat again. Finally, Richer had realized there was no other way.

"I want total anonymity for me and my entire family. *Total*, you understand? I want a new name, all references to my daughter and sister expunged from the file, and this entire experience, including every one of our conversations, completely removed. You got it?"

"Nobody will even know you exist." He disliked lying, but it was necessary.

There would, of course, be a file on someone's computer within the bureau containing all that information. The FBI never removed someone from the record entirely.

"And I want five million dollars."

"What the—"

"That's right. Five million dollars, deposited into an account I designate, spread out over ten separate $500,000 payments."

He was actually a little impressed.

Only an accountant, one who knew Sam Fisher or someone like him, could know that $500,000 was the FBI's regional branch expense amount limit. That wasn't exactly public information. Any higher than that, and he'd have to get director-level approval. Ten transactions meant a lot less red tape. Being impressed, however, did not make him willing.

"Just who the hell do you think you are?"

"I think I'm the one guy who can get you what you've been after for years. And that I'm worth every penny."

"You arrogant prick! I'm not paying you a thing. You hear me? Not one red cent!"

"Then find yourself another snitch."

Click.

* * *

He went through a tirade of curse words and pillow punches before the phone rang again. He didn't even check the Caller ID, certain it said UNKNOWN just like it did a few minutes ago.

"You listen to me you son of a—"

"No, you listen to me, because I'm only going to say this once." Richter's voice was calm and soft. "Maybe you'll get the PEACHES one day. I'm skeptical, considering your track record, but it could happen. But you can get them *now* for eight *ten-thousandths* of one percent of the Government budget. And I don't really care if I end up going down with them either, Mitchell. Because if I don't help them, I'm going down anyway, and their definition of going down scares me a lot more than yours."

"You snot-nosed little punk!"

"Are we talking business or name-calling? Cuz if we're name-calling, I've got a few of my own."

"I'm not paying you one red cent, Richter," he lowered his voice.

"You say that like it's your money. Uncle Sam's already trillions in debt. The least he can do is fork over a measly five million to nail a terrorist group you've already spent ten times that amount chasing. It'd be the best investment the bureau ever made. Come to think of it, I should probably be asking for more."

"What makes you think you're entitled to five million dollars?"

"I'm done talking about this. You know what I want, and the ball is in your court now. I'm going to read this account number once. If you don't catch it all, nice knowing you. If you decide not to pay, there won't be a second offer. You can call me any name you want...my mind's made up. Five hundred thousand dollars from ten different accounts wired by nine o'clock Friday night, or don't even bother coming to find me without the handcuffs."

"Mark, I can't just snap my fingers and get five million—"

But Richter had already started rambling off an account number. He scrambled for the pen on his nightstand, scribbling on his palm. It seemed to be a Swiss account, but he couldn't be sure. When Richter was finished, he tried to speak but got cut off yet again.

"One more thing: don't try anything stupid, Mitchell. You may know guns and bugs and terrorists, but I know accounts and money and transactions. If I don't have confirmation from the bank by nine o'clock Friday that a clean, verifiable transfer's been made to that account, we'll never speak again."

30

Moments after he hung up on Ron Mitchell for the second time, with a certain degree of satisfaction, he was already onto the next call. He needed Mitchell riled up, just a little, and that wasn't a challenge. It would be helpful later on, but it had to be carefully managed for right now. He doubted Mitchell would pay, but the clock was ticking and he had to try.

After one ring, Brad picked up.

"Mark?"

"Yeah, it's me. You okay?"

"I'm fine. Here in the hotel. I rented the office for a month."

"No problems?"

"No problems. There's no way anyone's watching that dump. The landlord's pretty desperate. I think we're his only client."

"Good, that means he won't ask questions. Did you get the stuff from Office Max?"

"Yeah. Fax machine, copier, printer, all in one. Pens, notebooks, everything else. I also got enough paper to clear out a rainforest."

"And you're not being followed?"

"I don't think so. At least I haven't seen anyone."

That was a definite "no." Mark didn't say it, but if the cops knew where Brad was, he'd already be in their custody. And if the PEACHES knew where he was...

"Great. Just lay low until Thursday."

"Got it."

"I mean it. Don't tell anyone where you are. Don't even go outside. Order pizza, pay with cash, watch TV all day, whatever. Just don't—"

"Mark...I got it."

"Okay."

"What about you? Is everything...okay?"

"We'll talk Thursday. Lay low until then."

"Okay bud. You got it."

"See you then."

One more phone call to make: the one he dreaded the most, more than the ones to Mitchell or even Tom. It was wrong and he knew it. There had to be another way, a better way, but he couldn't think of it. And Saturday would be here before he knew it.

He had to break his promise.

31

"I want you to take extra special care of each other, okay?" her fake, high-energy voice encouraged, covering her fear.

Will's response came immediately. "Yes, Mommy!"

"Yes, Aunt Caroline," Katherine's followed.

The two children, tucked into the back of her neighbor's Volvo, smiled and waved as Roberta backed up. She smiled back, fighting the tears until the car was out of sight.

Moments later, she stared out the two-story family room window at the vast array of high-reaching pine trees layering her backyard. She remembered how excited Richard was about those trees when they moved to Platteville. He wanted to get away from buildings and into nature, for Will to experience the country lifestyle. She had no objections.

That was almost five years ago. Will was still a toddler, Richard was still alive.

She missed the little things she used to take for granted the most. The comfort of his voice after a long day, relaxing walks through the countryside, the joy in Will's face when Daddy got home from work. Richard had a way of making everything okay. He handled stress better than anyone she knew. He was her rock, her lover, her best friend.

It made what happened that much harder.

It was a Thursday evening around five o'clock. In early October, the driveway was covered with red leaves. Richard had just gotten home from work and hugged her, flown Will around the room like an airplane, and asked her about her day. After listening to her recap every painful detail without a hint of boredom, Richard told her about a golf match that coming Saturday.

For some reason, a stupid one to be sure, maybe the long day, maybe it being that time of the month, maybe her being pissed at a client, she erupted. Even as she went on about the plans they'd already made for that Saturday, she knew she was overreacting. People sometimes forget. It happens. It's not a big deal. Richard could've very easily cancelled the golf match.

It was a non-issue, but she made it one.

The saint that he was, Richard didn't want to fight in front of Will. They never had, because he wouldn't allow it. Rather than get into a war of words even as she provoked him, he smiled and told her he was going to the store to get some milk, even though the real reason he was leaving was to get away from his screaming monster of a wife.

He tried to kiss her good-bye. She pulled back.

When an hour passed without his return, she grew upset. Two hours later, she was only that much angrier. It never occurred to her that something was wrong. She was livid, thinking of all the things she was going to unleash on him, when the phone rang. Caller ID said it was his cell, and she answered it harshly.

But it wasn't him.

When the police officer told her what happened, her knees buckled and she turned into a human waterfall, tears pouring from her eyes. Will, then only three years old, heard Mama crying and asked what was wrong. She didn't have an answer.

Now, alone in the house meant for her family, the pine trees reminded her of Richard and the words she could never take back. She wanted nothing more than to hold Will while Richard held her. She prayed she'd wake up from a bad dream next to both of them and promised God she'd never yell again if He would make that happen.

He never did.

* * *

The ringing phone Mark had given her snapped her back into reality.

"Hello?"

"Caroline, it's me."

"Mark, what's going on? You can't tell me to send the kids away and then not call for four hours!"

"I wanted—"

"Now they're 70 miles away in Mt. Sterling, and I still don't know why!"

"Did you move the equipment upstairs?"

"Yes, from the basement to the dining room, right in front of the window, just like you said. It took me over an hour, and I still don't understand why I had to do it."

She'd also locked every door and window in the house and killed the lights. When the sun went down, it would be pitch-black. There was no way a car could make it up her winding driveway without its lights on, not in rural Wisconsin.

"Did you pack the bag?"

"Yes, a week's worth of supplies. What's going on Mark?"

It was hard, painfully hard, to follow his instructions earlier with no explanation. But aside from Will, Mark was the only family she had left. So she did, because that's what people do for their family.

Now, however, it was time for answers.

32

The front entrance to Ogilvie Transportation Center on Madison Street had a dark-green metal frame and tall glass doors stretching from the ground to the top of four Ω-shaped concentric arches 100 feet above ground. Just three blocks north of the even busier Union Station, over 100,000 people buzz into and out of it every day, taking commuter Metra train lines back and forth to the suburbs of Chicago.

Mark strolled in acting as typically as possible on Wednesday afternoon to head home, a half-day of "vacation" ahead of him.

The station felt like ghost town at just before noon. Small shops and convenience stores were nearly empty, tall stacks of unread newspapers stood outside the Hudson newsstand and Waldenbooks. The food court behind the escalators, which offered everything from New Orleans Cajun Chicken to Panda Express to Mrs. Fields, was void of lines. It even smelled like a transit station to him, though he couldn't quite pin down what that meant. Some combination of floor cleaner, exhaust and sweat.

The second floor, on the other hand, had a lovely aroma of fresh sweets and pastries, compliments of Auntie Anne's. He walked briskly past GNC and Corner Bakery Café, glancing at the bridge that connected Ogilvie to Two North Riverside Plaza and the Chicago River Walk, a beautiful scene on a sunny summer day.

When he walked through the sixth of 15 revolving doors leading to the tracks, he took in the drastic change that assaulted his senses. Dim fluorescent bulbs that hung too high and an aroma that seemed like an equal mix of train exhaust and factory abruptly replaced bright lighting and the smell of fresh goodies.

The gray-and-tan checkered floor was twice as old and half as clean as its counterpart on the other side of the revolving doors. Poor acoustics muffled the announcements of imminent departures and schedule changes. A bright yellow sign hung in front of each train, indicating its destination.

The Union Pacific District Northwest Line was set to depart in a half-hour on Track 8 of 16. The line ran from Ogilvie to Harvard, a suburb 75 miles northwest of the city, a ride that took nearly two hours in total with 22 different stops. He withdrew his ticket to Arlington Heights and hurriedly boarded the metal vessel.

Every Metra commuter train is the same by design to both lower the railroad's costs and provide commuters with familiarity. Fourteen two-person blue-green seats behind eight singles on the first level; 25 singles on the second. Gray and black rubber floors. Metal-framed bars in between the two levels served as footrests for second-level passengers. The only light is that of the natural outside world and the emergency exit signs positioned around the perimeter. Rectangular-shaped plastic windows could be kicked out in case of an emergency.

Sam's caution had certainly rubbed off on him. He took an aisle seat near the rear door, left side, close to the emergency pull cord. He watched others board the train, not noticing anyone suspicious but painfully aware he likely wouldn't spot it anyway. People seemed to mind their own business. A lady with a crossword puzzle, a man already snoozing, a young mother reading a book to her two children. Everything looked normal.

But didn't it always?

The slow, creaky departure from downtown began at precisely 12:30 and lasted the usual five minutes, the train's wheels constantly rubbing against the rails. The screeching noise was bizarre to first-time riders, who seemed certain that derailment would occur, but regulars were inured to the high-pitched squeal. Before long, the train was zooming away from downtown Chicago.

He carefully removed his lightweight black jacket, the one he'd tried to wear as much as possible since meeting Ron Mitchell at The Hancock. He grabbed it by the arm, *not the collar*, and placed it on the coat hook, ensuring the collar was popped up just enough.

Just enough, that is, for the bug Mitchell planted on him at The Hancock to pick up the conductor asking for tickets and the announcements of the next stop. The business card Mitchell had given him was still in the pocket, and his was the only coat on the rack. Most Chicagoans didn't need coats in late May.

If someone from the FBI was on the train already, it was all for naught. They'd see and follow him, foiling everything. But if they were just following the bug, waiting for him to get off at the Arlington Heights Train Station at 1:16, to tail him from there, he had a slight chance.

After the Clybourn stop, he checked the passengers one more time. All still seemed normal. And Irving Park was next.

Sometimes you just have to jump.

Right on cue at 12:43, the train came to a slow stop at the Irving Park train station. It was smaller than Arlington Heights, only a few people detrained. He kept his head down and tried to be casual. He crossed the platform and stood behind the small train shelter before the train motored past.

Following Sam's firm direction to avoid Uber and Lyft and their digital footprints, the yellow cab he'd called was early, parked on Avondale Avenue next to the station. No one else was around, and the train was gone. He surveyed the scene for a quick minute: the side streets were empty, Interstate 90/94 was buzzing as usual to the north, an elderly man in a hat pushed a lawn mower with what looked like all his might, a middle-aged blonde woman walked her Cavalier King Charles, the mailman paced his route.

He climbed in the cab and slouched down, as if it would do any good if they were watching. If he was spotted, he was spotted. Slouching wouldn't change anything.

He shivered and thought of the irony. Even in May, with an appropriate gust of wind, or fear, Chicago still felt brisk without a jacket.

* * *

It wouldn't take long to find out if the plan worked.

At six o'clock that evening, there was little doubt that Mitchell would make it painfully obvious. The train he'd abandoned arrived at Crystal Lake, that particular train's final stop, at 1:55. That meant Mitchell had known for at least four hours if not more. Or, he'd been following him the entire time and was watching him in the hotel room at that very moment.

Either way, it was time to make the call.

He punched the number in and put the cell on speakerphone. There was no background noise, and the contraption to his right was in place on the desk.

"Mitchell," a frustrated voice answered.

"Hello, Ron."

"Richter! Where the hell are you?"

Well, that answered that.

"Nice talking to you, too. What, were you following me?"

"Don't play dumb with me, Richter. I'm at the end of my rope."

"And I'm at the end of mine. Don't you know it's illegal to bug someone without probable cause?"

"Not with the Patriot Act, buddy. I can do whatever I want."

"Like when you threatened to arrest Brad? I'm pretty sure the Patriot Act doesn't let you just throw a guy in prison when he didn't do anything wrong."

"First of all, don't you have enough to worry about without protecting your ex-con buddy?"

"And it's—"

"Second of all, I couldn't give the furry tail of a rat's behind what's legal and what's not. Don't forget, I'm the federal agent here! If I feel like pissing on your doorstep, I do it. If I have the urge to ride your ass all over this godforsaken city, I do it. And if I want to arrest your friend for no particular reason, I do it. I do what I want, when I want, got it? *I am the law.* You'd better start getting that notion through your thick skull. You belong to me, Richter. Rights? You don't have any rights. Don't forget who you're talking to."

"I'm talking to Mr. Ron Mitchell of the FBI."

"Damn right you are!"

"Listen to this."

He pressed STOP, disconnected the amplifier, rewound the tape, and played it for Mr. Ron Mitchell of the FBI. He only wished he could've seen Mitchell's face too. When the 30 seconds of leverage ended, he knew Mitchell's rage would be at its peak, he had to act now.

"Unless you want this tape to show up on the evening news, I suggest you make those transfers. You've only got fifty-one hours. I'll call you at 9:01 on Friday night."

"You really think a tape I'm sure I can prove is counterfeit puts you in the position to demand things? You don't have the first clue just how deep you're in. I'm trying to help you, and you're trying to strong-arm me? Think that one over, Mark."

A nice try, somewhat convincing, but clear desperation. Mitchell was busted and he knew it.

"You might be right. Maybe the tape won't do anything. Maybe all the major news networks will reject it. They hate things like FBI agents breaking the law and abusing citizens' rights. And maybe no one will listen to it on the Internet either. Social media never spreads a wildfire. But I don't think you want to find out."

"If you publicize that tape, you're signing your own death warrant. What do you think Albers and the rest of the PEACHES are going to do to you?"

"I'll worry about that. You worry about making those transfers."

"You've got your daughter. You'll never do it."

"Like I said, I don't think you want to find out."

He paused a few seconds to let the comment sink in...

"You're not gonna get to keep the money. You know that, right? You know there's no chance you're keeping five million dollars of the FBI's money. We're going to have enough tracers on that account to find Jimmy Hoffa. As soon as you try to use it, we'll bust you for extortion, and you'll be in prison and without your daughter. We're gonna watch that account like a very hungry hawk, Richter. *Try anything*...and I'll nail you."

"I wouldn't have it any other way. I'm always up for a challenge."

33

Thursday morning. Five after seven. Larry's Joint, a small diner across the street from Lafferty & Sons Accounting Firm. Sunny, about 60 degrees, intermittent gusts of wind from the east.

It was an understatement to say Mark had doubts about the plan.

Less than 24 hours after ditching the train specifically to get some privacy, he'd be walking right back into the spotlight the moment he set foot in Lafferty & Sons. Mitchell would puff his chest at first, Mark being back on the radar. But eventually, the FBI man would put his ego to rest and wonder why Mark went to such great lengths to lose his tail if he was planning to go to work the next morning. And what he did in the short time that he wasn't being watched.

That's why this had to happen today.

He saw Brad at a small table in the back, wearing a hooded brown spring jacket, blue jeans and green golf shirt, neatly tucked in. A half-eaten bagel next to him, Brad looked nervous, rapidly tapping the table.

"Hey, man," he said, scanning the room for onlookers, his head on a swivel.

"You're late. That's not like you," Brad replied.

"Got held up."

"You look terrible."

He was sure he did. A shower and shave and fresh clothes hardly outdid his sluggish posture, raspy voice and sleep-deprived body and mind.

"No one's following you?" he ignored the comment. Just then the greeting bell in front rang, and he nearly jumped out of his seat. After a long stare, he turned back to Brad.

"So, were you followed?"

"I don't think so, but the hell if I know."

"*Were you listening to me this morning?* If they find you, they'll arrest you on the spot. And they won't let you out until they get what they want," he snapped, forgetting who he was talking to.

Brad leaned back after the lashing, openly disappointed.

"Look, dude, I'm no expert. I think I'm alone. But asking me three times ain't gonna make me sure."

"Sorry man. I really appreciate your help." He sighed and put his head down. Brad had done everything he could possibly ask of him, and here he was barking at the poor guy. "So, you ready?"

"Ready as I'll ever be."

"What time you got?"

Brad checked the cheapo watch that Mark insisted he buy. Black Casio with a backlit digital screen. A real Walmart special.

"7:12."

"Check," he replied, looking at his own equally-chintzy watch. "You won't need a badge after eight o'clock. There's a guard in the lobby, but he's not very attentive. Act like you belong there. Come through the garage and they'll assume you're an employee."

They talked through the plan one final time, trying to convince one another that saying it again would help them flawlessly execute it.

"After you leave the building, you've *got* to stay out of sight. I don't know if they'll ID you from the cameras that soon, but they might."

"Oh yeah...*cameras*," Brad replied with a sigh of his own.

"No way around it, they're all over the place. Once we meet, split. Get in the car and head straight there."

"Got it."

"That's the trickiest part," he said. "Once Mitchell and the FBI see your face on the tapes, they'll rush to the building like the bulls in Spain. You've got to be long gone by the time they put two and two together."

Brad gulped what was left of his Dasani before fumbling to get it to sit on the table. His shaking hands made it hard to do.

"You sure you're okay with this?" he asked.

"I just want it to be over," Brad replied, handing him the key.

He could relate all too well. The anticipation was brutal, and it would get worse before it got better. He felt guilty to boot: this was *his* crooked plan, and he'd pulled an honest man into it.

"I'll call you when I can. Remember, quick and easy, and then get out of there. Don't use credit cards, don't get pulled over. Under the radar, okay buddy?"

As soon as he said it, he thought of Edward Doran. Not the kind of company he wanted to be in.

* * *

Mark finished his third tall glass of water at a quarter until nine. The conference room could technically hold 20 people, but after eight it felt claustrophobic. The content was dry and boring, and the six other people looked like they were ready to fall asleep.

He felt like he could run a marathon on anxiety fumes.

The weekly attendance chart posted on Monday indicated all five of them would be in the office, but he was terrified that things would change and one of them would be gone. It had been a Murphy's Law kind of week.

But fortunately, each accountant was actually there, strolling about as usual. Mark talked to them all briefly, forcing himself into further suspended hypocrisy. Jason was not in the office. He hadn't seen the security guard since Tuesday.

What a scam.

The guy had been walking around the office behind a flashlight and badge for the past five years, acting like the nicest guy in the world, talking like he was your best friend and laughing the whole time. He never swore, he never drank, he rambled on about his daughter like she was a princess, and he could do no wrong in raising her.

Yet beneath the Fugazi, he was really a heartless, ruthless killer who probably murdered his wife and would to the same to Mark and everyone else.

Time made matters worse, and he forced himself to concentrate on that. He knew he wasn't ready, and neither was Brad. Something would go wrong.

34

Hands in his pockets, Brad entered the building next to a middle-aged Korean man in a blue blazer and a woman in a pink blouse carrying a large Macy's tote bag and store-bought pound cake. They approached the guard side-by-side. He was a black man, about 60 years old, white mustache, adorned in a blue SECURITY jacket and hat, head down, glasses on, reading a magazine.

Monitors sat atop the desk, six of them, flipping through different images every few seconds. The guard looked up briefly, smiled at the two regulars on their way to work, and immediately went back to the magazine. The woman went straight and the man right. Brad took a left towards the elevators.

He tried not to scuff his feet on the floor or walk too fast or make noise or in any other way draw attention to himself. He made the hallway turn and saw the door. The quad consisted of a small sidewalk along the perimeter of a 400 square foot patch of grass. Past the sidewalk, opposite the quad, there was a large open area with four picnic tables, which wrapped around to the back of the building. It looked like a valley, with Interstate 90 a half-mile away on elevated terrain.

He sat on one of the comfy-looking-but-not-so-comfy-feeling navy-blue chairs opposite the cafeteria for a few minutes. He started to sweat, partly due to the jacket he yearned to remove. Wearing the White Sox hat per Mark's request, he rubbed the stubble on the end of his chin. Then he cracked his knuckles, bit his lip, and nibbled on his nails.

All the classic clichés that tell a person is scared.

8:52.

People buzzed around the cafeteria, stragglers just getting in for the day. The variety was uncanny. Some were in full three-piece business suits, some in business casual dress slacks and collared shirts, some in jeans and T-shirts. But they were all in a hurry to get where they were going. No one appeared to take notice of him.

8:54.

With the White Sox hat tucked over his head, he kept his eyes down as he tiptoed ever closer. No one was around, but he worried someone soon would be. No smokers were on the quad...yet. One of the four elevators dinged. He heard voices near the guard's desk but didn't dare look.

8:55.

He took a deep breath and reached out to the fire alarm, directly below a camera, yanked it down without looking up, and bolted out the quad door.

35

It blasted like a countywide tornado siren.

People instinctively covered their ears in shock. In the middle of her presentation, Samantha Ryan jumped back, dropped her bottle of water, and then rushed towards the door. The remaining four men and two women in the conference room reminded each other with concern aloud that all drills were pre-announced, but they were still hesitant to evacuate immediately. A whining comment or two about having to leave the office for no good reason was made, but as more people scrambled in the halls, and as line monitors continued to shout that this was not a drill, the six of them began to stir.

"Better to be safe than sorry," one of them finally said, before they all got up.

Mark hung back, letting them clear out in a nervous, chaotic and non-single-file line, contrary to the way they'd rehearsed it during the drill less than a month ago. Once they decided to evacuate, not one of them looked back. They were off to the races, scurrying towards safety and forgetting all about him.

Trampling feet rushed down the west staircase. Shadows he saw through the frosted conference room windows were pushing together, clustering and forming a bottleneck at the door before funneling through it. The east staircase was sure to look the same.

Elevators were off limits, and people had been instructed to leave everything behind. They had also been instructed to remain calm, stay composed, and be alert. But again, while they might've played it cool during the drill, this was real. People don't follow procedures when it's real. It was the first time the fire alarm had ever gone off without a two-day warning, and people responded the way you'd expect. Chaotically.

Which was exactly what he needed.

Two minutes later, he poked his head out the door and saw an empty office. He listened for voices but heard them only from the staircase. The annoying alarm got louder and his ears throbbed with pain. Confident he was alone on sixth floor, he rushed out of the conference room and headed towards the cubes.

The five keys were in different places. And over the years, as a fellow key holder, he had learned where. People either unknowingly revealed it to him, told him they needed to get it and where it was, or simply didn't try to hide it at all. In the long history of Lafferty & Sons, nobody had ever reported a missing file, and no problems had arisen. When there's no precedent, people let their guard down.

Accountants are cautious folks, but Mark hoped a surprise like this would make them drop their guard. There was no chance *he'd* be thinking about his file cabinet key if the building was on fire.

His only hope was they'd feel the same.

Dave, who was managing InfoHelp's file, always left it and his car keys in his jacket pocket, still hanging in the closet. He lost his keys too many times to put them anywhere else, he'd once told Mark. Bruce, handling Techbot, simply left it on his desk in plain sight next to a desk lamp. Why would he be afraid of someone taking it when he had such trustworthy coworkers? Lafferty & Sons didn't even use cameras.

Tony, who worked on Larry's Consulting, kept it in his unlocked front desk drawer. He'd seen Tony remove and replace it many times before, and prayed today was no different. Fred, the chief accountant for LPK, did the same. William, who rounded up the five by working on The McDougal Firm, was the most cautious. He kept his key in his locked desk drawer, but had shown Mark several times that the drawer key was in a coffee mug behind a stack of books on the desk.

He rationalized his action by saying that if the situation were reversed, he'd be happy to give his files to the others, which led him to question why he didn't just ask. But there wasn't time for debates or what-ifs or gut-checks. His daughter's life was at stake. He needed to act and react.

Hopping around the office like a jackrabbit, he gathered the keys one at a time, removing them from key chains and shoving them into his pocket. After he got the fifth, he breathed a sigh of relief they were all there and bolted towards the now-empty staircase. Jumping down each half-flight of stairs without touching any in the middle, his joints throbbed every time he landed. He had only minutes or it'd all be lost.

When the fire alarm is activated, the entire building evacuates. All nine floors, each of the 22 companies, every single person. That made for a chaotic and confusing evacuation on both the back east end and the front west ends of the building. He raced out of the same door Brad had raced out of moments before, opposite the Lafferty & Sons rendezvous point.

As he sprinted around the quad, he weaved through a maze of people crammed together, all looking up for smoke. Turning the corner, he saw Brad, without the green-collared shirt or the brown jacket or the White Sox hat, waiting in a squat behind a tree. His friend looked agitated: the minutes it took him to get the keys surely felt like hours to Brad. He jumped up and stuck out his hand. No words spoken, no looks exchanged; it felt like a baton pass at a track meet.

The handoff complete, he scurried towards the Lafferty & Sons team, gathered near the large floral arrangement on the front end of the building. He was 20 feet away when he heard the fire truck, making its turn onto the circle drive.

36

At 10:10 on a quiet Thursday evening, FBI Regional Director David Coldstone paced his cavernous Chicago office, Bluetooth headset clipped to his ear. Both of his hands rested on the waistline of his newest gray-striped Hickey Freeman suit. It was the only brand he wore, but now that Rochester had stopped making it, he'd never buy another. His short white hair and thick wrinkles revealed old age, but his mind still felt young and sharp. And with over 35 years of increasing responsibility and experience in the bureau, there were few others on the planet who understood terrorism and surveillance as well as he.

He spent his career blind to the possibility of failure, beginning at the lowest level and working upwards. When he got knocked down, he sprang back up. His drive was legendary within the FBI and his three divorces and two estranged children were evidence enough that he put work first. His womanizing didn't help those marriages, but ultimately it was his passion for work and neglect for everything else that brought them to crashing halt.

Yet even after all those years, after the six promotions, the five transfers, the countless eighteen-hour days, he was still hungry, and had no intention of slowing down. He could've retired years ago, but as long as he had that drive, there would always be a place for him.

The situation, however, had gotten way out of control.

"How is it possible to be so close yet so far away?" he spoke into the headset.

Ron Mitchell, the man leading the PEACHES investigation, didn't respond immediately. Mitchell was a promising agent but pretty rough around the edges. He had passion, which was critical, but his temper would compromise investigations if given the chance, and he assumed too much.

The very first rule he'd learned as Regional Director was the importance of empathizing with those around you. Only if you walked in the enemy's shoes, saw the situation from your witness's point of view, and understood what a suspect was thinking could you truly be effective. Mitchell was intelligent, inventive and resourceful. But he needed to work on his patience and empathy.

"I don't know, sir. But we've never been closer than we are now."

"Tell me more about this fire alarm," he said in a monotonic voice.

"It went off just before nine o'clock. The fire department combed the place but couldn't find any smoke or flames. Then security checked the tapes and saw that Brad Tarnow had pulled it."

"You're sure it was him?"

"Yes sir. No doubt about it."

"What did he do then?"

"Ran out the back door. The same back door Richter went out a few minutes later."

"Tell me about Richter's exit."

"That's where it gets odd. Most of Lafferty & Sons' employees evacuated together, like the other companies. They funneled down separate east and west staircases, but they all met up at the same point at roughly the same time."

"But Richter didn't?"

"No. He was about seven minutes behind everyone else. He also came down the east staircase even though his desk is on the west side of the building."

"Do you know where he was when the alarm went off? Maybe he was already on the west side."

"I haven't spoken with any employees, of course, and Lafferty & Sons doesn't use cameras. But I don't think he was at his desk."

"What makes you say that?"

"Call it a hunch."

"That's fine for your subordinates. With me, speak your mind."

Mitchell's cavalier attitude reminded him a lot of himself 15 years ago, but that wasn't necessarily a good thing.

"For him to be seven minutes behind, it means people didn't realize he wasn't there when they evacuated. If they had, they would've grabbed him. It's a small enough company for everyone to know everyone."

"What's that tell you?"

"That he was late because he didn't want to be seen."

Then again, Mitchell did have something working upstairs.

"Then what happened?" he asked.

"The outside security cameras aren't the best in the west. We know he was late in joining the other employees. But what we don't know is what he did from the time he left the building to the time he met up with them."

"What do you think?"

"Well, he didn't have a lot of time, only about two minutes. So he leaves through the back door, runs around the building, and then joins everyone out in front. Maybe he connected with Tarnow, but it couldn't have been for long. And I don't see why."

"Just because we don't see a reason doesn't mean it isn't there."

"Agreed."

"Then what?"

"All the employees waited together while the fire department did their thing, and then went back upstairs as a group to finish the day."

"Richter never left the group from that point on?"

"Nope. Stayed with them the whole time."

"What about later?"

"Went out to TGI Friday's for lunch around 12:30."

"By himself?"

"Yeah. Back at 1:30. Not typical, but not surprising. I can see why he'd want to eat alone."

"Did he meet Tarnow?"

"Not a chance. Sat at a table by the window and didn't say a word to anyone. Burger and fries with a Coke. No visitors, no phone calls. Then he went back to the office."

"When did he leave for the day?"

"Usual time. Around 5:15."

"Then?"

"He went downtown."

"And he stayed in the city the whole time?"

"Yeah, walked down Michigan Avenue for about an hour, and then grabbed a bite for dinner."

"And you're telling me he's at Lafferty & Sons *right now*?"

"Yes, sir. Since about eight o'clock."

"How can you be sure he hasn't left?"

"The lights in the office are on motion-sensors. No movement within 20 feet after a three minutes and they shut off automatically."

"There could be someone else there."

"There's no match on the entry log and no cars of any Lafferty & Sons employee in the garage. We've been watching the only exit point that's open after-hours, and no one from Lafferty has come in or out since six-thirty."

"Any sign of Tarnow?"

"Not yet. I haven't issued an APB because I was afraid the PEACHES would trace it back to Richter."

"Find him and arrest him, Mitchell. He's a civilian ex-con who shouldn't be eluding the Federal Bureau of Investigation."

"Yes, sir."

"It's over, Ron. Richter needed time alone in the office to steal the files," he replied, gripping the Scotty Cameron putter that usually leaned against his desk. "He cut a deal to save his daughter. Time to pick him up."

"Sir, if we pick him up now we'll lose—"

"We've already lost him. He's promising us results but also trying to extort five million dollars and dealing with the PEACHES. I'll tell you this: there's no chance he's getting that money. If this guy thinks he can play it both ways with me, he's got another thing coming. The deal's off. Pick him up, now."

"Sir, we *told* him to do what the PEACHES asked. We *told* him to play along, to make them think he was on their side, then to plant the bug."

"And he refused! Didn't even take the thing. Then he ditched the one you planted on him and did who knows what for a few hours before showing up in the office the next day. It's time to end his little game."

"Sir, I think we—"

"I'm not going to tell you again, Ron."

Something was off. Mitchell wasn't giving him the whole story. The agent seemed aloof, almost worried. No matter, he told himself. He'd find out what it was.

He always did.

***

10:42.

His cell phone rang unexpectedly, the wrong time for a call. Mark, pen in mouth, sifting through a stack of LPK, Inc. tax statements, ignored it. Ron Mitchell would have to wait.

Despite his paranoia, so far the plan appeared to be working.

Larry's predictable scan of the entire office and all client files after fire drills had given him only one option. All had to appear normal and nothing could be missing when the boss did his inspection. Brad made copies of the keys and hid them and the originals well, just above the third ceiling tile from the leftmost sink in TGI Friday's bathroom. Luckily, no one needed to hit the head as he stood on the counter to retrieve them.

It seemed that none of the five accountants recognized his key was missing after the fire alarm. That was why he made Brad wait until nine o'clock to pull it, to make sure the accountants had already taken the files they needed for the day and would have no need to return to their cabinet after the alarm.

He returned the original keys to their owners after he got back from lunch while they were in the first-floor cafeteria, and then waited for someone to say something. Something about the key not being in its exact location or some other tiny detail that would be just enough to ruin everything. But it didn't happen. When the day ended, all five of them, along with the rest of the employees, left smiling and unaware.

Yes, things were going along just fine.

Then it happened.

After exiting the building via the concealed rear service door and trudging through standing puddles of swampy water, tumbling over the tall metal fence and creeping through the same dark alley to the dilapidated office building Brad had visited a few days before, he made copies of everything. Then he scanned and e-mailed each one to Caroline. After making the return trip, the original files tucked neatly in plastic within his backpack, all he had to do was put them back in the cabinets and get the hell out.

Back to the "it."

Mitchell's phone call was first, which he ignored. Two files down and three to go, and all of the sudden a voice came from behind him.

"So...*that's* how you kept the lights on."

* * *

He didn't need to look to know who it was. Ron Mitchell strolled towards his desk, holding one of the five Neteast portable rotating fans that he'd duct taped to the walls under the lights' motion sensors.

He didn't think to ask how Mitchell got inside. He just faced him, trying to sit on the InfoHelp file on his desk and casually cover it up.

It wasn't so casual: Mitchell's stare told him he knew exactly what it was.

"We saw the lights hadn't turned off, and people thought you were still here. But I knew better, Richter. I knew you hadn't been here the whole time."

"What are you doing here?" he asked.

"What am *I* doing here? The real question is what are *you* doing here?"

"I'm holding up my end of our deal. How's your end coming?"

"It's not coming. The boss thinks you're full of it. He's not going to authorize the money. He's under the distinct impression you cut a deal to save your daughter."

Only his sweat pores responded, which he couldn't control or conceal.

"Did you?" Mitchell asked firmly.

If there was no money, there was no plan. His stare told Mitchell something he didn't want it to.

"I take that as a yes. C'mon, Richter. I told you we'd protect you."

"Ron, listen—"

"No, Richter. I can't listen anymore. I'm here to bring you in. You hear me? I'm here to arrest you. You pissed me off, and I dealt with it. But then you pissed my boss off, and that's the last thing you wanted to do."

"But I—"

"You also involved Brad Tarnow, which is the second-to-last thing you wanted to do. Now, you're both going down, and I can't stop it. We're going to put out an APB out on Tarnow and pick him up in a few hours. This is above my pay grade now."

"*You told me to play along! To make them think I was on their side!*"

"Nobody told you to demand five million bucks."

Mitchell withdrew a revolver and pointed it at his chest. Nobody, not Tom nor Edward Doran nor Jason Albers nor anyone else from the PEACHES, had held him at gunpoint. And now, someone from the FBI, supposedly on his side and supposed to protect him, was doing just that.

"Stand up and put your hands on your head. You're under arrest for extortion against the United States Government."

His entire plan was shot in an instant. He still hadn't warned Brad or Caroline. The files were sitting on his desk, out in the open. He hadn't hidden the key copies either. They were right next to the files. Desperate, he played the only card he had left, knowing it wouldn't win him the hand.

"You want that tape to go public?" he said with as much force as a surprised, out-of-his-league accountant could muster.

"That's beyond my control now. I guess I'll just have to improvise. Get up."

Out of options, he'd admitted defeat. After starting out promising, things had gone as wrong as they could've gone. There was nothing else he could do. Then he heard a voice that made things even worse.

"Mark, what are you doing here?"

37

Jason Albers approached them both from behind very slowly.

Mitchell quickly tucked his firearm into his inside jacket pocket, a less-than-obvious move he'd clearly made before. The agent's face was calm, his motions fluid. Even his breathing appeared regular and under complete control.

Mark's demeanor, however, was not so relaxed.

Jason Albers, the *leader* of the terrorist organization, his old friend, the definition of hypocrisy, was standing ten feet away. And the companies' files were on his desk next to an FBI agent.

The room, at that precise moment, got 20 degrees warmer.

Jason continued to move slowly, deliberately unhurried. He wore the standard blue uniform with the white nametag and clipboard, his graying salt-and-pepper hair again combed perfectly to the side. Nike gym shoes completed the uniform for the heavyset fifty-something-year-old, and with each step Jason winced with old-man pain.

"Good to see you man! What are you doing in the office so late?"

The walls were caving in. The room was in fact shrinking.

"Just finishing up some work," he choked out.

"There's Mark Richter for you, burning the midnight oil again! You're a champ, kid! Who's your friend?" Jason asked, motioning to Mitchell.

"I'm Walt," Mitchell responded, extending his right arm. "I'm in town for business and thought I'd try to give Mark a buzz. Surprise, surprise, he's hard at work in the office at eleven o'clock. I guess some things never change."

"It's nice to meet you. I'm Jason," the security guard answered, still smiling. "I'm just doing my rounds; pretty simple while no one's here. How do you two know each other? You're not from Chicago?"

"Oh, Heaven's no. I can't handle your winters. I'm from Dallas," Ron/Walt answered.

Mark found it amazing how easily, and convincingly, the FBI agent could lie. It seemed so natural, like it was boring chitchat between new acquaintances, not one between the head of a terrorist organization and the man in charge of bringing it down.

Mitchell almost played the part of a liar too well for his comfort, though at that moment he was grateful.

"You sure don't sound like you're from Dallas," Jason responded in laughter.

"Oh, I wasn't born there. I'm a transplant. Family moved around a lot as a kid, so I never did develop an accent."

"Funny. If anything, I'd guess you were from Chicago."

* * *

Mark froze.

Jason knew. He knew it was a lie.

He waited in pure angst for ugliness to ensue, for guns to bust out and for his life to end right there on the sixth floor of an office building. However, after a *long* moment of silence, the conversation continued.

"Well I can't explain that," Mitchell/Walt continued, "never lived here. I met Mark down in San Antonio a few years ago. Annual tax law seminar...those things could cure insomnia."

Jason chuckled. It didn't ease his tension.

"I could barely keep my eyes open, so when I saw Mark here taking diligent notes, I figured I'd sit by the smart guy in class. Been friends ever since."

"He sure is smart. One of the brightest guys here."

He forced a smile that was sure to appear far less genuine than Mitchell's.

"There's that modesty again," Mitchell/Walt said. "He'd never admit it, not in a million years! But I don't doubt it."

"So how long ago did you two meet?"

"About eight years ago, I'd say. That about right, Mark?"

He nodded silently.

"That's nice. What kind of tax law are you in? Corporate, like Mark?"

"You got it."

Jason could have been simply upholding his reputation as an overly amiable, chatty guy.

But he doubted it.

He worried the "security guard" would already have a list of every person he'd ever met in San Antonio and anywhere else and was referencing the list in his mind at that very moment. He pictured Jason mentally combing through his personnel file, line-by-line, letter-by-letter.

And finding out there was no Walt in his past.

"How's Katherine?" Jason asked, reengaging him.

"She's fine. She's at a friend's house tonight."

"A sleepover on a school night? That doesn't sound like the Mark Richter I know."

The Mark Richter I know?

"It's movie day in school tomorrow, so I thought it'd be okay," he responded, forcing back the urge to beat him to death with his broom. Anger and hunger for revenge greatly tempted him to satisfy that urge with the butt of Mitchell's gun.

"Oh, okay," Jason answered condescendingly, as if granting his approval. "I hear there was a little excitement this morning with the fire alarm."

"Yeah," he responded, clenching his fists.

"I hope they get those kinks worked out."

"Yeah...me too."

"So what are you guys up to now?"

It was the question he was waiting for but didn't have an answer to. Fortunately, Walt did.

"I just got into Chicago and thought we could grab dinner, but Mark's still got some work to do. Matter of fact, I better let you get back at it. And I should probably get to the hotel and prepare for a meeting tomorrow morning, anyway. Can you walk me down?"

"Huh?" he answered without thinking.

"Don't you have to escort me out after hours? Like the way you had to let me in?" the FBI agent responded without inflection in his voice, reinforcing his story and covering Mark's slip up.

"Yeah, no problem."

Jason smiled at both of them. Then he rested his hand on Mark's shoulder, and terrified him to no end.

"Walt, where are you staying? I can give you a lift if you like, since Mark here's still got work to do."

"Oh, thanks, but I'll just call American Taxi and get a cab. Might as well expense it since the company's paying. Appreciate the offer though."

"My pleasure, Walt. If I don't see you, have yourself a great trip," Jason said in a way that made him think the feds had to be wrong. There wasn't a hint of nastiness. Jason was friendly and gentle and it didn't seem possible he could be the monster the FBI said he was.

"Ready?" Mitchell whispered once Jason was down the hall.

"Don't—"

"Walk me down, Mark."

In plain sight of the FBI agent, he tucked the company files into his desk drawer and closed it gently. Then he and Mitchell left the floor together. Once inside the elevator, Mitchell faced him.

"Don't make this any harder on yourself than it has to be. You're innocent. I know it, you know it, and I can convince the higher-ups in the bureau. But you're gonna have to drop this five-million-dollar idea of yours, and you can't run. Running only makes you look guilty. Just come in, explain your side of the story, and you'll be okay."

Mitchell was full of it. The agent would never be able convince the FBI that he was on their side. Not after the fire alarm, and what had just happened. They'd send him straight to prison and throw away the key.

* * *

The sixth floor window offered a clear view of the circle drive.

The moon was out in full. No trees blocked his angle. Jason stood in the darkened conference room, one that didn't have portable fans taped to its walls, and watched Mark Richter and "Walt" standing on the sidewalk while they waited for a cab.

He already knew who "Walt" was, but even if he hadn't, their body language told it all. Even though they knew they were being watched, their posture told him everything he needed and then some. Very few people can control their body language.

First, there was Mark, who constantly shifted his weight from side-to-side. His hands dug deep in his pockets, the reluctant reckoner didn't say much. He wasn't smiling or frowning or reacting much at all to whatever "Walt" was saying. If he had binoculars, he was sure he would've seen uneven breathing, maybe even spasms.

"Walt," on the other hand, remained flat-footed. His lips moved at an average speed, and he waved his arms casually throughout the conversation, pantomiming the dialogue. His facial expression was happiness, not anger or frustration or fear. They were all easygoing gestures and loose movements, in stark contrast to Mark's stiff, unbalanced tension.

Case closed.

For one to be so casual and the other so tense, it could only mean one thing. He didn't need to see anything else. His reached into his pocket and pulled out a cell phone.

38

"*You've got to be kidding me!*"

First, the camel jockey took over an hour to get there. Now, he was getting pulled over. Ron Mitchell sat in the back of the rancid, awful-smelling taxi, pissed at the world. He'd just met Jason Albers in the flesh. The leader, the brains, the head of the snake, the head honcho of the entire PEACHES organization.

He felt like sterilizing his right hand after shaking Albers's. No, amputating it. He wanted to rip his bulbous head off and poke his fat cheeks with those big black glasses. After all his efforts for all those years, Coldstone's decision to cut their losses and put Richter away was going to let the PEACHES slip through his fingers *again*.

It didn't make any sense.

And now, Yusuf, his Muslim, non-English-speaking cabbie, full beanie hat and all, was getting pulled over for speeding, topping off an altogether awful night.

Coldstone was less than enthusiastic to hear the news and ripped him a new one over the phone. As if he *wanted* Jason Albers to show up. The Regional Director instructed him to arrest Richter at 3 a.m. to ensure it didn't tip Albers off. Another all-nighter to arrest the *one* guy who could help put the PEACHES away, but then just had to get greedy. But then Albers shows up out of nowhere, and just to make sure he didn't blow his cover, he not only didn't get Richter, but he couldn't even drive his own car home. And now some local flatfoot was pulling him over!

The night just kept getting better.

"No speed, no speed," Yusuf kept repeating to himself.

He shook his head in disgust as Yusuf turned into a vacant gas station, the cop following behind. Yusuf stroked his inch-long black whiskers. He wanted to yank them out one-by-one. When the police light turned off, it grew dark rather quickly. He just hoped this went fast.

But he knew it wouldn't. He could see it now. Yusuf would deny he was speeding, sputtering broken English and pissing the cop off even more. Then he wouldn't have all the documentation he needed, and it'd drag on and on and on.

He was wrong.

Soon after he heard the cop's door open, two silenced gunshots zipped through the window and into Yusuf. The cabbie let out a short yelp but didn't have time to say much before he hunched over the steering wheel, blood flowing from his back and neck.

Before he knew it, the back door was open and a white man dressed in all black fired a .357 caliber revolver into his left leg. He howled in pain, and the man fired another shot into his left arm. Then the man squatted down, left arm resting on the open car door, and tossed his gun on the ground.

His cries were then silenced not with bullets, but words.

"If you scream again, I'm going to do things to your wife and son that no wife and son should have to endure. And I'll let you watch."

* * *

Ron knew he had a reputation as a hot-tempered badass within the FBI. He'd gotten it because of a few, or more than a few, less-than-legal "voluntary" confessions, and his relentless pursuit of terrorists.

But now, his face was covered with tears and he whimpered for mercy. Mercy for his family. He thought of his wife and son, and finally understood why Mark Richter wouldn't play the FBI's game.

"It appears you do have control when you need to have it," the man whispered. "Now, this is not going to end well for you. I'm sure you understand that. But we can keep your family out of it and make it relatively painless if you give me straight answers. What is your real name?"

Ron knew it was over, but he'd been trained for years to study aggressors, and some habits are impossible to break. The man's face was smooth, no prickly stubble, moles or freckles. His short, black hair didn't need to be combed and wasn't. Of average height and build, he didn't fit the generic description of a hit man.

He remained silent, which led to another gunshot wound, this one in his right leg. He bit through his tongue and felt the blood slowly trickle down his throat. He searched for anyone who might be nearby. But no one was in sight at nearly 12:30 early Friday morning. The cars were well off the main drag, no houses were within a hundred feet, and there were only empty roads and sidewalks.

"You're going to tell me what I need to know."

Ron's training prevailed once again. He regained focus for his last chance in his final minutes. His motivation was simple: the longer he stayed alive, the less likely it was that his wife and son would.

The assailant had fired two gunshots to kill Yusuf, and Ron had sustained three. That meant there was one more round in the .357 before he'd have to reload. The man had taken his gun, eliminating retaliation. But he also threw it on the ground, which would require him to pick it up before use.

Ron summoned a courage that only people facing death can. His old partner had told him ten years ago that it can't be learned or taught or experienced otherwise.

Now, it was his turn.

"My name is Walt kiss-my-ass Whitman."

The bullet ripped into his left leg, his third gunshot wound in 30 seconds. He didn't yell in pain, but instead channeled that urge into his uninjured right arm, reaching into his right jacket pocket and withdrawing his cell phone. He pressed the Emergency button on the locked screen before smashing down the call button. Then he held it as far away as he could, in his outstretched right hand, towards the rear passenger-side window.

"No!" the man yelled, realizing that reaching for the phone would take too long. He dropped the .357 and grabbed Ron's gun from the ground instead, quickly elevating and firing it at the same time. The loud shots rattled the silent evening. Bullets ripped through Ron Mitchell's chest and face, one after another.

* * *

The man reached across the corpse and grabbed the phone from the dead agent's hand, disconnecting when he heard the operator. Moments later the callback came, and a woman informed him that a 911-call had been placed from that number.

He apologized, chuckling, explaining that he'd accidentally dialed the numbers. To which she replied with her own brief chortle, explained that it happens all the time, and urged him to stay on the line in the future.

He apologized again, thanked her for her time, and said good-bye.

39

It took Brad a little over two hours to make the normally three-hour drive. Despite Mark's insistence that he not get pulled over, his already-lead foot only grew heavier.

He left around ten p.m. per Mark's request. Staying in Chicago all day wasn't exactly ideal for his nerves, but he agreed nighttime was the best option. In the hotel room Mark had rented for him, every time he heard a siren, the Channel 9 news came on, or he heard voices outside his door, afraid they were coming for him.

What scared him most about that was the fact they were looking for him when he didn't actually do anything wrong. One of the things he learned from his old cellmate, Francisco, was that when the cops come after you, you sleep better at night if you're guilty. You know why they're chasing you and what will happen if or when you get caught. When you're innocent, when there's no reason to be on their list, you have no clue what the future holds.

After an hour-and-a-half, the streets turned more rustic. Many had no signs or signs that were uprooted and lying on the ground, victims of teenage pranks. He followed the directions as best he could but several times felt lost. Dodging fallen corn stalks and roadkill on winding, undulating country roads, all he could see in every direction was blackness. The breadth of stars and glowing moon above were beautiful but provided insufficient light, and it seemed there was nothing but cornfield after cornfield on the long, lonely stretches.

When he finally arrived, he noted that the driveway was a half-mile long according to the odometer, lined with cornfields and grass on either side. Its hard gravel texture abruptly met a smooth concrete surface when he reached the house.

It was a large, rustic-contemporary home, somewhat out of place in rural Wisconsin. Made of red brick and white siding, three mini triangular roof structures jutted upwards, each with a window in its center. To the left, a steep hill lay parallel to six concrete steps. A small sidewalk met those steps that connected all the way to a front door and elevated porch with two wooden rocking chairs and three hanging plants.

To the right, a gently-sloping hill emptied into an open lawn maybe half an acre in size. Large pine trees that reminded him of fairy tale pillars sprung up from behind, well over the top of the house. Straight ahead was a three-car garage housing an old red pickup truck with a basketball hoop above it.

All the windows facing the driveway were dark except for one. It looked like the dining room, a large glass and wooden hutch on the right side. She stood in the center of the large window, waving her arm and smiling. Brad parked the car and prepared to say hello for the first time in many years.

* * *

Caroline seemed almost too cheery considering the danger they were both in. She gave him a big bear hug and smiled wide. Despite his concern, her positive attitude reminded him that some things never change. He faked a bit of his own optimism and wished it could be genuine too.

But some things do change.

And one of them was how good she looked. Her body had grown even shapelier over the years, and her hazel eyes were large and inviting. She'd grown out her brown hair and pulled it back in a ponytail, the perfect complement to a few adorable freckles doting her cheeks. His best friend's sister had grown up in a big way.

The inside of the house was even more impressive than the outside. An ornate chandelier hung high above the wood-floored foyer and pristine white walls leading to the family room displayed classic artwork from artists he didn't know. The living room was spotless, clutter-free and well kept.

"Is everything okay?" she asked. "Mark told me things went well this morning, but is everything still okay?"

Now she looked nervous. She was nibbling her lower lip and breathing rather rapidly.

No, she looked *terrified*.

Then it hit him why she seemed so happy when he arrived. It wasn't that she wasn't concerned or scared or worried at all. She was horrified. But she'd been dealing with it all alone, without answers or closure, and a familiar face can make a big difference.

At least now she wasn't alone.

He gave her another long hug and felt her shaking arms. She squeezed back tightly, pressing herself into his chest and interlocking her hands behind his back. Her grip was that of a woman who mowed the lawn and killed the spiders as the get-stuff-done head of the household, while at the same time being a loving mom who'd always cared for others above herself.

He couldn't deny that he liked the way it felt.

"Everything's fine, Caroline. We're going to be okay," he said.

Now, if only he could believe it.

"Mark sent me some files a few hours ago," she answered, slowly breaking free of their embrace, somewhat to his dismay.

"Any issues?"

"Not so far. But I'm still waiting for the rest."

"That's all we can do."

It was the only thing he could think to say.

"I'm going to get some coffee. Would you like some?" she asked, blending her pragmatic and sweet sides seamlessly.

"Caroline..." he began but did not finish.

"Yes?"

"I'm sorry about Richard. And I'm sorry I didn't say it sooner."

She forced an obviously insincere grin, her lips pushed together and unnatural. He heard her swallow and watched her eyes grew watery. He regretted saying it, but he had to. He'd felt guilty for years that not only had he never met Richard, but that he didn't tell Caroline how sorry he was. The accident happened smack dab in the middle of his prison sentence, and he hadn't so much as called her since being released. He'd put his embarrassment in front of her feelings, and he needed forgiveness.

"Thank you, Brad. And I'm sorry about what happened to you."

Even facing the memory of her husband's death, she showed empathy and compassion towards him. Yet another example of how caring she was. Another thing that didn't change.

"How about that coffee?"

"Yes, please."

He further surveyed the house when she went to get the beverage. A large blue duffle bag was lying on the floor against the wall, zipped up and bulging at the seams. In the dining room was the fine-oak hutch he saw from the car in the driveway that his decoratively challenged mind thought was exclusively for bedrooms, but looked perfect right where it was.

The table, in stark contrast to the rest of the house, looked like a remote NORAD missile control station. A computer, desktop printer, scanner, and a few other gadgets he couldn't readily identify covered almost every inch of it. Cords lay intertwined behind the machines, plugged into surge bars on the floor. Pages and pages of what looked like income statements were spread across the floor.

Clearly work was being done, but he didn't have the slightest idea what.

Suddenly his cell phone, the one Mark had given him, began to vibrate. So did Caroline's. They stared at each other for a brief moment before checking the short but informative text message.

TAKE WHAT YOU NEED AND GET OUT. THE COPS ARE COMING FOR YOU.

40

Four a.m. The wretched roosters weren't even up yet, and he was already 20 minutes deep into a conversation with The General. Three cups of coffee and a Red Bull didn't offset nature's demand for sleep, but this was The General. You fought through exhaustion when The General wanted to talk, and you did it with zest.

"Tom, don't forget that the primary objective of this conversation is to determine what to do with Richter," The General reminded him after they got slightly off-track.

"He's too much of a risk, sir. By lying to you about who Mitchell was, he proved he knows who you are and is working with the FBI. We should get rid of him as soon as possible."

He'd thought it through carefully, considering all alternatives, just as The General had taught him, and that was the only decision that made sense. It felt like a no-brainer: there was simply too much risk to do anything else.

The General, however, seemed less than certain.

"Take a step back," The General said. "Revisit the facts and make logical deductions. Let's assume Richter understands our capabilities and knows not to cross us. What's the first thing he does?"

"Sends his daughter away."

"Correct. He protects his most prized possession and gets her up to Wisconsin."

"He has to know she's not really safe there."

"Sure he does, but he knows she's safer there than here. Or at least that's what he tells himself. Either way, he's removed precious baggage. Trust me, she's the first thing on his mind."

"But he still called Sam Fisher, even after we told him to keep quiet."

"He did that well before the FBI was involved. And let's think about what he did? He asked an old college friend he knew was into surveillance to find out about a man who offered him three million dollars to steal files. It's a logical thing to do, and Richter's always going to do what's logical. That's why he's so predictable. But we didn't lose anything. It was all a part of the plan."

"General, sir, permission to speak freely?"

"Of course, Tom."

"Richter going to the feds wasn't part of the plan. And I'd think if he really didn't want to cross us, that's the last thing he'd do."

The General chuckled softly as Tom stared in confusion, only able to wait for an explanation. After a sip of water, The General provided it.

"He didn't go to the feds."

He stared back, squinting his eyes in question.

"They came to him, no doubt using Fisher's death to try to scare him into submission. They probably told him about us and offered protection for him and his daughter, maybe even money. Puppets on strings move where instructed." The General then smiled, confusing him a bit, though he decided to keep quiet. "But Richter's smart, and he knows that dog won't hunt. He knows we'd find him, that we'd find his daughter. Richter's not giving them a thing."

"What makes you so sure?"

"Empathize with your subject, Tom. He's got the feds watching him and us demanding that he break the law. If he gets caught trying to steal the files, sure, he goes down. But if he doesn't help the FBI, even if he doesn't get caught, he'll still go down. The FBI is telling him they're close to catching us, and that if they do, he'll go down with us unless he helps them. He's being cornered and pressured by people he knows can't protect his daughter, his top priority."

Tom now saw where The General was headed.

"On the other hand, if he doesn't do what we ask, his daughter dies. When we eliminated Fisher, he became a believer. So he's trapped. Screwed if he does and screwed if he doesn't. When push comes to shove, fathers protect their daughters."

***

"Yesterday," The General continued, "we learned that Mark Richter understands helping us is what's best for his daughter, but also that the FBI can significantly delay Project VIXEN if we don't do something soon. We can't allow that to happen."

"What about Richter talking to—"

"Project VIXEN is the top priority. It cannot be compromised."

"I understand, sir. But with all due respect, the decoy we used yesterday won't throw the cops off forever. We do have to put some distance between you and Richter."

"Damn feds could lose a caged animal at the zoo."

"Bitch," "damn," and a handful of racially derogatory expressions were, as a general rule, the only curse words The General ever used. Typically, Tom would mirror the dialogue with a similar expletive of his own, but he needed to understand The General's decision first.

"That doesn't change the fact Richter was talking to the feds. I don't understand, sir. All it took to move on Edward was news from the informant that the feds had connected him back to you. And just like that, he's gone. Yet Richter is not only on their radar but also openly communicating with them, and we're not doing anything?"

It wasn't like The General to keep liabilities around. Usually he erred on the side of caution, conservative to the end in every walk of life. Silently, Tom wondered if The General had grown too close to Richter and just didn't want to do what he knew had to be done. Did that have something to do with The General's coy smile earlier?

"Tom, you're going to lead this organization one day, so you need to ramp up your learning curve. Edward's the reason they know about me, and his death is his own fault. I told him many times that one day his notoriety would jeopardize the mission and that when it did, he'd be eliminated. Our informant confirmed that happened."

"But Richter—"

"The question isn't whether or not to remove him. His exposure to the FBI is reason enough to do that, I agree. But we still need the information to keep VIXEN on track. Right now, he's stealing files to save his daughter. When he's finished, he'll refuse to join the cause and we'll have no choice but to eliminate him. But why shoot a working horse?"

He cursed himself for doubting The General's loyalty to the cause. How could he question the man? He'd lash his arm later to pay for that ambiguity. The General then rose from his seat and pushed two fingers between closed blinds, peaking through with his large, brown eyes.

"What about Brad Tarnow? And Richter's sister?" he asked.

"Get our man up to Wisconsin and tell him to sit tight. As soon as we're finished with Richter, we'll deal with them and the children in that oh-so-secretive hideout they'll leave for as soon as Richter tells them to abandon the house, if he hasn't already."

"The children?"

"Leave nothing to chance. I don't want Will Hubert growing up with revenge on his mind. Haven't you ever seen *Godfather Two*?"

41

Thirty grand isn't as much cash as you'd think.

After giving Brad and Caroline more than half and using most of what was left for necessary purchases, Mark realized the stash was getting quite small, only $6,500 remained. But he didn't have the time or energy to worry about "that" money.

It was the "other" money that he couldn't stop thinking about.

The night before was one to forget for many reasons. Stealing the files, Ron Mitchell's surprise visit, Jason Albers showing up, etc. But the FBI's decision to arrest him and not pay the five million was the biggest blow, and now he had no idea what he was going to do. The whole plan depended on that payout.

It also meant that possessing the confidential information and tax filing records for five companies, documents that could put him behind bars for fraud and larceny and a host of other things, had nothing to show for it. Nothing but an arrest warrant and pissed off cops and criminals. He was officially WANTED by the FBI.

The federal government of the United States is after me.

And Tom's deadline is tomorrow.

Even so, he still couldn't fight fatigue. He catnapped on the floor, flat on his back, his face absorbing what little it could of the sparse northern sun. He couldn't ever remember being so tired, hardly able to keep his eyelids open despite knowing the floor had more germs than a dumpster. On-and-off five-minute snoozes kept him going, regulated by his watch alarm and the nightmares he had when he drifted.

Three 20-ounce bottles of Coke sat atop the desk amongst a maelstrom of paperwork. His head propped up on a briefcase, he stared at the full-length cracks of the office walls. Wondering how they formed, he drifted off once more.

At 11 a.m. sharp, his cell phone started ringing.

A man who despised cell phones, Mark now had four, all from different people. His original was long gone, along with the rest of his old life. And like that life, it was never coming back.

The continuous ringing came from the mobile Ron Mitchell had given him, free of tracking bugs according to Sam's anti-surveillance technology. He jotted the number down and grabbed the phone he used exclusively for placing calls. After splashing his face with water from the glass next to the Cokes, he dialed the digits to call Mitchell back.

I have to convince him. I need that money.

"Hello?" the male voice answered. It didn't sound like Mitchell.

"Ron Mitchell, please."

"*Who is this?*"

"Who is this?" Mark replied.

"Is this a secure line?"

"It is."

"Are you sure?" the voice asked, this time deeper and softer.

"As sure as I can be."

"This must be Mark Richter."

* * *

Mark didn't respond.

The phone pressed to his left ear, he waited for the man to reveal himself first. The voice was deep and without accent. Crackly. It sounded like it belonged to an old man, but what can you really know from a person's voice?

"I take it from your silence that you are in fact Mark Richter. The same Mark Richter who has been communicating with Mr. Mitchell for the past two weeks."

Tempted as Mark was to simply say yes and find out just who the hell he was talking to, he silently reminded himself that it could've been someone from the PEACHES.

Pillar #3, Clarity, he reminded himself.

"Who is this?" he whispered.

"My name is David Coldstone. I'm the Regional Director of the FBI, Ron Mitchell's former boss."

"Former?"

"I have some news that will likely come as a shock. Ron Mitchell is dead."

His physiological response was the same every time he learned someone he knew had perished. And within seconds, he felt his widening eyes, his churning stomach, and his trembling hand. Small beads of sweat formed around his hairline; his heart rate accelerated, speech went away.

And even though he had no reason to believe this man was who he said he was, or that this news was true, that reaction still set in like clockwork.

"What?"

"Ron is gone. He reported to me for over seven years, Mark. My direct subordinate. And I'd gotten to know him personally as well as professionally. And now he's gone. He's been murdered."

"Murdered? How?"

"Last night at just past 12:30, Des Plaines 911 emergency response received a call that was traced to Ron's mobile phone. The caller hung up as soon as the operator answered, and on the callback he claimed accidental dial. It was a male voice, but we don't know anything else. We haven't been able to map it to anyone with voice recognition software as of yet."

"But how—"

"I heard the tape this morning, and it wasn't Ron's voice, so I did some investigating. The last I heard from him, he'd gotten into a cab at around midnight yesterday. Sound right to you?"

He was finished trying to verify David Coldstone was who he said he was. He needed answers, and he needed them now. If the caller was someone from the PEACHES, so be it. He simply didn't have the energy anymore.

"Yeah, it was around midnight."

"Ron also said he'd waited forever for the cab? Did it seem like a long time to you?"

"It took a little longer than usual I guess, but it was twelve o'clock at night. What does that matter?"

"We contacted American Taxi. Someone called the cab company five minutes after the car was ordered and told them to come a half-hour later than previously requested to the same location."

Now Mark saw the relevance.

Ron Mitchell didn't make that call.

There was only one other person who could have.

"Jason Albers had Ron pinned from the start, Mark. He delayed the cab ride to give someone time to get to your office and follow him. I'm not sure of the details after that, but you get the gist of what happened next."

Mark recalled, sadly, that Ron, at the time going by Walt, had specifically stated he was going to call American Taxi for a cab.

Why did he have to do that?

"Did you get the number that called the cab company?" he asked Coldstone.

"Unlisted. But when I learned that a few Des Plaines residents ten minutes from your office reported what they all said sounded like gunshots, we did a little more legwork and found out that the cab driver never reported earnings after his shift ended. First time in over six years that Yusuf Haseem failed to report his evening earnings. He also didn't come home, another first, and his wife hasn't seen him since he left for work. The cab is nowhere to be found."

He tried to absorb the overload of information being thrown at him. What Coldstone said made sense, and it also answered some questions he'd had earlier. He'd expected to hear from Mitchell later that night, but never did. When he snuck out the back door of the building fifteen minutes after Mitchell got in the cab, he was sure the agent would be there to arrest him, yet he walked away free. And while he wasn't going to look a gift horse in the mouth, it didn't make sense at the time. Mitchell's death explained it now.

That didn't make it easy to hear, however.

"Think this through for a minute, Mark. They killed him because they knew he was FBI. And if they didn't know in what capacity before, they sure as hell do now. They know you've been talking to us. They're going to kill you if you don't come in."

He wanted to ask a million questions. Why didn't they kill me already? What do you want? Why can't you arrest Jason? How did you get this number? The list could go on indefinitely.

But he couldn't show his hand to Coldstone. Ron Mitchell was dead, and he felt terrible about that, but it wasn't he who decided Ron should show up at his office. Come to think of it, Ron had said that it was his *boss* that didn't approve of the five million dollar payment and had ordered Mark's arrest.

When he put two and two together, he realized he was talking to the man who'd done more to cause Mitchell's death than he had. Or so he told himself.

"Mitchell tried to arrest me last night." He tried to remain stoic and unreadable. He couldn't know for sure if it was working.

"Yes."

"He told me you gave the order."

"Ron said a lot of things," Coldstone replied.

"Is it true?"

"That's beside the point."

"No, that's precisely the point. What he told me was to play along, to get them comfortable with me. Make them feel like I'm on their side. And that's exactly what I did. And that's exactly what I'm doing. And for that, you ordered him to arrest me?"

"Nobody told you to demand five million dollars."

"You're right. Just like nobody told you to send Ron to my office last night."

"There's no other way out of this. You've got to see that."

"Listen to this."

Mark retrieved the small tape recorder that held his only leverage on a man now deceased. Rest in peace, he thought, but for now I have to exploit you.

"You think that's bad, you should hear what he had to say about his boss. Wait, didn't you just tell me that *you're* his boss?"

At first, his impression of Coldstone was very different from that of Mitchell. The Regional Director was calm, concentrated on the facts. He seemed void of emotion, even over Mitchell's death. And he didn't show too much excitement one way or the other in stark contrast to Mitchell's mercurialness. But first impressions often don't last.

Especially when money is involved.

"You're not getting away with blackmail and extortion, Mark. I can tell you that right now! I'm not giving you five million dollars so you can go help the PEACHES. Ron's dead because you wanted to play games. I'm not going to play games with you."

"Ron's dead because *you* screwed up. *You're* the one who sent him to my office. *You're* the one who put him in harm's way. You can try to guilt trip me all you want, but we both know who made the call that led to Ron's murder. If you uphold your end of the deal, I promise you'll get what you want. If not, find yourself another rat and either come arrest me or leave me the hell alone."

He surprised even himself. His willingness, and ability, to play hardball had increased with frustration and exhaustion, two things he had plenty of at present. He had Coldstone on the ropes. The Regional Director controlled his temper better than Mitchell, but he too was a loose cannon. Both men shared the same weakness.

The director regained control quicker than Mitchell would've, but the damage had been done.

"Sooner or later, you're either going to be dead or in prison. Is that really how you want to play this? Think of your daughter."

"I am, Mr. Coldstone. Believe me, I am thinking of her. And if I thought there was any other way, any safer or easier way, I wouldn't be doing this."

"Your time's running out, son. Don't make this mistake. We can protect you."

"How can you say that? Mitchell's dead...and you're claiming you can protect *me*? I don't think so, bucko. It's *your* time that's running out. I told Mitchell that I needed the money by nine o'clock tonight, but now I'm talking to someone with more authority. You've got until noon, or I go to the papers."

"No you won't. You'd be dead as soon as you did."

"According to you I'm good as dead anyway, so I might as well bring you down with me. I *will* go to the papers, and the newsrooms, and the Internet. And when I do, I'll bring this tape and expose you for what you are. I'll show the world what kind of a unit you really run and how safe people in this country really are. Then I'll tell them how all that mattered to you was your money and your warped ego. I think the media would gladly show the taxpayers what they're paying for."

There was a delay. He'd actually caused Coldstone to think about it. He pictured an old man with black glasses staring at the ceiling, running through the certainties of getting the money back: the tracers on the account, the protection encompassing the cash, the analysts watching every transfer on a computer screen.

He could see Coldstone nodding his head, sure it was safe. One hundred percent certain that he'd get his money back.

"Noon is in 50 minutes, Mr. Richter. That's cutting it a little close."

"Then you'd better stop wasting time talking to me."

42

The white, four-cylinder, 2010 Nissan Altima moved better than he expected.

Despite looking like a lemon, due in no small part to the duct taped front fender, numerous dents and scratches, and the plethora of stains and tears on the upholstery, the engine ran smoothly and it accelerated nicely.

Brad found out quickly he wasn't the only one with a lead foot and held on for dear life the entire trip. Caroline pushed the pedal to the metal like she'd done it many times before. The speedometer lingered around 85 miles per hour for most of the trip, surely the car's max.

They drove to Madison, Wisconsin, a 75-mile trip that would've taken most human beings an hour and a half. Caroline had them there in 55 minutes. US-151 N ran more east than it did north and the wicked early two a.m. hour meant traffic was light, even as they approached the greater Madison area. He tried to lighten the mood once by comparing her to Danica Patrick and discovered she didn't take that as a compliment.

Write that down, he'd told himself.

In the hotel room, to his left sat a determined, focused woman. Her dichotomy was still in the back of his mind, but it was her intensity that had taken over the front. She was at the desk, glued to her laptop, scanner, and the files she'd gathered from her home before leaving. She brought a video camera per Mark's request, but all her other equipment and personal possessions, including pictures, homemade videos and Will's adorable refrigerator art, were quickly abandoned.

There were no last looks or doubts. They'd left the house in less than one minute.

The text's urgency didn't exactly encourage a long, drawn out good-bye, but it was more her resolve to do what needed to be done than fear that got them out so quickly. He reminded himself that Caroline lost her husband very unexpectedly. There was no chance for final adieus, no promise of closure. You don't get through something like that without having the fortitude to leave a house and some possessions.

Mark's text had shaken them both up, and he questioned why. The cops were coming. So what? Shouldn't they be *happy* the cops were coming? Wouldn't innocent people who'd done nothing wrong welcome the police with open arms? Even with everything that was happening, it felt awkward to him to run away from the cops instead of toward them, even as an ex-con.

There was no shortage of hotel vacancies in the mid-sized college town during the summer, even at this late hour. They checked into a Holiday Inn & Suites right off Highway 14, paid cash, $100 per night for four nights, and "unloaded" all of three bags. Exhausted but unable to sleep, Caroline had connected her computer to the Internet only to see there was no e-mail from Mark.

"How much money do you have left?" he asked her.

"Five hundred. You?"

"About a grand."

"Will that be enough?" she asked hesitantly.

"How's Will?"

A smile, followed quickly by a frown, crept across her face. Caroline had called the Mount Sterling hotel the kids were at as soon as they arrived, just to make sure Will and Katherine were okay. She'd told Brad that the 110-mile, two-hour drive that separated them was the farthest she'd ever been from her little boy. She didn't say much on the call and Will did most of the talking. But what she did say sounded like it came from June Cleaver. Her voice was soft, her inflections caring.

"He's happy. Roberta's letting him get ice from the ice machine. He loves getting ice when we stay at hotels."

He chuckled. A little bit of innocence in a very guilty world went a long way. He could just picture the little guy sprinting down the hallway, ice bucket in hand.

"He's handsome," he said, pointing at the wallet-sized picture she held.

"Thank you. He reminds me of Richard."

Not where he wanted that to go. Not where Caroline wanted it to go, either. She quickly changed gears, figuratively, and got up to use the bathroom. When she came back, he knew she'd wiped away tears.

"You called Mark?"

"No answer. Left a message and told him we were here, but he said he'd be out of touch for a bit."

"It's pretty late. I'm going to try to close my eyes for a bit."

"Good idea. Get some sleep."

"Wake me up as soon as he calls. I need to work on that as soon as he e-mails it."

"Will do."

Caroline finally drifted off a little after three o'clock, but he still couldn't sleep. He stayed up and watched her, her soft face angled towards him, one arm tucked under the pillow and the other down her side, her mouth open ever so slightly. He felt guiltier and guiltier watching her sleep, thinking of what would happen next.

"Mark," he whispered to himself, "I sure hope this plan of yours works."

He had no idea he was being watched.

43

He would get the money back. That much was certain.

David Coldstone squeezed the Scotty Cameron putter tighter at the very thought of giving into Richter's demands. His navy blue, Hickey Freeman suit jacket was folded neatly over the chair, white dress shirtsleeves rolled up to the elbows, silk tie loosened at the neck. The $300 golf club on his left shoulder, he stared out the two-story window.

Logistics, of course, had not been a problem in the least. That was his specialty. He made a few phone calls, pulled a few strings and, poof, five million dollars from ten different accounts appeared. Richter was right about one thing: he did have a lot of pull with the FBI.

A lot of pull.

Each account was also secured with three surveillance tracking mechanisms tied to the unique PIN numbers. He'd ordered a team of computer lab rats, also known as analysts, to do nothing but stare at those ten accounts all day long. If Richter so much as thought about dipping into them, they'd be on him like white on rice.

The truth was, five million would be a small price to pay. Abacus Boy really wasn't asking for too much if he delivered what he promised. Hell, they'd spent more than that the past few years just watching the PEACHES.

Plus, it was worth repeating to himself as he dialed the number, he'd get the money back.

Every penny.

No answer. He hung up. It was 11:54.

Six minutes early and the son of a bitch wasn't picking up.

He couldn't blame Richter for questioning the bureau's ability to protect him and his daughter. The accountant's skepticism was more than justified. Nor could he say he'd play it any different if he were Richter. Abacus Boy had shown a healthier set of balls than he'd expected. But none of that mattered. It didn't make a difference if Richter had a point, or that deep down he agreed with that point or the demands.

What did matter, what he made well known throughout the entire organization, was bringing down the PEACHES once and for all.

His office line began to ring.

"Coldstone."

"It's almost twelve o'clock. I was getting worried about you," Mark Richter responded.

"Don't you have enough to worry about?"

"Tell me about it. So it's done?"

"Five hundred thousand from ten different government funds has been wired to the account number you gave. The transfer took place eight minutes ago and is now available for verification."

"I'm glad you came to your senses."

Anger bubbled. Richter's condescending remark almost forced it to surface, but now was not the time. Now was the time to play along, to let Abacus Boy think that money was actually his. It was the lesson Ron Mitchell never did learn.

"I'd like to know your plan for nailing Jason Albers."

"Leave that to me."

"Richter, I've got more than enough skin in the game, five million bucks' worth to be precise. You got your money, by noon, without telling me your plan first, which is very atypical. But now, I need to know precisely how you're going to hand Albers over with enough evidence to put him away for good."

"It sounds like this is personal."

"You bet it's personal. I want Jason Albers in a six-by-nine cell for the rest of his natural life with the nastiest, meanest inmates having their way with him night after night after night. I want to hear him howling from 200 miles away and live the rest of his life in agonizing pain. Now when are you coming in to get the wire?"

"I appreciate your passion. But I'm not coming in."

"You sure are. I need irrefutable evidence, and I'm not going to pay you now only to find out later you blew your wad and we won't have anything to show for it when this is over."

"First of all, I'm still taking all the risks, so we're still doing this my way. Second, you already told me you're watching the money like a hawk. I'm sure you'll be able to get it back if you don't get your man."

"That's beside the point, Richter!"

"Here's the plan. I'm going to verify that you wired the money. After I do, I'll let you know where you should put the wire for me to pick up on my own terms. The rest of the details we'll square away soon."

This guy had no idea who he was messing with, but he soon would. He held back his anger yet again. Ron would've lost control, which was what Richter wanted him to do. But Richter wasn't dealing with Ron anymore.

"If that's the only way you'll play, you aren't leaving me much choice. But don't try to screw me on this, Mark. I'm warning you."

"I won't. I promise: if I'm alive at the end of this, you'll have your man."

"I better have him."

He could care less if Abacus Boy was alive at the end of this.

* * *

Mark sat in the rented office, arms folded and resting on the table, fidgeting, counting the zeros on the screen once again. It didn't seem real, but it was as real as it got: $5,000,000 was now in the account Trevor had set up for him in Switzerland. There was something unsettling about all those zeros. They didn't offer him the warm and fuzzy blanket of reassurance he'd assumed they would.

Instead, they made him more nervous.

After five minutes, the screen hadn't changed. Thinking of Costa Rica and the slim but still present chance he'd actually get to see it, he took a long swig of warm Coke and dialed Brad, still ever grateful to Sam for providing him with untraceable technology. His friend had proven to be a lifesaver from the grave more than once.

"Mark," Brad answered.

"You okay?"

"Yeah, a little freaked out by your text, but we're okay."

"Sorry. Couldn't help it. You're in the hotel?"

"Since early this morning."

"Were you followed?"

"I didn't see anyone, but that doesn't mean we weren't."

Always the realist.

"Just tell me what I want to hear, dude."

"Who are you, and what have you done with my friend?"

Brad was right. It was one of the last things he'd ever expected himself to say.

"Indulge me," he replied.

"We weren't followed."

"That wasn't so hard, was it?"

"Not at all." Brad actually eked out a chuckle.

"Caroline okay?"

"Mark, we're fine. What's the deal?"

"Get ready to go. Hopefully, you'll get an e-mail from me soon."

"They actually wired the money?"

"All five million of it," he replied, unable to completely conceal his giddiness. Even with the danger involved, the threats on his life and his family's, and the helplessness he'd felt the past 14 days, it was tough to not be a little excited about those zeros.

"No kidding?"

"What, you didn't think they would?"

"No clue, man. I'm just glad they did."

"Me too. I'll let you know one way or the other very soon."

"We'll be waiting."

44

Although he hadn't seen him in years, Trevor Malowski considered Mark Richter a good friend.

They'd first met in an accounting night course at Northwestern University and found out immediately they had several things in common. Recent college grads, single, tagged as future leaders in their industries, highly intelligent, and eager to have a drink after a long night of lectures. Both grew up lower middle class, had fathers not worth their salt, and got where they were for the most part on their own. From there, the mutual respect they developed for one another professionally led to a personal relationship. They shared similar tastes in beer, watched White Sox games, and grew relatively close during the twelve-week course.

But there was one notable difference between them.

Trevor had worked on the ground trading floor of the Chicago Mercantile Exchange, starting shortly after it merged with CBOT back in 2007, putting in 18-hour days, getting up at three o'clock every morning to be ready for that opening bell. He was hungry, and unwilling to let his ravenous appetite go unsatisfied. Everyone around him said he'd burn out, but he never did. And he didn't slow down. He couldn't. He was too fueled by the promise of success.

Mark, on the other hand, had lived a much more relaxed lifestyle, content to let each day come and go. It was a mistake in Trevor's eyes, and something he tried to rectify. He'd urged Mark to leave his accounting firm and join him on the trading floor. They could room together, work together, then grab beers together when the day was done. And Mark would've blown him away on the trading floor. The guy was as sharp as a tack and quicker on his feet than anyone he knew.

But it was a dead issue before it began. Mark wasn't interested in the least.

Then he tried to get him into investment banking, where Mark could've quadrupled his salary. Again, not interested. For a solid year they hung out every few weeks, and he tried fruitlessly to get Mark to join him in one endeavor or the next.

Then he ran out of time to keep trying.

Thirteen months to the exact day after "Accounting Information Systems" ended with a horrendous final exam, he was offered the opportunity to go to Europe and learn the banking business from the best, the crème de la crème, the revered Credit Suisse Group. His mentor at the CME Group, it's name after the merger, had put in a good word for him, and the opportunity came on a Wednesday night to start work the following Monday.

That was his first lesson in the power of networking. His second came when he convinced the hiring manager at Credit Suisse that it'd be prudent to bring over two young Americans, one with some floor-trading experience, the other a brilliant CPA with a savvy business background.

From that Wednesday night until Saturday afternoon, he'd used every means possible to get Mark to tag along. Mark was still single, had no home to sell, would make a ton of money, and they'd tackle Zurich as a team. *Zurich*, he'd said, *the place to go for banking*. Everyone knew that Switzerland was the place to be, where real studs cut their teeth. If you didn't like it, you could always head back, he'd rationalized. But with no strings attached and no compelling reason to stay in brutally cold Chicago, why not give it a shot?

He failed to convince him.

Mark stayed put and he headed for Switzerland. And though their relationship could most aptly be described as a 16-month fling rather than a lifelong friendship, they still talked to each other every couple months and congratulated each other in person when their daughters were born. They both still cherished those 16 months.

Once he got to Switzerland, he never came back. He lived in the Lindenhof quarter of Altstadt, known as District 1. It was close to the

Limmat River, not far from the mountains. Enough distance from the yuppies of Oberstrass and Unterstrass in District 6, yet close enough to go there for coffee and danishes with his clients. Lindenhof was a small community, only 6,000 residents, roughly two percent of Zurich's total population.

Just the way he liked it, perfect for his native wife and baby girl.

Europe's looser lifestyle and laxer schedules gave him an almost unfair advantage. You can't just start relaxing because you moved somewhere that maxes out the workweek at 45 hours and averages just over 40. It's not realistic to all of the sudden start taking long lunches with cocktails instead of devouring a sandwich in minutes while staring at a computer screen. You can't just flip a switch and turn that drive off.

As a result, he'd risen to become Vice President of the smaller yet no less prestigious Discount Bank & Trust Company. And because of that prestigious title even more people came to him for favors, and his position only grew stronger.

***

Their history aside, it was still an odd request, coming from Mark.

But Trevor got where he was by respecting such requests and not asking too many questions. As long as they didn't break it, bending the law was the key for many of his clients to get even richer than they already were. Tax law had a very fine gray line, so they turned to him to help draw it. He didn't mind doing so as long as he reaped the rewards too and didn't have to do anything illegal.

Rich people didn't have a problem with that arrangement.

He was also extremely loyal to his friends, which most certainly contributed more than anything else to his ascension in the banking industry. The business was based on favors between friends. Even with all the classes and the knowledge and the strategic planning and forecasting presentations, the primary driver of success was still basic relationships. It had always been that way, and it always would be.

Mark's particular favor came in three parts.

The first was relatively simple: set up an untraceable, safeguarded checking account at the bank. Those were set up every day and no biggie. Campfire stories about anonymity and tax protection of Swiss bank accounts were 100 percent true. People who really wanted to protect their money and identities came to him and people like him in Switzerland.

But that didn't mean it was a typical request.

In the 18 years he'd known Mark, not once had he heard him concerned about secrecy. Mark's motto, admirably, was if you don't do anything wrong, you don't have to keep secrets. His friend had also never asked him to set up an account of any kind since he'd been in Switzerland. Not for kicks when he first arrived, not for a trust when Katherine was born. Yet suddenly Mark needed one and needed it now. It didn't add up.

Still, it wasn't his job to pry for reasons, and there was nothing illegal involved. He complied with Mark's ask and set up the account personally instead of delegating. When he called Mark a day later to confirm it was done, he half-expected a thank you and retrospective explanation. What he got instead was more confusion.

The second part.

Mark wanted another account created with even higher levels of security and protection than the first. And his old buddy wanted him to be ready to transfer money from the first account to the second on a moment's notice.

He nearly balked at that. Not only was the first account still empty outside the small minimum opening, but usually only high net-worth folks with something to hide requested such things. Yet again, there was nothing illegal about it. He took care of it and stayed out of the details. Mark didn't say why he needed it, and he didn't ask.

But at 6:47 p.m. Zurich time (CEST) that Friday, he got a big hint.

The transfers coming in did a few things. First, they caught him well off guard. Mark was an accountant with a steady paycheck, not a banker with crazy bonuses deposited once a year. The sources of the money were sure to be the reason for all the secrecy. It meant there was trouble. He didn't know what kind or how much, and it didn't fit Mark at all, but his experience prevented naiveté.

Those deposits also made him think about Mark's second request some more. If Mark wanted the money transferred to the new account on command, he didn't want people to know where it went. Those "people" were perhaps the ones who deposited it in the first place. Was it possible they would want it back? Was Mark trying to prevent that with the second transfer?

His bank executed huge deposits on a daily basis, much, much larger than five million US dollars. But it wasn't the amount that concerned him. It was the combination of the amount, the person behind the requests, and the unusual behavior for his character.

The final thing those ten equal transfers did was make Trevor seriously reconsider Mark's third and final request, which was by far the riskiest.

Yes, it was highly atypical and not something he wanted to do.

Yes, he initially agreed to do it.

Yes, it could be, and likely would be if ever exposed, construed as illegal.

After seeing the transactions, he decided he had to back out. That gray line was thinner than ever before, and since Mark wasn't exactly an expert at walking it, he didn't plan to oblige with the third part.

It simply couldn't be worth the risk.

He e-mailed the address Mark had given him over the phone, a standard Gmail account. Convinced the memo would go straight to spam, he marked it urgent and requested a phone call.

After he hit SEND, he just stared at the screen. This was Mark Richter, he forcibly reminded himself.

Moments later, his cell phone began to ring. The number was unidentified.

***

"This is Trevor."

"Trevor. Mark."

"Mark, what's going on here?"

"You asked me to give you a call."

"I mean what's going on with this account. Five million US dollars? Ten different transactions? What's this all about? Where'd it come from?"

"That's obviously what I want to know."

"I'm not doing this trace, Mark. I know I said I would, but I can't. It's too dangerous. I'll transfer the money from the first account to the second when you ask me to, but I can't do anything else."

"Trevor, I need your help."

"I need answers."

"No, you think you *want* answers. But you don't. Trust me. Remember what you told me about knowledge?"

He remembered all too vividly, and Mark's reference to it scared him. Ten years to the day after he'd moved to Switzerland, as his position and reputation grew, he called Mark with a lesson he'd learned vicariously through others who'd learned it the hard way.

"Yes, I remember. What you don't know can't hurt you."

"Trust me, Trevor. You don't want to know."

"Mark...I've got a family. I know we're friends, but if this is going to incriminate me—"

"I wouldn't do that to you. Just do exactly as I ask. Once you send me the information, wait for my signal. Don't jump the gun. As long as you wait for me and do it as soon as I ask, that won't happen."

"I can't, Mark," he repeated. It was the hard but correct decision.

"Trev..." Mark whispered, his old nickname bringing back memories of those 16 months.

"Yes, Mark."

"It's Katherine. If you don't help me, she's..."

His old friend didn't finish. Instead, his voice choked up and silence ensued.

"Something will happen to her if you don't help me."

Speechless, he thought through his loyalties. He scratched the top of his balding head. He stared at the picture of Lara and Nina on his desk. He imagined Lara being in danger, the situation reversed. He thought of Mark and Katherine and what his friend would do for him. Then he put the phone down, buried his face deep into open palms, eyes closed. When he reopened them, he put the phone to his ear and heard silent fear.

"I'll e-mail you as soon as I can, Mark."

45

She nearly jumped out of the red-leather hotel seat when she saw the message.

After an hour of refreshing the screen every 30 seconds, the TV on pointlessly in the background, the broken, old A/C unit recycling stagnant, room-temperature air, there was finally a new message in her inbox. It was from Isaac Gutman and addressed to only her. No subject. Time of delivery: 2:32 p.m.

Mark.

It had to be Mark.

She opened it, Brad standing behind her, close to her shoulder. His extended right arm leaned on the desk to her right, exposing forearm muscles that bulged from his skin. Part of her wished it leaned on her instead.

Brad's presence was soothing and comforting. She'd slept as well as she could've hoped to considering the situation, and she credited Brad for that. She knew she couldn't feel safe, not until this was over, but his presence helped a lot more than she'd expected.

"Open it," he urged, just as impatient as her if not more so. His stubble had grown over the past few days. He rubbed its prickliness, and it sounded grizzly and manly.

As she double-clicked the message, the cell phone began to ring, an UNKNOWN number. No one, aside from Mark, had called it. After less than a full ring she put the phone to her ear and greeted her brother.

"Mark. I got your e-mail."

"Good. Can you work your magic?"

"Give me 20 minutes. I'll e-mail you back."

"Just be careful. It has to look legitimate."

"Mark, who are you talking to?"

"I know. But it's important."

"I know." Sometimes, siblings just know things without saying it. Other times, unnecessary assurances make a world of difference.

"How's Brad?"

She smiled hesitantly. She was quite good at knowing the right "when" and "where" for things, and this wasn't either. But there was no denying in her heart that she felt the attraction.

"He's fine."

Mark paused, then moved on to the question he really wanted to ask.

"How are Will and Katherine?"

She pitied her brother even more. He didn't have the chance to talk to the kids that she'd had. He didn't hear his daughter's voice or listen to laughter that made all seem right in the world. He was hours away and in considerably more tangible danger.

"They're both okay, Mark. Katherine's keeping a good eye on Will. And Roberta's keeping a good eye on Katherine. They both told me to tell you that they love you very much."

White lies can be good things. Anyone who disagreed didn't have kids.

"Tell them I love them too."

"I will. I'd better get to this," she interrupted the emotion.

"You're right. E-mail it to me and be careful. If anything goes wrong—"

"I know, Mark."

"Okay. Put Brad on," he replied, back to business.

She handed the phone to Brad, who paced towards the bathroom. He had the nervous habit of pacing while on the phone. Richard used to do it too. *Put the emotions away,* she ordered herself.

Then she cleared her throat and went to work.

***

"Brad, everything all set?"

Brad held his breath, then sighed, then sucked in a jagged breath again. He looked through the spotty mirror above the sink at

Caroline. She was hacking away on the computer, engrossed in the screen. Not looking at him anymore, she displayed a focus and level of concentration that was impossible to miss. Why wouldn't she?

She trusts Mark. And she trusts you.

"Are sure about this, Mark?"

"It's the only way to know for sure. You're in danger right now, bud. And we're running out of time."

"But why not tell Caroline?" he whispered so softly he questioned if Mark could hear it.

"She's got to focus on what she's doing right now. That's the most important thing. We can't afford to take the risk, and you know it. She's better when she doesn't think. She'll worry for the kids and for you and for me. She just needs to react. Honest innocence is the best defense."

"That doesn't sound like you."

"I know," Mark said, almost lamenting. "It isn't."

"This could really backfire, you know. Are you sure it's the only way?"

"I know it could. And yes."

Just then he heard a phone starting to ring on Mark's end.

"Brad, I've got to go. But I need to know if you're on board or not?" his best friend said in a hurried, frantic voice.

"I'm on board."

46

He hadn't given the number to anyone, but he knew who it was.

"Mark Richter. You've been a busy man."

Despite what the FBI told him, nobody from the PEACHES had confirmed who they were or mentioned what they thought he knew. Nor had referenced his conversations with the feds or indicated they were aware he knew who Jason Albers really was. In fact, they hadn't even contacted him since before Ron Mitchell was murdered, so Mark reminded himself not to say too much.

"Hi, Tom," he whispered, pacing the rented office.

"How are you, Mark?"

"I'm okay. What do you mean about me being a busy man?"

"Well with all the sneaking away from your house and fire alarm pulling and working at the office late at night...it seems you've been busier than a one-armed paperhanger. I'm just glad I got you."

That could've served as confirmation of Jason's involvement, Mitchell's murder, and the PEACHES organization watching him that very second. He opted not to think about it.

"Have you obtained the information?" Tom asked pointedly.

"Yes."

"Excellent. We knew you would. You're a winner, Mark, plain and simple. You're intelligent and resourceful, a real team player. We knew you'd get it done."

Team player?

"We?" he said in lieu of that thought.

"Edward and myself, of course."

"I see."

"And, well, you know...whoever else might be involved."

That was as much confirmation of Jason's involvement as he would get.

And it was all he needed.

"I see."

"So, Mark, how's eight o'clock tomorrow morning sound?"

"As good as any time."

"That's what I like about you. You're as kind as you are honest. You don't want to meet me any more than you want to lose your left testicle, but you still found a way to agree to my proposition without insulting me."

"Where do you want to meet?"

"Straight to business. I should've remembered, you're not much of a gabber."

"Not with you."

"Touché, Mark. A little bit of smartass has developed in you. I like it! Eight o'clock tomorrow morning it is. Arlington Heights Train Station."

"I'll be there."

"Of course you will. And you'll remember the files for each of the five companies. And you'll make sure the files list account numbers, including copies of the notarized seals, and verify authenticity with the necessary background information."

"I'll give you everything Lafferty & Sons has. Just don't hurt my daughter."

"If you give us what we want, we won't harm a hair on her pretty little head. Trust me."

Trust you?

"I'll bring it all."

"I know you will. And Mark?"

"Yes?"

Tom's voice changed from lackadaisical and carefree to stern and serious. Suddenly the spurious greetings of friendship were gone, and all that remained was honest, grim reality.

"Don't try anything stupid. No cops, no FBI agents, no wiretaps, no Brad Tarnow showing up at the last minute. You understand? Not one thing. If you know half as much we assume you know, you know we're not going to fall for a trap. Don't be stupid and try to set one. If you do, it won't work, and you'll be in a world of pain you can't even imagine. You've got three million reasons waiting for you if you play this right. Don't risk paradise and your life to be a hero."

Then Tom hung up, uninterested in his reply.

***

"He says he has all the files. Everything we need."

Tom leaned back in the leather chair while The General bit a fresh honeycrisp apple slice in half from behind his mahogany desk. He'd already informed The General over the phone, hence there was no need to say it, but he often used the obvious as an icebreaker.

"Do you believe him?"

"Well, like you said sir, when push comes to shove, he's going to protect his daughter..." he shrugged his shoulders.

"Check with the informant to make sure no surprises pop up this time. And keep an eye on Richter's house, just in case he has unfinished business there."

"Yes, sir. What about our guy in Wisconsin?"

The General rose from his chair and walked towards the fish aquarium, tapping the glass gently. He looked like Marlon Brando when he did it, such an innocent act for such a powerful man.

"When did you last speak with him?" The General asked.

"Earlier this morning. Said Richter's sister's house is crawling with cops."

"They still don't know where Tarnow and the woman are?"

"Not a clue. Our man has been watching the cops for a while, and they don't have any leads. They're looking for a hideaway, some sort of panic room. But you'd think that by now they would've searched every nook and cranny."

"I wouldn't put it past the police to miss a bright red 'SECRET DOOR' sign," the general pantomimed the air quotes. "Either way, there's not much we can do right now. Tell our man to sit tight. You focus on tomorrow. I'll confirm where they are and contact him directly."

The General would find out, too. The boss always managed to somehow obtain information it seemed he shouldn't be able to obtain. Classified, Top-Secret, Level Five, none of those terms stopped or even fazed him. He didn't know how The General did it, but the man always got what he wanted.

"Does the fact Tarnow and Richter's sister are missing concern you, sir?"

"It proves Richter's playing games with the feds. With us, he's getting the information we requested and meeting us on our terms. He expects it to end tomorrow, which it will, one way or the other. The feds want to bring him in, but they wasted too much time and missed their chance. Unless they go national, which they won't."

"Why not?"

"There's too much at risk for them to do that now. Fisher helped him outsmart them and they blew it. But he's not smarter than us and he knows it. Either that, or he's not willing to bet his daughter's life otherwise. But in any event, all it proves is that he's a step ahead of the feds. But that's about to change."

Tom had absolutely no clue what that meant, but it seemed like an intentionally vague statement. The General said such things from time to time, things that didn't make sense until later, sometimes much later. Past experience had taught him not to probe.

"Do you think he'll comply?"

The General dug his hands into his light-brown, double-pleated dress slacks, then turned away from the fish and towards him, eyes pointed towards the ceiling as usual when in deep thought.

"Knowing Richter...no, I don't. But it's worth a try and we'll make a great deal of money one way or the other. Even more than we anticipated. That's important. Operation VIXEN is a game-changer. It needs luscious funding. If he doesn't comply, you know what to do."

He smiled, thinking of the possibilities.

47

The cracked, cobweb-laced drywall and shaggy dark-blue carpet were the standout features of the shoebox-sized room Brad rented that Mark had called home for the past few days.

The room replaced his spacious two-story house with clean floors and curb appeal. His windbreaker, wadded into a ball, replaced a queen-sized bed with silk sheets and memory foam pillows. An old bathroom designed for communal use with a toilet that flushed when it felt like it and a floor he wouldn't dare walk barefoot on replaced a private bathroom, scrubbed clean once a week, with plumbing that worked every time.

Yet it was a great trade.

Luxury was unimportant. He was free of the cameras and the bugs and the wires and the surveillance. The miniscule room led to bigger things. Things he'd always taken for granted but never would again if he lived past eight o'clock tomorrow morning. Papers were scattered across the desk and floor; empty Coke bottles piled up beyond the wastebasket's rim. All the cell phones lay side-by-side along the wall opposite the desk.

He risked bacterial infection to take a much-needed shower before changing into a fresh set of clothes for the first time in two days, gratefully throwing the old ones into the trash. The duffle bag felt nearly empty after he removed the khaki pants and white golf shirt.

He reran everything once more in his head, looking for the flaw. The meeting tomorrow, Brad and Caroline in Wisconsin, the FBI contact, the folders and paperwork. Everything.

It was a long shot, but still a shot.

After he kneeled and prayed and knocked on wood that it would all be okay, that he'd see Katherine again and watch her grow up, he grabbed one of the phones and dialed David Coldstone's number. He was as prepared as he could possibly be.

First ring.

"Coldstone."

"This is Mark Richter."

"It's past four o'clock."

"I said I would call."

"You're a man of your word, or so I'm told."

He had no desire to discuss honesty with Coldstone. He was tired, agitated, and felt like a hypocrite.

"They contacted me about tomorrow."

"And?"

Coldstone either wasn't as interested as he thought the director would be, or he hid it quite well. Mark wondered which.

"Tomorrow morning. Nine o'clock at Ogilvie train station."

"Tomorrow...nine o'clock...Ogilvie." Coldstone repeated it very deliberately, as though writing it down. "Did they say anything else?"

It wasn't a blatant question, as though Coldstone knew he was lying, but it was a clear test of Mark's resolve and faith in the plan, whether Coldstone knew it or not. He swallowed hard, reminding himself of the risks involved with lying to the Regional Director of the FBI.

"No."

"Okay," Coldstone replied, accepting his assurance. He seemed to be in the clear.

At least so far.

"You can leave the bug at the ticket desk in Ogilvie. Second story, across the tracks. Middle window."

"What if they don't—"

"I'm pretty sure a man of your position will be able to convince a cashier to hold something for the FBI until I come pick it up."

"I suppose you're right."

"Drop it off late tonight. Don't be anywhere near the ticket office tomorrow morning."

"This isn't how we usually do things, Mark."

"It's a pretty unusual situation."

Coldstone paused longer than he expected. The director was really trying to sell the genuineness. Mark waited it out in silence, knowing where it would inevitably end.

"Fine, but I have a few conditions of my own."

"So you're going to be there tomorrow?" he asked, ignoring the comment.

"Yes, but we'll keep our distance until the exchange is made. What precisely will be exchanged?"

"I can't say for sure if they'll have anything for me. They said they would and if they do, it'll be a gym bag filled with money."

Or a loaded gun.

"How much?"

"None of your business."

"You're just swimming in moolah these days, aren't you? Five million bucks from the Federal Bureau of Investigation, bags of cash from terrorist organizations...talk about playing both sides."

"We both know I'm not keeping anything they give me. And that I'd give it all up in a heartbeat to have my life back."

Mark quietly refrained from saying what he really wanted to say. Coldstone's temper had to remain in check.

Pillar #1, Composure. Keep it under control, he ordered himself.

"You're right, and I'm sorry," the regional director choked out. It was clearly a bit forced, but a good sign nonetheless. Coldstone was playing right along.

"Forget about it."

"What about you? What will you bring them tomorrow?"

"Five folders of paperwork."

"What kind of paperwork?"

"You'll find out when you arrest them."

Sam's description of the three pillars echoed in his mind:

Don't give too many details. Don't incriminate yourself over the phone. Be short, be simple, be slick. Don't use twelve words when six will do. Don't get emotional unless emotion serves a purpose.

He'd written those guidelines down and pinned them to the wall as soon as he arrived at the rented office. He stared at them every time he spoke.

"I guess that's the best I'm going to get."

He didn't respond.

"Back to my conditions, Richter. First, if anything goes wrong, you need to tell me as soon as possible. Speak into the bug, call me, text me, whatever you have to do. But let me know, and let me know right away. Second, should something happen that prevents me from getting my man, you have to agree to testify after we make arrests."

"But—"

"All the chips are on the table now, Mark. If this doesn't work, we're moving forward and making arrests with what we have, and you'll take the stand. If you do your part, you'll get your life back and have a five million dollar head start. If you cross us, we'll yank that money back; yes, we can do that. Then I'll personally throw your ass in jail. Those are my terms, and they're non-negotiable."

What a scam.

First off, if the PEACHES found the bug, the last thing he'd have to worry about was testifying, or breathing, at any point in the future. Coldstone knew it and he knew it.

Next, testifying was nothing more than another form of suicide. Anyone who agreed to speak out against the PEACHES in court simply wouldn't be alive come trial time.

Finally, nothing was documented, meaning the whole thing was a sham. The only things that were real were those in writing, and sometimes even those were a mirage. Agreeing to anything over the phone was as pointless as forging someone's name on a contract, with less chance of success.

Coldstone didn't think much of him, he concluded. And that was fine by him, if not preferable. He needed to be underestimated.

He needed every advantage he could get.

"Okay. But you better back me up on this, I'm scared as hell," he said, finishing the sale. Coldstone was no doubt shaking his head, probably smirking too. But he was under control, exactly where he needed him to be.

"We'll be there, Mark. Don't worry."

Don't worry...what an asinine and counterfeit thing to say. It was followed by a more sincere comment, a few words of encouragement from the FBI Regional Director.

"We'll drop the bug off this evening. Don't screw up, Richter."

48

In the 21 years she'd spent in the graphic design industry, the last twelve as owner of a small business, Caroline had seen a great deal of change in the industry. Computers, software tools and even AI had re-identified the marketplace and transformed customer expectations. And if you worked in the field and wanted to be good, you either had to embrace those changes or move on to something else.

She was one of its best embracers.

Her counterparts often shunned new technology, preferring the stability of sticking with what they already knew. That surprises most folks, who assume designers are always into the latest and greatest. In reality, many of her old coworkers' aversion to technology reminded her a lot of Mark. Most people want to leave well enough alone in life. Why force yourself to learn a new tool every six months? Or stay current on several new inventions that will only lead to more problems and headaches?

She looked at it completely opposite: why let the technology of yesterday hold you back? Many of her old coworkers, like Mark, were Laggards and Late Majority users. She was an Innovator, an Early Adopter, which made the task currently in front of her far from cutting edge.

She reviewed the files once more, making sure there wasn't more to it. Brad sat on the bed, pretending to watch TV but really eyeing her. She liked it. And she'd taken off her sweatshirt to tease him with a tight-fitting T-shirt just before she got to work. But her attention was now fully on the computer, and the job appeared to be done. All five files were complete. She needed less than half the tools she brought, let alone everything still at her house.

Mark had told her to be prepared for anything. And part of her, she couldn't deny, was actually excited for the challenge despite the circumstances. She couldn't just turn off her passion for difficult tasks. Once the work was in front of her, the job was all that mattered. When the world didn't make sense, when she couldn't make heads or tails of the unfairness in it, graphic design came to the rescue. It took her away from an unjust place and put her into one where she *actually* reaped what she sowed. Shortcuts and laziness led to crappy outcomes. Hard work and persistence resulted in quality. Getting lost in her work was her escape. She had relied quite tremendously on it when Richard died, and she leaned on it now as well.

A half-hour after she received Mark's e-mail with the rest of the information, she hit REPLY and typed a quick note:

Mark:
Review the attachments, let me know if they do the trick.
Please be careful. I love you.
Caroline

Seven minutes later, a message from Isaac Gutman arrived.

Caroline,
These work. Thanks for your help. I'll be careful...you do the same. Keep an eye on Brad. He needs it. I'm so sorry I got you involved in this. Be careful. Stay strong like you always are. Hope to see you soon, but if not, you know what to do. Love you, sis. Take care.
M

She read it for the fourth time and closed her eyes, fighting back the memories of losing Richard again. After a moment to herself, she decided to respect Mark's request and joined Brad on the bed to keep an eye on him.

49

It was 9 p.m. in Washington, DC, a good time for that city, at least in the eyes of Milton Montgomery, National Director of the FBI.

The politicians were home for the night. The sun was down, city lights sparkled, airport noise was minimal, usually gridlocked streets wide open, the pedestrian congestion nonexistent. He stared out the window of his requested standard-issue office. He didn't need 1,000 square feet and leather couches to do his job, and he didn't need them to feed his ego either.

Beyond the top few levels, easily found on the Internet, the FBI had no defined hierarchy that the public was aware of. Part of that was due to the sensitive nature of such information, but mostly it was because the 35,000-person network was simply too expansive and there were too many other more important things to do than publish hundreds upon hundreds of organizational charts for no real reason. With over 55 regional headquarters, some 400+ resident agencies, and upwards of 60 legal attaché offices overseas, it was a confusing web of responsibility and accountability. And trying to capture it all in one PDF was as arbitrary as it was challenging. One thing, however, was quite certain, known to most US citizens and every nation's leader around the globe:

Milton Montgomery was in charge.

In the fifth year of his ten-year term, his accomplishments didn't meet his high aspirations. It wasn't that people didn't like him or felt he was doing a bad job or weren't satisfied with the results. To the contrary, public opinion polls were the highest they'd been for an FBI director in over 30 years. Security had tremendously improved since he took over, and he'd made more headway on the "FBI's Most Wanted" list than most directors did throughout their entire tenure. The President had repeatedly and publicly credited him for enhancing safety in the United States, and his subordinates truly respected him and admired his passion. He was an outsider to Washington, and the public loved him for it. Everyone seemed to be pleased with the job he'd done the past half-decade.

He was not.

He came to Washington to solve problems and drive change. To enhance the quality of life for the average citizen and bring a new level of integrity to an organization that had a less-than-pristine reputation. With everything from the J. Edgar Hoover tales to the Hanssen traitor scandal, brought to the public's attention by the movie *Breach*, to the presidential runs ins of late, it was clear that the public rarely remembered the FBI's successes but couldn't forget its failures. Past administration's interrogation techniques and highly questionable domestic espionage strategies had generated a thick cloud of doubt over the FBI's general credibility, and he'd planned to change that five years ago.

Others warned him that his goals weren't merely lofty, they were unattainable. But he tenaciously pressed on with blind faith, as critics often labeled it. And the difficulty of those challenges did at times make him feel like the first half of his term was a failure. Perception of the FBI hadn't changed enough. Despite high ratings for its leader, phone surveys still revealed people's palpable lack of trust for the organization assigned to protect them. Nations around the globe still questioned its honesty.

And now he had to deal with *this*.

His jacket on the hook behind the door, the window cracked halfway open, he leaned back in his brown-leather chair with a glass of bourbon in his left hand and Mark Richter's file in his right. Feet propped up on the desk, he read every word twice, committing much of it to memory.

Which wasn't that hard because there wasn't much of a file.

Richter was the kind of guy he never read about. He dealt with terrorists and killers and mass murderers, clear threats to the nation's safety. He rarely interacted with honest, trustworthy citizens who didn't have a mile-long rap sheet and a story with more holes than a strainer. Day in, day out, he saw the worst specimens of humanity. That morose reality came with the job, and he accepted it, but the files of people like Mark Richter didn't belong on his desk.

Richter was a Chicago suburb resident and had been all his life. Arlington Heights. Forty-one-years-old, single father of an eight-year-old daughter, CPA for over 20 years, tax-paying, law-abiding, US-born citizen with a mortgage, a car payment and a 401(k).

Simple.

He didn't have any felony charges or misdemeanors or speeding tickets. The file was a razor-thin biography of an average guy who didn't have any conflict with the local police, let alone the FBI, until a few weeks ago.

He plopped the folder down on the desk, removed his $10 black-rimmed Foster Grant reading glasses, and aggressively rubbed his eyes. Staring at him, the way it always did, was ultimate accountability, hanging on the wall, motionless and silent. The dark-brown oak wood plaque and inscribed acrylic plate looked cheap, especially for a Director's office. But gaudiness didn't matter. What did matter were the three words stenciled into the plate in pyrite:

Fidelity, Bravery, Integrity

Those three simple words were the powerful meaning behind the acronym that everyone knew, yet most couldn't define.

The FBI motto was on the official seal but hardly noticed, often overshadowed by the flag background, the laurel leaf and the peaked, beveled gold edging. It's what all FBI employees pledged to practice, and what they should be committed to. It required their best effort and commanded their full respect, yet he knew when he became Director that many of them were just as ignorant as the average citizen.

His first call to action, therefore, on Day One, was to require every single employee to undergo training on the meanings behind the features of the seal and, most importantly, the significance of the motto.

That plaque, the chintzy-looking, underestimated collection of cheap wood and pyrite, was the main driver of his work ethic. It was bigger than he and the President and the Cabinet and the 35,000 employees. It represented what the people of the United States of America deserved. It never stopped watching or judging him.

It never rested. So neither would he.

Thus, when he was tempted to ignore someone like Mark Richter and the events that led to his file ending up on the desk, all it took was one glance at the plaque to remind him of his duty. His ringing phone interrupted that very thought.

Nine-fifteen on the dot. Just as promised.

* * *

"This is Milton Montgomery."

He never revealed his title. There was no need to; people who called him knew who he was.

"Mr. Montgomery, thank you for your time this evening."

"Not a problem. I presume this is Mr. Richter?"

"It is."

"Well Mr. Richter, I was informed that you initially contacted Special Agent William Hunt, our Chicago branch administrator, to request this meeting. May I assume you're calling from there now?"

"You're not tracing this call?"

"No, Mr. Richter. I've been told you specifically requested that I not do that."

And he wasn't. Hunt had told him the trace they ran from the Chicago office didn't work, so it probably wouldn't work this time either. He decided he'd play it Richter's way for the time being. There was little downside, and he wanted to see where this was going.

"Yes, I did. But that doesn't mean you listened."

"Then I suppose you can either trust me or hang up the phone."

A brief pause followed. Richter wasn't expecting such an honest, frank comment, at least not so early in the conversation. He sensed the surprise through the silence.

"I guess you're right. Let the trust begin."

"So you're calling from Chicago?"

"Yes."

"Mr. Hunt also informed me that you have some information I would find especially interesting, concerning a variety of topics."

"Correct."

Very short answers, stoic and unwavering. It didn't sound like a man who feared for his life. It also didn't sound like someone who'd never broken a law, or a man who should be scared to death to be talking to the Director of the FBI. That meant two things: Richter had been given some good guidance, and he'd had to conceal his emotions before. Both aligned with the story Richter had told Hunt.

It also supported that Richter was likely as intelligent as advertised, but he knew that before the call. Not only does it take more than a smile to be a CPA, or to have the kinds of investments this man had at his age, but it was also extremely impressive that Richter had gotten up the FBI's food chain as quickly as he had.

With 335 million citizens to protect and a schedule that has to accommodate such protection, he was simply a hard man to reach. Richter had used a recorded message of Ron Mitchell very wisely, and his words, while brief, were impactful. David Coldstone and he had discussed the PEACHES a handful of times in the past, but Richter's unique tie to the terrorist group and his delivery of certain information to Hunt were very well-placed and executed.

That, combined with the accountant's background, and his theory, implausible as it may be, was why they were talking.

"May I call you Mark?"

"Sure."

"Mark, it's my understanding that you feel hesitant to help the FBI."

"Can you blame me?"

"I guess not. I've been briefed on the situation, and I suppose it's a bit of an understatement to say that we've handled this situation poorly."

"Have you heard the tape I played for Mr. Hunt?"

"I have. Mr. Mitchell was out of line, rest in peace. There's no other way to say it. And I apologize for his abuse of power. It's something I discourage from all FBI employees, and you shouldn't have had to hear it."

"And Mr. Hunt told you what I believe?"

"He did. Though he didn't mention any evidence you provided to support it."

"I couldn't risk sharing that. It's nothing against Mr. Hunt, but Chicago's a corrupt city and I don't know how deep the rabbit hole goes. Those details are for your ears and your ears alone."

"Fair enough. I'd like to discuss them, but first I have a question."

"What's that?"

"I was wondering why you feel comfortable talking to the leader of an organization you don't trust and feel is corrupt."

The silence that followed implied that Richter either didn't expect such a candid question, or that he wanted him to *think* he didn't. He leaned towards the former, given Richter's initial awkward pause to his earlier bluntness.

"Because I think the last thing you want right now is a public frenzy about dishonest FBI agents who abuse their power and aid terrorists."

Before speaking to Richter, he'd assumed the man was smart. Now, he thought he was a certified genius. His primary focus the past five years had been restoring as much integrity to the FBI as he could. News like this would crush that effort, and Richter not only knew it, but used it very well.

"Yes, you're right. Short of another terrorist attack, that's the last thing I want."

"As long as that's true, and your actions back it up, I promise it won't happen."

"And why should I believe you?"

"I'm talking to you, aren't I?"

Silence. He put his finger to his mouth in contemplation.

"Mr. Montgomery, you can believe this or not, I really don't care anymore. All I care about are the people I love. Helping you helps me protect them, so I'm all for it. We all have mutual interests. That's the only reason I called."

Now *that* was an honest answer. Richter let it sit for about five seconds before following it up with a question he'd already asked himself.

"Besides, do you really have a choice?"

Richter was, in fact, holding all the cards, and five million dollars of the Bureau's money. If the accountant's somewhat-radical-yet-not-impossible theory was by chance correct, he certainly wanted and needed to know about it, and he had to play this Richter's way to get it. He leaned forward in his chair, bent at the waist, phone pressed to his ear, lips calling for the bourbon.

"What is it that you'd like to tell me?"

"We don't have much time, so listen to me very carefully. Got a pen?"

50

Saturday morning. Doomsday. Six a.m.

The breeze off of Lake Michigan made Chicago's early June feel like mid-February in the south. The sun had already been up for some time. Thick dew layered postage stamp Chicago yards, parked cars saturated street sides but both lanes were empty. Pigeons cooed freely and often, the city's version of the rooster.

Mark watched a beat-up Honda Civic cruise down the street with the hazards on, accelerating quickly and breaking just as fast, the driver tossing fresh copies of *The Chicago Tribune* out the window in between bursts. Some throws landed right where intended in the center of the sidewalk or driveway, others didn't even clear the curb. Mexican music blaring from the speakers, the driver never stopped to rectify an errant toss.

Wearing the light pillowdy windbreaker, he left the building that had, with any luck, safely concealed him from both the FBI and the PEACHES. Inside that 800 square foot palace of freedom, the papers had been collected, the trash disposed, the desk organized. It looked virtually identical to the way it did before Brad rented it, except for $5,000 worth of equipment and one bright-green folder atop the old, broken desk. The small desk lamp was on, illuminating that folder and that folder alone. The rest of the office was dark and empty.

He wore gym shoes, a bit out of place with his khakis and white golf shirt, but he wasn't going to a fashion show. Four cell phones weighed down his pants pockets. A black computer bag hung over his left shoulder.

Hair combed to the side, he marched through Chicago breeze towards the office. Entering the building via the familiar back door, he kept his head down and tried to look like one of those young, hungry CPAs coming into work on Saturday that he used to laugh at. Security was lax, but the motion-sensitive cameras would still turn on.

Walking up the stairs, his mind regressed. He thought of Saturday morning pancakes with Katherine, movie nights, root beer floats with extra whipped cream, and the smiling face of the most precious thing in his life. He hadn't seen her in a week, the longest he'd ever gone, and knew he might not ever see her again. At the second-to-last stair, he stopped to reflect one last time, picturing his baby.

Then he slapped his face, literally. He didn't in general have Caroline's focus, but today it had to be there. By the time he reached Lafferty & Sons' sixth-floor main entrance, an office he knew he'd never set foot in again after today, he was as focused as could be.

Two lights unavoidably turned on when he entered. He walked to the east side of the floor, hoping the sun's blinding reflection off the thick-glass windows would prevent anyone who might be watching at a distance from noticing them flicker on. The west side, where his desk was located, was off limits. He needed to stay as far from his own space as possible.

The air conditioning didn't kick on until noon on the weekends, so it already felt warm inside. He removed his windbreaker and tied it snug around his waste, reluctant to set it down for fear of somehow leaving more evidence of his happenings behind than was absolutely unavoidable. It was bad enough that just entering the building left a digital footprint.

The first stop was the break room.

He walked into the unlocked, spacious, windowless kitchen and immediately shut the door. On the far back wall, equidistant from the copy machine and refrigerator, sat a gray, wall-mounted mail chute. It looked back at him, as if asking if he really wanted to do this.

The brown manila envelope was addressed to Larry McDougal, whose office was 30 feet down the hall. He'd thought about sliding it under the door, but Larry sometimes came in on Saturdays, and he couldn't see this until after today. He again considered not sending it at all, just ripping it up and going back to Milton Montgomery with everything he had. But Katherine wouldn't make it, and that made the decision all too easy. There was no going back now. He held the envelope over the chute and released his hand.

It was done.

Finality set in, and Mark acknowledged to himself that he couldn't undo it now if he tried. There was absolutely no point in stalling anymore.

He scurried towards the filing cabinets, filing cabinets he'd never forget. They too offered a silent stare of judgment, but he was too hardened by then to care. The first one in line was Bruce's, and he extracted the Techbot file from the computer bag, ignoring his reluctance.

The file wasn't any different than what he took two days ago. He'd copied it page for page, cover to cover. He even used the same weighted paper. There was no difference whatsoever.

Yet it still felt different.

Doing the wrong thing always resulted in doubt. It felt innate. And when he finished the fifth file, he was all but certain this wasn't going to work. But what choice did he have?

Back in the break room only a few moments later, he placed the remaining contents of his computer bag into the supply cabinet's bottom drawer. Tucked under unopened office boxes of Staples printer paper, the original Lafferty & Sons client files called for their home in the fireproof filing cabinets. Their silent screams were the loudest yet, and he shut the door on them.

He left the break room and bolted for the east stairwell exit. He needed escape, he needed to breathe cool and fresh and free oxygen, if only for another hour. Earlier, he thought it would be hard to say good-bye to the company he'd worked at for 23 years. But ever since he dropped the brown manila envelope down the mail chute, he wanted nothing more than to leave it forever. He needed to bust out that door and never look back. He needed escape.

He didn't get it.

Twenty feet from the door, a mere five or six steps from that escape, he saw something his eyes and brain couldn't reconcile and dove into the cubicle to his left. He inched up slowly, his eyes just above the cubicle's black metal frame. When the rest of the lights flickered on, they confirmed what he couldn't believe he just saw.

* * *

He hunched down out of sheer, instinctive panic.

It didn't appear that Jason saw him, but he couldn't be sure and tried not to think about it. Under the desk with his knees tucked into his chest, he saw Leo's chair five feet away, meaning he was exposed. When Jason passed the cube, if the heavyset security guard were to turn around and bend down, even halfway...

The room got hotter and his sweat got stickier. The loud whistling and heavy footsteps approaching, he decided to just hold his breath altogether. Time stood still. He was in a static state of trepidation, unable to fast forward.

He forced his eyes open against their puerile tendency to clamp shut just as Jason walked past the desk and into his line of vision. It was only a brief moment, but it was long enough. Jason wore dark blue jeans and a black jacket with white gym shoes. He thankfully never saw his face. But that moment felt like an eternity. It finally passed when Jason's slow stroll made it beyond the cube's outer wall.

Relieved but far from out of the woods, he closed his eyes for a moment to consider his options. Duck out of the cube and tiptoe to the staircase? Run as fast as he could and hope he didn't make too much noise? Sit tight and wait for Jason to leave? But what if Jason didn't leave until he was supposed to be at the train station?

He checked his watch: 6:35.

Could he risk waiting this out?

No, I can't.

All the pondering and uncertainty led back to the same question: why was Jason there in the first place? Just as he was connecting all the other questions back to that one, he heard a strangely familiar jangling sound from the other side of the hall. It was a noise that couldn't be mistaken. He didn't want to believe it. It just *had* to be something else. He needed to make sure.

Dreading every inch moved, he quickly but quietly bear crawled from beneath the desk to the cube across the way, still out of Jason's sight. Hunched down, he rested his right arm on the desk and his left against the cubicle frame, slowly lifting himself up from a squat to the point where his eyes were just above the wall. Once positioned, his knees still bent and locked, his quads began to burn with pain.

But after getting a clear look, he soon forgot about the burning.

The sounds could only be a rattling file cabinet, the same cabinet he'd opened just minutes ago. Jason stood in front of William's personal cabinet, still whistling like a sweet old man in the park. He pulled out a folder, Mark couldn't see from across the room but had a pretty good idea which one, and moved to the next cabinet.

Once there, Jason withdrew a set of keys from a large key ring that Mark was sure didn't come standard with personal filing cabinet keys included, even for security. Within seconds, the next cabinet drawer was open and another file was gone. Jason went down the line to three more cabinets, the same five Mark had visited minutes before, surely with the same five files that he'd replaced, before walking towards the break room with the folders tucked under his arm.

He ducked down just before Jason made the turn at the hallway corner. Shortly after, he heard loud beeps.

Beeps from the Xerox copy machine.

Replacing the files was supposed to be an unnecessary precaution. How did Jason get the keys? He wondered in what other ways he'd underestimated the security guard. He stared at the east window from the ground, swallowing, sweat drenching his neck and white undershirt. Still hearing beeps, he realized this was his only chance. Against all desire to stay put, to remain tucked under the desk in the fetal position for however long it took Jason to leave, he slowly got up from the ground.

He scanned the hall...no one in sight. Jason was making copies and there was nobody else in the office.

Now or never he told himself.

He bolted into the open hallway towards the staircase, opened the door slowly and quietly, and then ducked behind it as soon as he could. He shut it just as silently.

He could've stayed to see what else Jason was doing. He probably should have. Maybe he would've seen something else he didn't expect. Maybe he'd learn more information about the imminent meeting with Tom. Maybe he was leaving valuable intel on the table. But he didn't care. He could barely stand he was so terrified. Escape was the only thing he could think about. He walked down the first flight cautiously and sped down the rest like a bat straight out of hell, skipping three steps at a time, hopping from floor to floor. As he did, he repeated the same wicked, frightening truth to himself over and over.

Jason Albers has copies of the files.

51

This Candlewood Suites was not a five-star establishment.

But it beat the pants off the Comfort Inn six miles away that he and Caroline were staying in. There were bellboys, a decent front lobby, and three floors of somewhat clean, generally well-decorated rooms. When Brad checked in and paid cash, the young girl behind the counter gazed in awe at him. Generation Z hardly knew what cash was, let alone used it to pay for hotel rooms.

It made him think about how true the threat of digital money was.

His visit to Room 155 was brief. He grabbed a few cans of Pepsi from the soda machine, opened and emptied them into the sink, then tossed each onto the two beds he then unmade. He ruffled the pillows and pulled the bedspread down to the ground, tossing the decorative pillows on the chair in the corner. The sheets were tucked in tight along the sides of the bed and bottom. He ripped them free.

He also turned on all the lights and flipped on the bathroom fan switch. He spread out a few copies of *USA Today* and *Wall Street Journal* across the matte blue-carpet floor. After he splashed the mirror with water, a thin stream of liquid trickled down its length. He shut the curtains, opened two drawers of a dresser that hoisted a TV on low volume, and tossed the satellite channel guide and basic hotel room welcoming papers across the top of the desk. In minutes, he'd turned a clean, fresh room into one that looked like it'd been lived in for days.

Then he did the most important thing.

He held Moultrie's motion-sensitive 14-Megapixel digital camera that Caroline brought from her house and searched for the best spot. She used it to capture nature for some of her advertising projects. Deer approaching the saltlick in her backyard was the most common trigger to start the recording, she'd said. She asked him on the drive to Madison why they needed it, and he told her he didn't know, that Mark had just said so. He intended for that to be his last lie. But then he told her another when he left the hotel 20 minutes ago to "get pizza." That, he swore to himself, was it. No more lies.

Famous last words.

He plugged the camera into the wall and set it on top of a small, wooden table next to the brown-cushioned Providence Lounge chair, or so the tag told him, adjacent to the desk. The camera pointed at the door, he checked the view from behind. Perfect. The light from the three lamps and overhead bulb was plenty. He grabbed a fresh towel from the bathroom and draped it gently over the camera, exposing only the lens. Then he tucked the cord behind the chair, out of sight.

***

Twenty minutes later, he handed the cabbie $50 to stay put while he made the call. The cabbie didn't complain. Tips like that were few and far between in the college town, especially during the summer. The Yellow Taxi was parked alongside the curb just outside the hotel, a short walk from the payphone. He was surprised there even was a payphone, assuming they had all died with the explosion of cell phones, but grateful nonetheless. It made the call more realistic. He needed to appear stupid, but not too stupid.

The Nissan Altima sat in the guest parking lot, its final resting spot. Its dented exterior frame looked lonely and abandoned. The sky was overcast, clouds as far as the eye could see, but not yet raining. It was cool now but was supposed to heat up to about 80 later that day. In a pair of jeans and a plain green T-shirt, he felt okay, but far from comfortable.

He watched two cars pull into the circular entrance, people casually stepping out of and walking into the lobby, bellboys greeting them at the door with smiling faces. He looked across the street and didn't see anything out of place either, just a few restaurants and a hardware store with very little traffic. After giving the immediate area one final scan, making sure this was the right time and place, as best he could tell, anyway, he picked up the receiver and punched the digits to one of two phone numbers written on a piece of scrap paper.

He'd replayed the conversation in his head a hundred times. But even all the planning and preparation and practice couldn't get him ready for this phone call. And Mark had warned him that it wouldn't. "Sometimes," his list-driven, OCD best friend had told him, "you just have to jump."

And jump he did.

Actually, he took a gigantic leap of faith off the high dive with his eyes shut, and pressed the final number. The tape recorder on, his nerves as controlled as they could be, he waited only moments. After two rings, the man picked up and answered just as abruptly as Mark said he would.

"Coldstone."

Time to swim.

* * *

"Mr. David Coldstone?" a quiet man's voice on the other end of the line asked. A slight hum lingered in the background. He couldn't quite place what it was.

"That's right. Who is this?" he leaned forward in his desk chair, not recognizing the voice, either. And he was good with voices.

"My name's Brad Tarnow. I have a message for you."

Tarnow! He leapt up from behind his desk, his dark olive green Hickey Freeman suit wrinkled from the past hour of sitting. It was a little after 7:30, less than two hours before Richter said the meeting would take place.

"Mr. Tarnow, we've been looking for you for some time now."

"That's what I hear. May I ask why?" His tone wasn't cocky, but direct. It was forced confidence, like he was trying to push through nervousness.

"We're looking for you because you are currently aiding and abetting someone wanted by the FBI."

"Who is that?"

"Don't play games with me."

"What's Mark done to be wanted by the FBI?"

"Mr. Tarnow, I'm not at liberty to discuss the details of an ongoing investigation that doesn't concern you. What does concern you is the fact that you've assisted the suspect and are accountable for your actions."

"I think you've abused your power by coming after me."

The conversation was certainly being recorded. This ex-con was fishing in an empty pond.

"As I said, Mr. Tarnow, you are wanted by the FBI for aiding and abetting a fugitive of the law."

"What do you want from me?"

"I want you to tell me where you are."

"So you can come arrest me?"

"That's correct."

"I don't think so."

That's what you think. He needed just a few more seconds and it'd all be over. Tarnow would be out of the picture, and so would Caroline Hubert. Then he could focus entirely on Richter.

"It's only a matter of time, Mr. Tarnow. Given your experience, I'm sure you know that. Fugitives never make out in the long run, not even in the movies. Eventually, we *will* find you. And the longer it takes, the harsher the sentence. Works that way every time, son."

"But I didn't do anything wrong."

"Then the courts will exonerate you. It's not my job to judge the law. It's my job to enforce it. And according to the law as it's written, that means I need to bring you before those courts and let them to their job. If you're innocent, you have nothing to worry about."

"But it'll look bad that I ran, won't it?"

"A little bit. But it's not anything that can't be explained. Natural reactions and nervous decisions never outweigh the facts. And the facts decide your fate, Mr. Tarnow. But since you brought it up, if you're really innocent, why *did* you run?"

"You pretty much said it. I was scared. I didn't want to go back to prison because of Mark. So I did the first thing that came to mind."

"That seems reasonable to me, and defendable as such. Do you know where Mark is? Has he told you everything he's gotten himself into?"

"Yes, and I'm pissed at myself for listening."

I would be too. Brad Tarnow's fate was sealed. There was no hope for him now. The first mate was going to go down with the ship, whether he surrendered or not.

"Well, given all that, if you really haven't helped him, I don't see any reason why the courts wouldn't be lenient. Especially if I put in a good word for you."

"You'd be willing to do that?"

Now he owned him. He'd gone from alienating him to getting him to ask for his help. Tarnow's tail was between his legs, and he was begging for a bone of mercy. He wouldn't get it, but there was no reason to tell him that now.

"I would be if you came in. Listen, Mr. Tarnow, the more you cooperate now, the more leeway I'll have with the courts later. If you keep hiding, it's going to be pretty hard to cut you a break when we do get you."

"But I—"

"And you're a smart guy," he lied, barely containing a chuckle, "so I'm *sure* you've come to terms with the fact that we *will* get you. It's best to just turn yourself in now."

Finally, he saw the green light flash from the corner of his eye. Time was up, whether Tarnow came in or not, Richter's best friend would be his within the hour. He sat back in his chair, smiling. This was outstanding.

Tarnow still hadn't responded, but soon would. He'd seen too many cases and worked too many suspects to not see it coming. Experience was the best teacher, and it told him that Tarnow would walk in freely, which was still preferable. All it would take was one more nudge.

"May I call you Brad?" he asked, sounding sympathetic.

"Sure."

"Well, Brad, the first thing you said was that you have a message for me. What is that message?"

"I wanted to tell you that I'm not talking with Mark anymore."

"We have reason to believe you're with his sister, Caroline. It's hard to swallow that you're not speaking to him while running away with her."

"She's not talking to him either," Donavan quickly replied in a sort of rushed stutter. He began to slur as he spoke faster, trying to pedal his way up a steep hill of questions in low gear.

"He wanted us to help him. But we don't want anything to do with him or all this trouble. She's got a son...and she's worried that Mark will get him into trouble or hurt."

That meant Caroline Hubert knew it all too. Another fate sealed.

"What did he want you to do?"

"We hung up before he could ask."

"Then you ran away together?"

"We just want to be...left alone. We...we like each other."

What sentimental hogwash. A love story affair in the middle of an already messed up situation. He muted the phone and smirked out loud, tapping his fingers against the desk in both disgust and levity. He had what he needed and wanted to put an end to a long chapter of an even longer saga.

"I'm happy for you Brad. I've seen pictures. She looks beautiful."

"She is. She's amazing."

"Listen to me, son. It's your choice, and of course you've got to think through what you want to do. But I can tell you this: the best play you've got, if you really want to be with her, is to tell me where you are so I can have you safely picked up. Once you come in, you cooperate, give us a statement, I'll do everything I can for you. And for her. It sounds like you both just got caught up in your friend's mess. Believe me, it happens more than you know. Speaking from over 35 years of experience, the best thing you can do right now is cooperate with the FBI and tell me where you are."

A brief moment of silence was followed by the inevitable.

"We're in Room 155 at the Candlewood Suites. It's in Fitchburg, Wisconsin, just outside Madison. Caddis Bend Drive."

"You and Caroline are together?"

"Yes."

Even better.

"You're there now?"

"I'm calling from a payphone outside the hotel. I wasn't sure what you were going to say or what I was going to do, so I thought..."

"You didn't want to call from the room because you thought we might trace it," he finished the sentence, as if it even mattered where Tarnow called from.

"Yeah."

He could tell Tarnow was impressed. Impressed with his ability to know what he was thinking and beat him to the punch. And he was relieved. Relieved to finally tell the truth and stop running. Now he didn't have to worry. And he didn't have to hide. Most criminals felt the same relief when they finally took that step, even if they did so by getting caught.

"Okay, Brad. Here's what you need to do: go back to the hotel room and stay where you are. Don't leave your room for any reason. You understand? *Stay put.* Someone will come by soon."

"Thank you, Mr. Coldstone."

The idiot was actually thanking him.

"Just doing my job, son."

52

When dial tone returned, he checked the source of the green light atop his desk. State of the art technology had the trace complete long before Tarnow even mentioned the hotel, pinpointed to the exact street address.

Marvelous.

Coldstone smiled, considered his play once again, finger stroking an imaginary mustache, and then decided that one more verification couldn't hurt. A few strokes on the keyboard, and boom, he was ready. Dialing the number, he laughed to himself at how well things had fallen into place.

"Candlewood Suites. Front desk. How may I help you?" a young-sounding woman answered, too much perk in her voice for the early hour.

"I'm trying to reach Brad Tarnow and forgot what room he's in. Would you be so kind as to refresh my memory?"

"Yes, absolutely," she began. Seconds later: "He's staying in Room 155 with us. Would you like me to connect you?"

"No, that's okay. I'm in the area. I'll just pop in and say hello. Thank you very much."

"You're welcome, sir. Have a pleasant day."

***

Brad didn't even hang up the phone.

After finishing the call with David Coldstone and wiping an impressive collection of perspiration from his forehead with a hand towel he'd borrowed from the hotel bathroom, he stared at the same piece of yellow scrap paper that had Coldstone's number on it and dialed the other one written underneath. Even though this one was a personal cell phone, he expected serious difficulty getting through. He was wrong.

"Is this Brad Tarnow?" the voice answered, sounding rushed and panicked.

"Yes. Been expecting me?"

"That I have. What can you tell me?"

"Candlewood Suites. 5421 Caddis Bend Drive. Room 155."

"You made the call?"

"Just now."

"Any surprises?"

"Sadly, no," Brad answered, sighing into the phone, still not truly believing he was having the conversation he was having with the person with whom he was having it. "Are you ready?"

"I've been ready for an hour. I've just been waiting for your call."

"Then I'll let you do your thing and get out of Dodge."

"Go. Don't show yourself in public any more than you have to. Keep your cell phone on you. I'll be in touch."

"Good luck." Was all Brad could think to say. Ending the call and wiping another round of sweat, this time from the back of his neck, he stared down at the ground and his untied shoelaces, shaking his head in suspended disbelief.

Is this really happening?

53

Trevor Malowski sat in his second-story home office, eyes glued to the screen, hand gripping a cell phone. His desk was empty, all the work files were put away, no loose papers sat on the floor, only one Google Chrome window remained open on his computer screen.

The only entity that broke his concentration was Lara's boisterous voice from the kitchen, where she helped Nina prepare dinner. It penetrated double-thick walls and a steep flight of stairs. He loved her to death, but that child did exercise her larynx. Always had too, ever since she was a baby. First-time expecting parents will tell you all they want is a healthy child, which is certainly true. What they don't tell you, because they don't know, is that the next item down the wish list is restrained demonstration of those healthy lungs.

He seemed to lose more hair every time he refreshed the screen or checked his cell for a text but still got nothing from either. He quickly guzzled what was left of his third bottled Gerolsteiner mineral water in the past hour. Solitaire didn't work, reading was pointless. He'd been waiting in that room at that desk all day long contemplating the stupidity of his decision. The waiting killed Type-A personalities like him more than the danger did. He wasn't a religious man, but he found God in the purgatory of anticipation. What he didn't find, however, was patience.

But at 2:45 p.m., 7:45 a.m. Chicago time, it finally arrived.

A short text message from an unidentified number. The wait was over. That didn't mean the danger was gone, not by any stretch. But it meant that purgatory would end.

The message read:

EXECUTE TRANSFER AT 4 P.M. SWISS TIME.

54

The Arlington Heights train station was located on Northwest Highway, or US-14, in the heart of downtown, two blocks away from a garage that provided plenty of parking. Its four-story red brick pillars and distinguished white trim with gray roof shingles stuck out in the center of the quaint, progressive community that surrounded it.

Buildings across the street were clean and fresh. No pollution or garbage in sight. Parking on the street was prohibited, resulting in open roads. It had a feeling of newness, a ubiquitous freshness that stemmed from the town's revitalization initiative a few years ago. A few years before, it'd initiated Arlington Alfresco, a program designed to encourage open air outside dining by using space usually reserved for street parking for restaurant dining tables instead. The program was so successful that nearby suburbs soon followed, and several had extended the duration to beyond that of just summer.

The train station itself was nicer than many other stops. Six bike racks sat under a small roof just outside a three-foot, stone-enclosed section of trees, mulch and dirt. The grass was watered daily and bright green as a result. Matching fresh brick floors led to tall archways in the outdoor waiting area. A red-framed, one-person rain shelter no larger than a phone booth stood just outside the entrance.

The inside of the station, surprising to most folks the first time they saw it, was even nicer. It had a large waiting room with two snack vendors, used books on display and lotto tickets for sale. It was heated in the winter and air-conditioned in the summer. Twenty leather-padded light-wood benches offered plenty of seating capacity and comfort. The clean, light-green tile floors were well-kept, and five modern LED lights hung from a vaulted ceiling. The walls were brown paneling on bottom, fresh white drywall on top.

The people inside always seemed friendly and innocuous to Mark, too. Businessmen on their way to work, moms taking their kids into the city, teenagers headed downtown.

Fresh-made pretzels and muffins made the room smell like a bakery, and it was perfectly decorated for the seasons year-round. The large windows and three skylights were always spotless, the upkeep impeccable. He'd been there more times than he could count in the past ten years, and he always enjoyed the wait. There's nothing like a warm pretzel with cheese and an ice-cold Coke to pass the time.

Arlington Heights's family feel permeated its train station, and folks like he and Katherine always showed up a few minutes early when they took the train.

But on this Saturday, the seats felt hard, the vendors were gone, and the safe, inviting feel of the station was replaced with terror and reluctance. At 7:50, he took a seat on his usual bench, far-back row on the north side, opposite the tracks. The next train didn't arrive until 8:32, which meant he'd be alone when "they" arrived.

Whoever "they" might be.

His cell phones, except for the one in his hand, were gone. Ditched in a trashcan, memory chips and SIM cards removed and destroyed. His computer bag rested next to him, containing his end of the deal that would hopefully save Katherine's life. Three million would be nice too, but her safety was all that mattered.

The windows, layered with dew, didn't offer much of a view. The chilly outside air would grow warmer soon, but for now it required his windbreaker. The sun was up but mostly obstructed by clouds. He fidgeted with his phone, trying to distract himself from the fear.

Then he heard a car pull up next to the station.

It could've been anyone...a resident checking the train schedule, someone picking up a free coupon book from the stand, an early drop off for the 8:32...but he knew it wasn't. His instincts, the very things he'd avoided like the plague until two weeks ago but had since relied on more than any actuarial table or spreadsheet, told him it was so.

He hated being right.

"There he is!" an exuberant Tom shouted while walking through the door.

He wore dark pants with a tucked-in, short-sleeved, white-collared shirt, no jacket. He carried nothing, both arms hung free in the air.

"Hello, Tom."

"Hello, hello! You ready, my friend?" Tom clapped his hands enthusiastically.

"Are we going to a pep rally?"

"You *have* become a smartass! I like it! Let's have a look at you."

Tom proceeded to pat him down, his arms spread and legs open. He took his time, starting with Mark's ankles and moving up slowly. When he reached his windbreaker pocket, he found the cell phone stuffed inside.

"Won't be needing this," Tom said casually, dropping it to the ground and stomping it fiercely with his right foot. It shattered instantly, fragments scattering in every direction across the floor.

Mark figured that would happen. The only numbers he'd need were committed to memory. He knew that from the moment they met, everything important would need to be between his ears. When Tom finished patting him down, he unfolded a small, baton-like contraption from his back pocket and held it in front of his chest. No thicker than a small Fungo bat, it was about one-and-a-half feet long. It looked like one of those minor league baseball giveaway bats from the Kane County Cougars. Except that at the bottom of it, there were three unlabeled buttons with pairing LEDs.

"Meet the latest and greatest in surveillance detection. Tracks everything...even things not on the market. Can never be too sure, you know?"

He couldn't prevent the natural reaction that followed: holding his breath and biting his lip. And it was way too late by the time he realized it. Tom surely knew how nervous he was; he just hoped Tom didn't know why.

After again covering every square inch of his body, Tom finally folded the device back up. Mark stood like a statue, his short-lived composure long gone after only a few minutes with Tom.

"Relax, Mark. You're clean! You don't have anything to worry about. Or do you? Hmm...nah, I'm kidding. Relax."

He didn't relax.

"I assume that bag has our information?" Tom asked, pointing to the black computer bag on the bench.

He nodded, then picked it up and offered it to Tom.

"Hold onto it for now. C'mon, let's get out of here."

"What? Where are we going?"

"It's a surprise. Bring the bag," Tom said with a wink.

* * *

They exited the formerly friendly confines of the train station and stepped inside a parked car, the engine still running. It was a black Lincoln, a car Chicago interstate drivers saw heading to and from O'Hare airport all the time. Unassuming and innocuous, no one would think anything of it or the people inside.

It didn't work that way in the movies. There was always *something* to tip good guys off that bad things were happening. *Something* led to a 911 call and the modern-day John Wayne showed up just in the nick of time.

But there, sitting in that unassuming car, on that day, at that time, the DANGER signs were nowhere in sight. The telltale indicators were gone. There would be no police intervention, there would be no John Wayne.

"Like I said...relax, Mark. We'll be there soon. We'll trade some bags and be on our way."

He could only hope. He leaned back in the seat, jittery.

"Why didn't we just trade at the train station?"

"Partly because we want to test the information, partly because we have a surprise for you. The train station wouldn't accommodate either."

They were going to verify the information live?

That could only mean one thing. Edward had said when they first met that they'd need verification, but he never thought of *this*. His stomach churned as he stared at the bag. It was nearly empty, but his realization made the five folders feel heavier than bricks.

They were going to transfer money on the spot, in his presence.

* * *

It was a short drive.

There were no interstates or four-lane highways; the car never went over 40 miles per hour and obeyed all traffic signs. The entire trip took less than 15 minutes. He relished the silence; it couldn't have lasted long enough.

With no blindfold, much to his surprise, Mark watched the driver turn south on Arlington Heights Road. Four stoplights and two miles later, he made a sharp turn onto Algonquin before taking a quick left into the Courtyard Marriot hotel.

He stared, perplexed. He drove by this place every week on his way to the Meijer grocery store. He'd had several offsite business and client meetings here. It was for vacations and occasional meetings, not illegal transfers and money exchanges.

The hotel's large signature red-and-green sign screamed *family hotel*. Fresh blacktop with crisp, white lines layered a parking lot packed with mini-vans and SUVs. Screaming kids and water splashes echoed from the outdoor pool. A small lemonade stand stood in front of the main entrance, operated by children.

This *couldn't be* where their meeting was. Mark was surprised enough he wasn't blindfolded or bonded, but this was too much. No secret location, no dark office. Instead: the Courtyard Marriot, frequented by families.

Children.

"Let's go," Tom said.

As they walked towards the front door side-by-side, the driver exited the parking lot. Mark held the computer bag and his wadded-up windbreaker, still in disbelief. Tom walked freely, the detection device creating a slight bulge in his back pocket.

The sun had crept its way out from behind the clouds; no breeze accompanied it. The humidity had started to show itself, at least in how warm he now suddenly felt. Walking between cars and keeping quiet, he swallowed fiercely to counter his nervousness. Each step towards the entrance felt longer and more uncomfortable.

Tom walked through the automatic sliding front door like he owned the joint, confident and causal. He followed, jittery and awkward. They took an immediate right and walked down the hall, past a continental breakfast buffet, to the last door on the right, labeled CONF. A.

Tom opened the door and motioned him to walk in first.

55

"Hi, Mark."

He stared back, watching Jason without blinking. It didn't matter if he wasn't supposed to know who Jason really was. He couldn't hide the fact that he did.

Actually seeing him face-to-face paralyzed him. Unable to find the words, already something he hadn't planned for had happened.

Jason had replaced his blue jeans from earlier with tan dress pants and a blue dress shirt. His hair now gelled, he cleaned his glasses and stared back. The Nike gym shoes had also been removed, freshly polished brown loafers in their place.

After the moment of shock, Mark studied his surroundings. It was a standard conference room with a projection screen, side table filled with coffee and doughnuts, and no windows. Only half the lights were on, creating dimness.

Jason sat in the last of three chairs on the left side of a six-person conference table. In front of him was a pad of paper and a pen. To his left, a half-filled glass of water. To his right, an overflowing candy dish. Two seats down, a Dell computer rested on the table next to an upright, closed briefcase. He didn't see any bag big enough to hold three million bucks.

"Aren't you going to say hello?" Jason asked.

"Jason..."

"I suppose that's as good as I'm going to get. Have a seat," Jason said, pulling the chair next to him out from beneath the table. It wasn't an offer or a question, and Mark slowly walked towards the seat cautiously. Tom took the final seat on that side of the table, to his right and behind the computer.

"Mark, I know you know who I am, so let's not pretend you don't. Let me start by asking if you have any questions."

There was only one that came to mind.

Of all the things he'd thought and wondered and pondered over the past few weeks, from Sam's disappearance to Ron's murder to Edward's death, only one question made it to the surface. Only one begged for an answer.

"Why, Jason?"

"Why?" Jason repeated, leaning back in his chair, hands folded. "That could mean a lot of things. But if you mean why am I involved with the PEACHES, it's because I care about our children's future. I don't want them to grow up in a world run by animals that aim to destroy us. You may not agree with me; I'm not here to convince you, but take a good, hard look at this country's crime and tell me who commits it. And be honest. We're the victims. A growing group of animals that brings violence to what was once a safe place to live are the aggressors."

"You commit *crime*, Jason."

"I commit crime to prevent crime. My atrocities, if you want to call them that, prevent genocide over time. I'm a utilitarian. I care about the greater good."

"You only care about yourself."

"That doesn't even make sense, Mark. I don't do what I do for money, and obviously I don't do it for fame. I do it because when I look at this city, this *country*, I see the minority filth that kills our children every day. And nobody does a thing about it. People don't have the fortitude or the resolve to stand up for what's right, to do what needs to be done. They'd rather sit on the sidelines and watch it happen. Fine, that's their prerogative. But not me."

"Is that what this is all about, Jason? Blowing up a health center is actually you taking a stand for good? And killing innocent people, including my friend, was for some greater cause? You're out of your mind."

Jason slammed his fist on the table. "Don't you *dare* question my intentions again. Eliminating my employee, Edward, was unfortunate but necessary. Sometimes difficult decisions have to be made. Like I said, I'm a utilitarian. I'd kill myself in a heartbeat if it'd further the cause. But not so with your friend, Sam. That was an easy decision and he got what he deserved."

"You're insane."

"That's your opinion. But at least I'm answering your questions honestly."

"I'll bet you're not so proud to tell Kristina what you've done. I'll bet she doesn't have a clue what you are."

His fear was still there, to be sure. Palpable and undeniable fear. But they were having a frank conversation and for some odd reason, he knew that's what Jason wanted. He wasn't worried about upsetting him or getting shot. Not yet.

That worry would come later.

Jason nodded slightly, not thrown off one iota by his candor. He remained cold as steel, pragmatic. There was no emotion whatsoever in his words or body language.

"It's true, she doesn't know. But not because I'm ashamed. She's just too young to understand it all right now. She hasn't seen the real world. She still lives under the sheltered and ridiculous notion that most people are by nature good people. She's fed lie after lie in school about slavery, equality and civil rights, not to mention evolution."

"You—"

"But when she starts to see the harsh realities of this world, when she sees gang killings and murders on the news, and she reads about them in the papers, when she sees that we live in a country that celebrates BLM and Muslims and illegal spics, the very people who kill, torture and endanger people like herself, she'll respect what I've done and what I'm going to do. So will Katherine."

* * *

His teeth dug into each other. Every muscle in his arms flexed.

"Leave my daughter out of this!"

Unfazed by the noise, Jason looked back, still stoic.

"If you recall, Mark, I'm not the one who brought our daughters into this conversation."

"Just leave Katherine out of it. You want to raise your daughter to think like you, I can't stop you. It's a free country. But let me raise mine the way I want to."

"It bothers me that Kristina talks to those filthy children in that school, that she doesn't see the truth yet," Jason went on, ignoring his demand. "She's just a girl, though. That's what I remind myself. She'll learn what's important when she gets older. She'll realize her mistakes and pay for them by furthering the cause, by keeping up the fight. And so will Katherine, if you know what's best for her."

He shook his head, slowly and deliberately, making it clear there was no chance that was going to happen.

"We're a family, Mark. The PEACHES don't want to cause you any harm. The problem is that doing nothing is hurting both of us. Think about this country's history, from the sixties to tons of stories like the Jena Six to all the gangs to the unfair double standards and quota setting for kids getting into college. If we don't stand up now, we won't have a leg to stand on by the time Kristina and Katherine bring children into this wretched world. I won't be a bystander to our genocide, Mark, even if you will.

"Look at the world's terrorism, from Al Qaeda to ISIS to Boko Haram to the Taliban to the Hamas animals. Do you see a common thread of peace in those groups? Do you really want to just let them try to kill all the good people of the world? Because they won't stop on their own, Mark; their sacred book tells them to kill us all."

Until that exact moment, he thought it was possible Jason was motivated by money, power, or fame. That he had a different version himself, a Mr. Hyde, that coveted popularity and authority, contrary to the honest, blue-collar Dr. Jekyll that didn't care about such things. People want to feel important. And what better way to feel important than to be worshiped as the leader of a group? He thought that maybe Jason just got way, way too carried away...

But now he knew that wasn't the case.

Jason was truly insane, twisted by his own emotions, drinking his own Kool-Aid. He could never be cured of his hate. Rehabilitation would never happen. He would never change.

"I just want to give you the files and get the hell out of here."

"Don't question me, Mark. I warned you."

He looked back at the man who'd just used derogatory names the way most people use verbs and saw no wrong in it. But what he said was somehow an issue, worthy of a tongue-lashing. Jason only saw what fed his creed. The pitcher of Kool-Aid would never run dry.

"I just want to give you the files and leave," he said, amazed he was actually rushing *towards* the moment of judgment.

Jason stroked his chin, staring at him with unblinking eyes and a still-expressionless face. He let the question linger, just for a moment, then nodded and looked at Tom. When he did, a strange and, to Mark a very unexpected, thing happened. Jason's lack of emotion suddenly changed back to wearing them on his sleeve. Yet it was different. The security guard looked tearfully sad, as if let down. It wasn't anger. It was disappointment.

"Let's see the files," Tom said.

He grabbed the computer bag on top of the windbreaker at his feet and quickly withdrew the five folders and offered them to Jason, who deferred to Tom with the point of a finger. After giving the files to Tom and seeing on the Dell the same gray box that he saw two weeks ago, he thought he was going to lose it.

"Okay," Tom said, looking through the pages. "Let's find out if you've done your job."

Tom typed in the information for the first transfer, referring to the InfoHelp file for the SOURCE input and the DESTINATION input from memory. Then he slowly types the AMOUNT: $50,000. Several small transfers as opposed to one large one, just as Edward Doran had said.

But Tom didn't press ENTER. The page sat there, a click away from judgment. Mark tried not to show his anxiety or eagerness, but it was hopeless. He tapped his leg and fidgeted and bit his cheek until it hurt.

Instead of pressing the button and sealing his fate one way or the other, Tom reached into the briefcase that sat innocently on the table. Turning the small combination dials on both ends, he finally snapped it open and withdrew another pile of folders. He licked the tips of his fingers and sifted through the pages until he found the one he was looking for, removed it, and perused its contents.

Mark couldn't see, and the file wasn't labeled, but he knew what Tom was looking at. And knowing that caused him to hold his breath. His lungs would have to wait.

Seconds later, Tom looked at Jason.

"Exact match, General. Employer ID, Tax Identification, routing, Account numbers...they're all good."

Jason said nothing, and he let a little air out from his aching lungs. But that wasn't the ultimate test.

When Tom pressed ENTER, he thought through the plan he'd spent so much time developing. The help Sam had given him, the risks Brad had taken, the faith Caroline had placed in him, the long shot he'd pinned his hopes to, the hope of seeing Katherine again. It all came down to this moment, to this instant in time. One stroke of bad luck, one glitch in the system, one thing that he hadn't planned for, and it was all for naught.

The beach ball icon spun forever, unwilling to free him. But then, when the screen finally changed and the pop-up window proclaimed TRANSFER COMPLETE, he let out the rest of the air in his lungs and instantly felt dizzy.

He'd just helped fund a terrorist group.

56

The Nissan Altima's Illinois license plate, rundown condition and faded white color matched the file precisely.

That was the car. This was the place.

Parked under the red and blue Candlewood Suites sign, the van's engine idled, just in case a quick getaway became necessary. Sheets of thick, steady rain now hindered his view, but through binoculars he saw everything he needed to.

He got the call at 7:40 a.m. and left the winding country road two miles from the house immediately thereafter. His news that the Platteville, WI residence was covered with cops was not well-received, but he'd been told to remain nearby and stay out of sight. It was the first time since working with The General that he'd been sent to a job in which the police were already there, and although he wasn't given details and didn't ask, he knew it had something to do with an unexpected FBI decision. He was told an updated assignment would come soon, so he bided his time.

And now, at 8:50, he was ready to complete that assignment.

The two targets, a male and a female, both middle-aged, were staying in Room 155 and didn't have a weapon, at least according to Tom. Even if they did, he was told, they were inexperienced at using them. No military or weapons training. Neither had a registered firearm or hunter's license. Years ago the man had served a brief prison sentence for involuntary manslaughter, but the crime was reactionary in nature, and the weapon of choice was a convenient beer bottle. It wasn't as if he'd used a sniper rifle to pick someone off from 1,000 yards away in high wind.

He also had the element of surprise in his favor. The targets had run from the female's house in the country but didn't know their location was pinned. They weren't expecting him or anyone else to do them harm. Their guard was down, and they were vulnerable.

Just the way targets should be.

He'd asked Tom over the phone if they were lovers, and Tom replied with a snide question about why it mattered. Now, overall, he didn't care for Tom. Tom was a brown nose who only wanted to rise up by kissing The General's butt. And yet, he *had* in fact impressed The General, which indicated Tom was either exceptionally skilled at the act or actually had something to offer. He had no choice but to assume the latter. He knew Tom didn't like him much either, but he could care less. They had, more or less, agreed to disagree and put their differences behind them out of mutual respect for The General.

But that snide little suck-up could take his disrespectful question and shove it up his ass, which is precisely what he'd told him to do. It matters, he'd explained, because if they're lovers, they'll probably be in the same bed. If they're platonic, they'll be in separate beds if not separate parts of the room altogether. He needed to know all the details, no matter how tiny or irrelevant they seemed to Tom. The devil was in those details, and the more he knew, the more effective the operation would be. He concluded that conversation by telling Tom that if he ever questioned him in that manner again, he'd make him the next target on his list.

That shut the little brown noser up pretty quick.

His trustworthy .357 revolver hidden in his inside jacket pocket, silencer attached, he dropped the paperwork and exited the van, the engine still running. Wearing a pair of dark-blue jeans to go with his zipped-up black jacket and Green Bay Packers ball cap, he jogged through the rain, hands in pockets, feeling the reliable sensation of the gun's steel against his chest.

He kept his head down and walked straight through the lobby to the public restroom. Once inside, he wiped the water from his face and checked the gun one final time. Cocked and locked. Then he moved the weapon from the jacket's inside left pocket to its outside right, holding it as he walked.

He didn't like executing missions during the day, in plain sight. Hotels might have cameras, people are up and more alert, folks have sharper hearing. It wasn't the way he preferred to work. But Tom said The General insisted it be done as soon as possible. And even as arrogant at Tom was, he wouldn't lie about something like that. The mission obviously couldn't wait until tonight. He'd have to work without the customary and trustworthy darkness.

He exited the bathroom and searched for a sign. It took less than a few seconds to find. Thankfully, Room 155 was on the first floor, at the end of the hall opposite the public restroom. He took a deep breath, composed himself, and started walking. No one in the lobby stopped him. People didn't say hello. They were too busy to notice a man who looked like he belonged there.

The hallway had stereotypical dark-blue carpet and white-yellow walls that held up chintzy paintings no one ever looked at. Seven doors down the left, at the hallway's end, adjacent to the emergency exit he planned to use, Room 155 awaited. A small display table and mirror were opposite the room. This was it. He loved this part and lived for it. The butterflies. The excitement.

It made the job worth doing.

He withdrew the "master key" from his left pocket. One of Edward's claims to fame, rest in peace, it was a magnetic key card that looked like a standard room key but was distinct in one very important way: it could open any hotel room, in any hotel, with two swipes. He'd asked Edward to improve it so it would work on the first try, but even Edward Doran had had his technological limits. In all seriousness, one try or not, it was an incredible invention that had yet to fail.

He slid it in the reader as slowly as he could to avoid making any noise. Red light. His right hand gripping the gun through his jacket pocket, he checked the hallway once more, *empty*, and slid it down again.

The cherished green light flashed brightly, and he walked through emphatically and withdrew the .357. Shutting the door behind him, he moved into attack mode, storming past the bathroom, peeking briefly inside, and quickly aiming the gun towards the two beds on the other side of the wall.

They were empty.

He checked the floors beside them, nothing. He looked in the bathroom again but didn't see anyone. Someone had obviously been staying there, papers were scattered all about and lights were on throughout the room. Trash was all over the floor and in the garbage cans. The TV hummed on low volume. He faced the window, his left arm down his side, his right still gripping the gun.

How could this be? He'd missed them. Maybe they left to grab a little food? Could they be hiding in the hotel business center? *No!* Something was wrong. He was told they'd be in their room. Alone, and in their room. The FBI had instructed the targets to remain there. To not leave for *any* reason! What the hell was going on? Where were they?

"Freeze, dirtbag!"

* * *

Four p.m. Time stood still. Trevor couldn't sense anything but the doubt that infiltrated his mind. Lara's earsplitting voice and laughter were gone. Even the smell of freshly baked homemade chocolate chip cookies with Swiss chocolate chips, his all-time favorite, had ceased to register. He couldn't hear Outlook dings that told him he had new e-mail. He couldn't feel the sweat he knew was on his arms and head.

He sat in front of the screen, motionless and petrified, unable to think about anything other than the worst-case scenario. He'd done these transactions a thousand times before, but never like this. Vice presidential authority gave him access, but it didn't offer immunity. This was his own neck on the line. And if things went sour, if laws were broken and people found out, it'd be in a noose by the end of the day. A career's worth of hard work and sacrifice, nullified by one split-second action.

It was his last thought before he pressed ENTER.

Seconds later, the transfer was complete.

He thought he'd feel better, relieved it was done. Elated that the moment had come and gone, and he was still there. He thought that when the anticipation went away, it would take the fear with it. He expected to feel light as a feather.

Instead, he felt as if he had an anvil around his neck.

* * *

The words "freeze, dirtbag!" caught him by more surprise than anything in his entire life.

He knew immediately it didn't come from either of the targets. He didn't hear the door open, but it was obvious there were several people behind him, and he saw enough through his peripheral vision to know it was the police. His heart sank as he quickly contemplated his options.

"Drop the gun, now! Now!" the voice yelled with confidence.

He saw a flash of yellow through the mirror behind the TV. Not much, just a brief hint of the bright primary color. Just enough to know the three simple letters.

F-B-I.

These folks, unlike the targets, *were* trained with weapons, same as he. And they would fire as needed.

And with that, he realized he had no options worth contemplating.

He dropped his trusted .357 and was immediately overtaken by three men with cuffs. *Unbelievable*, he thought over and over. After all these years serving The General, after so many missions, successes, and advancements, he was finished. The feds dug their knees into his back. One of them mentioned Ron Mitchell, his final target. He felt the piercing pain of a gun barrel push into his neck shortly after.

This was all Tom's fault. That prima donna and his pathetic so-called intelligence. He cursed himself for listening to the nitwit. How could he be so stupid?

He was gonna get Tom if it was the last thing he did.

57

"Congratulations, Mark."

The five transfers had been completed. Each one brought more nervousness than the last and the five companies Lafferty & Sons serviced were now anywhere from $50,000 to $70,000 poorer, and that was obviously just the beginning. Now that Jason and Tom had information they knew was accurate, more transfers were coming.

He wasn't quite sure how to reply.

"Mark, you've done a good thing. The money will go to a good cause instead of to some rich executive's second yacht. You should be proud of yourself."

"I just want to get out of here," he said, feeling sicker by the minute.

"And I must say," Jason continued, "I'm impressed you got the files without anyone noticing. Made copies, put them back in the cabinets, got out...all without a single person catching on. That fire alarm bit was good. You're every bit as sharp as we thought you were."

He didn't respond.

"But there's one thing you haven't asked that I thought you would. Best I can figure, it's for one of two reasons. You're either so scared you haven't thought it through, I don't believe that for a second, or you already know the answer."

"I don't know what you're—"

"Why would we ask you to steal these files if I could get the information myself?"

He felt deflated. He knew it would come at some point. He didn't know when, but he knew it'd show its ugly face. And that he wouldn't have an answer.

"I don't care."

"Sure you do, Mark. Why would we put you through this, and add to our own risk, if we didn't have to?"

Those were Ron Mitchell's words, almost verbatim. Mark thought back to the River Walk in San Antonio. To Boudro's Restaurant and to Ron's at-the-time-outlandish theory. He thought about how crazy it seemed then, how unrealistic and misplaced it felt at the time.

"Yes, Mark, that's right. We'd like you to join us in our fight for what's right. We're impressed with you, always have been. We're a small family, Mark. We only have a few members, and we choose very carefully who we ask to join us. We'd like to ask you."

"You're not a family, Jason. You're a horrible group of people that does horrible things. I don't want any part of it."

Jason leaned back in his chair, arms extended behind his neck, right leg crossed over his left knee. Then he smiled.

"You're already part of it, my friend."

"At least I haven't killed anyone."

"What's worse, the shooter or the guy who buys the gun? Thanks to you, we've already got funding for several more operations lined up. Your work will help fund the largest initiative in our family's history. Bombs and small hits are nice, but Operation VIXEN is going to change the world. For the better."

"Operation VIXEN?"

"No need to get into details, let's just say we've got some exciting plans for the future thanks to your support."

He felt every ounce of decency abandon his body at that moment.

"And we're going to get more funding before the day is over. You've stolen from legitimate companies and handed financing over for VIXEN. Your hands are already dirty, Mark, at least from the FBI's perspective. I don't see what choice you have."

* * *

There was one overarching, undeniable problem.

Everything Jason said was true.

Mark could finagle and justify and explain everything he'd done in his own mind, but at the end of the day, the security guard was right. In the law's eyes, he was guilty and would have to pay the price.

But there was no way he was about to give Jason the satisfaction of acknowledging it.

"I don't care, Jason. There's a difference between killing people and being forced to steal."

"Not to the FBI, there isn't."

"I'm not the FBI. There is to me. I was told I'd get three million dollars and our partnership would end."

Jason stared at him, blankly. No words uttered could've been more frightening. That look in Jason's eye, that deep, unflinching, penetrating look, was relentless, incomparable to anything else he'd experienced.

Jason got up from his seat and faced the wall, slowly shaking his head. Mark again saw saddened eyes as Jason poured two cups of coffee from the breakfast tray and brought them to the table, setting one in front of him, holding the other.

"Mark, Mark, Mark. You surprise me, friend."

He just looked back.

"I knew you'd be disappointed when you first found out I was involved, but that happened a while ago. And I knew you'd have your doubts about the PEACHES. It's a gray world, with hard lines. But I thought you'd be open to reason. I thought you'd see the good as well as the bad. I had high hopes. You've got leadership potential written all over you. And you've got so much at stake, your beautiful daughter, just like me. A precious little girl I didn't think you'd want to grow up in a world of such filth. You've got the brains, the looks, the demeanor. You've got it all, my friend."

"I'm just not a killer like you, Jason."

"To whom are you referring, exactly? Let's look at who, or what, we've purged the world of before we point fingers. Pathetic women who bring bastard kids into the world just to raise them on dope and welfare? The same ones that end up joining gangs and killing white teenagers as part of their initiation? Or did you mean the wretched illegal-alien spics that use US taxpayers' hard-earned money to buy alcohol and drugs? Those are the folks at that health center, Mark."

Tom shifted in his seat, smiling. The guy hadn't said a word and wasn't going to. This was Jason's show. Jason was in charge, and Jason would be doing the talking. Tom was merely a spectator.

Mark knew there was no hope convincing Jason the bombings were wrong. The man he'd known for five years was too closed-minded, too lost, and never coming back.

He didn't even try.

"What about the FBI agent you murdered? He was white, and he was making an honest living."

"Oh, you mean Ron Mitchell? The FBI agent who tried to coerce you into giving us up by using deception and blackmail? The FBI agent who sent the police after your best friend for no good reason, and then threatened to do the same to your sister? Yeah, we took him out. I didn't love it, but he gave us little choice. If he'd been a gook I would've done it sooner, but I wanted to give him a chance. All he had to do was back off on you. It would've made you happy, it would've made us happy, and it would've saved lives. And he knew it. He'd been given the warning. But he was on his high horse and just *had* to play superhero. People get hurt when superheroes show up. This isn't Hollywood."

Mark remembered thinking that very thought at the train station. It wasn't any more enjoyable the second time around. In fact, it was worse.

"I don't want this, Jason. I don't want anything to do with it. I just want to be left alone to raise Katherine. You can keep your money. Just let me go home. Please."

Jason leaned back in his seat a final time and looked him straight in the eye. He stared for what felt like hours on end. No blinking, no movements, no gestures. After terrible awkwardness, Jason smacked his lips nonchalantly and rolled his eyes, as though he'd given up. As if he too had accepted something; accepted that there wasn't use in trying.

"Okay, Mark."

At that moment, Tom, the one *not* involved, the one *not* a part of the conversation, stirred in his seat, moving his arms just enough to catch Mark's attention.

When Tom swiveled on the chair towards him, he saw a gun with a long silencer attached to it resting across his stomach in his right hand. He tapped on the trigger with his index finger. His left hand was under his chin, its elbow on the armrest. Leaning back in the chair, he looked relaxed, unfazed, and experienced. The dimple on his right cheek was fully exposed, the result of the large smile that covered his face.

"The General tried to reason with you, Mark," Tom began. "I didn't think it would work, but The General wanted to try, and who am I to argue? He wanted to give you the chance to do the right thing. But you didn't. So now you're my problem."

He stared into the barrel of the black weapon. It was sure to be heavy, but Tom made it look like a feather. He didn't know what kind it was, but it didn't really matter. It was a gun.

"Here's the thing Mark: if you don't join us, there's simply too much at risk to keep you alive."

58

He didn't expect this.

Not right now. Not this way.

Not in the Courtyard Marriot conference room.

It would've been wishful thinking to assume they'd just give him the cash and let him walk away. He reminded himself he wasn't that stupid, noting his "plan" as evidence. But now they were going to kill him right there, right in the middle of a crowded hotel. They weren't afraid of getting caught. They weren't afraid of someone hearing.

They weren't afraid of anything.

He stirred in his seat, still staring at the black gun in Tom's lap, trying to think a way out of it. He couldn't believe it was happening. It came out of nowhere, but he hated himself for not seeing it.

"Mark, listen to me," Jason said calmly, "you need to think long and hard about this. You have to think about how thorough I am, and about how I can't know for sure you didn't tell your sister and Brad Tarnow about us. And that you didn't tell Katherine."

"But I—"

"You have to consider the fact that I'll have no choice but to assume you told them all. And that means that after this, we'll have to turn our attention to them. I don't want to, but the cause...the cause is just too great. Think of your family. I'm giving you a choice here, just like Ron Mitchell had a choice. Think of your loved ones and all that's at stake. Don't make me do this, Mark."

He started heaving when Jason finished and found it hard to control his shaking legs. Hearing Katherine's name broke Mark. His vision became blurred with tears and mental images of her smile. He had only seconds, and he knew it. Tom's finger was already getting itchy. He couldn't think of what to say or how to say it, but he knew he was running out of time.

He took two deep breaths, with Jason waiting for the response he indicated he'd give by holding up his index finger, asking for a moment. His head down, he swallowed and prayed, then looked up to respond. He didn't have a choice. This was life and death.

"Whatever you want, Jason. Just don't hurt them."

Jason smiled and took a deep breath of his own, as if he cared. The man was evil and ruthless. He'd murder his own daughter for the "cause." And he felt no relief for Mark, only relief for having a new member in his wretched family of criminals.

"Excellent, Mark. I'm so glad you made the right decision."

Just as Jason began leaning forward to stand up, he saw the silencer shift away on Tom's lap, and he gave it everything he had.

He grabbed the boiling hot cup of coffee and thrust it towards Tom's face with his left hand, reaching for the computer bag with his right. Tom howled with pain when the steaming hot liquid reached him and instinctively dropped the gun to cover his eyes with both hands. He then swung his computer bag as hard as he could at him, striking him in the face and knocking him out of the chair.

Then he ran.

59

He didn't have time to look at Jason.

If Jason had a gun and withdrew it quickly enough, he'd be dead. He jumped from his chair and bolted through the conference room door without looking back, computer bag in hand. As he sprinted down the hallway, he heard both Tom and Jason scream from within the room. He'd made it to the end of the hall before they regrouped and started their pursuit.

He dropped his bag for more speed, bumping into two people along the way, pivoting off their unstable bodies to keep his own balance. He stumbled to a knee and got up quickly, people pointing and screaming as he dashed through the front-door exit. Tom and Jason were then within sight, close behind him and pushing through bystanders to get even closer. He didn't get a good enough look to see if the gun was in Tom's hand.

He burst into the parking lot and nearly got hit by a Chrysler Pacifica minivan turning in off Algonquin Road. Sprinting due east, through The Red Roof Inn parking lot, a car wash to his right, he then darted across the very busy Arlington Heights Road, dodging car horns and screeching tires. He looked but didn't stop as another car, a sedan this time, nearly ended his life. A quick glance behind told him that Jason had climbed into a parked car, but Tom followed him on foot, rushing into the crowded street just as fast if not faster than he.

Running for dear life through a chocolate factory parking lot, he crossed Tonne Drive and cut northeast through a condominium complex, rushing past a sanctuary and silently praying for survival. There were far less people around now, and he wondered if Tom was going to start shooting.

After darting through another parking lot, he saw a St. Mark's High School sign about 100 feet ahead on the other side of a small alleyway. He ran towards it with all his strength, his lungs begging for air, his legs pushing through pain. Tom was close behind, but what scared Mark even more was when, out of nowhere, a silver Chevy Malibu zipped down the street just in front of the school.

He heard squealing tires, then saw the car speed into reverse, peeling out. When it was in front of him, the driver slammed on the brakes and stared.

Jason.

Flustered, he took his only option, a hard left north, straight towards the high school. Jason got out of the car and followed on foot, gun visibly in hand. Tom was five seconds away. The school parking lot was empty and there were no homes in sight.

No witnesses.

He climbed the fence desperately, his fingers grasping the hard metal for dear life. He hopped over it just as Tom approached the other side, dashing to the right behind a large bush just in time to miss the silenced gunfire that shattered branches. Then he continued sprinting north away from the school's main entrance, hogging air and heaving, using the bush and a large row of trees as best he could to impede their view.

The private high school comprised three buildings with a small quad in between. Two of the buildings were connected, the third stood isolated on the far north end of the campus. He ran towards it up the west side of the property, 300 feet away, pumping his arms for speed. When he got there, he ducked behind the brick wall entrance and stopped to look behind. Tom was dangerously close, maybe 30 feet away.

He didn't see Jason.

After sprinting to the back side of the building, he came to a dead halt. The Malibu pulled up on the street just past the fence enclosing the campus and abruptly halted.

Jason had driven around the block and cut him off for the second time.

Once again, he had only one option. He saw a metal-framed door with a glass interior. It was locked on a Saturday morning in the summer. But bricks lined the landscaped perimeter of the building, and he grabbed one and threw it into the glass.

It shattered instantly, making a hole big enough to climb through, and he bolted inside.

* * *

When Tom reached the door, he saw the broken glass and looked at Jason, who'd already used his gun to remove the lock on the metal gate enclosing the school. The school's alarm had been activated, but that was okay. On average it took eight minutes for the police to even be notified of an alarm breach, before dispatching units. That alone would be enough time. Jason directed him to follow Richter through the same northern door and began to walk around the building to the south side main entrance.

Tom smiled, rubbing his reddened cheeks and surveying the building's perimeter as Jason paced towards the front. There were no east or west access points to the inside. They had him surrounded.

Mark Richter was trapped.

60

That third building on the high school quad was a woodshop, which explained its disjointedness from the other two. Mark rushed inside to unexpectedly find he was in the back of a 10,000 square foot space with sawdust covering the floor and a poignant smell engulfing humid, sticky air.

The room was dark, illuminated by only a few rays of sunshine through two small windows near the ceiling. The lack of light and high windows reminded him of an old factory floor. Straight ahead were matching rows of six two-person tables and narrow aisles, met at the front of the room by a teacher's desk on the south end. Above the desk was a large loft, about 15 feet off the ground with sheets of plywood in storage. Stairs leading up to it were to the right of the desk, opposite the main southern entrance.

He kept moving, rushing towards the desk, sweating profusely in the stuffy workshop heat. When he reached it, he saw there was no phone. An archaic-looking dusty yellow computer sat on the desk, but the power was off and he didn't have time to boot it up. He saw an intercom on the wall by the door, but it was Saturday in the summer, and no one would be in the office to hear a message.

He eyed the door connected to the outside quad, planning to exit the building via the south, when he saw Jason approaching from the outside, gun in hand. Stepping back immediately, he swallowed hard and turned towards the back of the room where he just was. And he knew any second Tom would be walking through the same door he just had. They were pressing in on him from both sides. Panicked, he quickly scanned for a side entrance but couldn't find one. There was no other way out that he could see. He was trapped.

Pressed for time and out of options, he ran towards the loft and sprinted up the stairs, reaching the top just as he heard Tom enter the classroom through the back door and, at what felt like the same exact time, Jason walk through the front. He tried to breathe softly, but found that impossible, still recovering from a near dead sprint to get there. He grabbed an old rag resting on a table to mop his sweat, but it was soaked instantly and the sweat wouldn't stop coming.

"Marrrrky, come out, come out, wherever you are," Tom called from the ground floor. He was lingering near the back, checking the corners near the door and the small storage space in the northeast corner.

His heart relentlessly pounding, Mark ducked down behind one of the many sheets of plywood and peered around it for a quick appraisal of the loft. There were a few rows of disorganized plywood, some resting on large dusty metal carts with wheels, others resting on each other. Up towards the ceiling were large shelves filled with different kinds of wood, but no windows or exits to the roof. In the center was a large table and saw used to cut that plywood down, evidenced by the pungent layers of sawdust covering the floor. Just in front of that was an old cracked wooden railing that separated the 15-foot drop to the main level.

He crawled on all fours, perspiration dotting the floor in front of him. Slowly, he made his way towards the center of the loft, hands covered in sawdust. He heard Jason almost directly underneath him, poking around the teacher's desk. Then, a few moments later, he heard footsteps on the loft steps.

"There's no use in hiding anymore," Jason said monotonically, trudging up the wooden stairs.

Panicked, he searched for anything he could use. He scurried behind the metal carts, as far away from the stairs as possible without being in plain sight. Jason reached the top way too quickly, and he peeked out from behind the wood sheets to see the security guard holding a gun with both hands. As Jason approached the table saw, Mark maneuvered around the wood sheets to stay concealed from him. He tried to think light, quick. No sounds, no rustling.

But it was only a matter of time. Jason kept walking, systematically inspecting every square inch. Jason had a gun. He didn't. Jason could afford to be careful and slow and exposed. He could afford none of those luxuries. When Jason reached the end of the table saw, he moved behind the cart and plywood, Jason now only five feet and a corner's turn away that he was sure to make in seconds. His heart thumped with fear, and his stillness went away. He tried to wipe his sweat so it didn't splash on the floor and make noise, but Jason was so close it was almost pointless.

Just then, Tom found the light switch.

* * *

The incandescent lights hanging from the ceiling turned on instantly, and he realized that Jason was even closer than he thought. When the one bulb above the loft flickered on, it flashed even brighter than the others. And when as it did, Jason instinctively looked up.

This was his only chance at a surprise attack.

He lunged at Jason, catching him off guard, and instantly grabbed his arm as a struggle ensued. The grunting and howling from both men alerted Tom, who was still in the back storage area on the north end of the room, and he began to rush towards the loft.

Their hands locked together, each man fought with all his might, bumping into the plywood, Mark first. His back didn't appreciate the blow, but his concentration was on Jason's right hand and the gun it held. Jason was stronger than he looked and tried to force-aim the weapon towards him. Two shots went into the ceiling in the struggle to gain control of the gun. Jason's face was tight with flexed muscles, his teeth gritted, his eyes pure evil behind his foggy black glasses. Sweat dripped from his forehead as well, and both men grunted with exertion.

They pushed and leaned into each other, gripping one another's arms in an unstable fight for balance, until Mark's final push off the floor led to a burst of momentum that neither one of them expected. They lunged towards the front of the loft, losing balance together, just to the right of the table saw. Jason was in front, and the inertia from the push propelled him forward.

Mark abruptly released his grip and pushed off Jason, sending him and his heavy body tumbling towards the railing. Unable to stop his forward momentum and with nothing to grasp, Jason crashed through the old wood, and fell to the ground floor. Mark heard a loud crack followed by a dense thud. Then, it was quiet. He rushed towards the railing to peek over.

Jason's body was on the ground, blood streaming from his head, the glasses broken on the floor. The corner of the first student desk was broken off. Jason's head was turned almost three-fourths around. He lay motionless, the gun on the ground a few feet away from his snapped neck.

Tom hollered expletives and started firing gunshots.

* * *

In the heat of the battle with Jason, Mark had somehow forgotten about Tom. But the loud screaming that followed, and the sound of a gun being fired rapidly reminded him.

Bullets ricocheted off something behind him as he dove behind more sheets of plywood.

Here we go again.

Tom was now racing up the stairs with vengeance on his mind, shouting vehemently.

"You...you killed him! I'm coming for you, Richter! You hear me? I'm coming for you!"

Tom's curt voice couldn't have been more disparate than its tone of friendliness the first time he met him in the limousine. That Tom was gone: this Tom would do things he didn't want to think about.

As Tom stormed up the stairs, Mark eyed a 2 x 4 on the floor behind the metal carts. Next to it was a small piece of scrap wood that he threw as hard as he could into the lone light above the loft. It shattered the bulb and provided some darkness.

Not nearly enough.

Grabbing the 2 x 4, he checked around the loft as his lungs sucked air greedily. He thought of jumping to the ground level, then considered how that worked out for Jason.

Tom had to have noticed Jason's gun on the floor by his body, which meant Tom knew he didn't have one because they'd patted him down in the hotel. Tom had nothing to fear and was at the top of the loft within seconds. Shots hit the plywood just above his head. Bullets were getting closer each time. Tom walked on the other side of the metal pushcart, looking between aisles of plywood sheets, approaching the point where Jason had fallen through the railing.

As Tom approached him, Mark moved in the opposite direction towards the stairs, gripping the wood stud as if it would defend him against a gun. When Tom stepped to the back side of the cart, he quickly dodged to the front and heard gunfire riddle his previous hiding spot.

Panicked, he grabbed a handful of sawdust from the floor and chucked it haphazardly towards Tom, hoping to toss it into his eyes. It hit with surprising accuracy and he immediately ducked behind the cart when the retaliatory shots followed. Mark then threw his shoulder into the metal transport, pivoting the wheels, and slamming it into Tom.

Bullets whizzed by his head, Tom screaming in pain and firing off more shots. Mark stayed ducked behind the cart and, low to the ground, pushed it like a football player used a tackling dummy. But after a few shots, he heard the click he was waiting for. Tom's gun's chamber was empty.

As Tom began to reload the weapon partially blind from the sawdust, Mark jumped up and swung the 2 x 4 into Tom's right arm hard, breaking it instantly. His gun fell to the floor, and now it was open season. Tom howled in what had to be excruciating pain, trying to recover, but his follow-up swing hit square across the face, knocking Tom backwards into the plywood. Tom rolled off the cart, unconscious, as he tumbled to the floor, landing on his back.

Blood streamed from Tom's face. But just to be sure, Mark gave one more strong kick into his chest. The body didn't move, despite the blow having been strong enough to crack a few ribs.

Then, realizing what he'd done, Mark dropped the 2 x 4 like the murder weapon that it was. His knees buckling, he dropped down onto all fours. He stared at Tom's motionless body once more, then clamped his eyes shut and buried his sweaty, throbbing head in his dusty hands with a loud sob.

A bigger puddle of blood now encircled his head.

He rolled over onto his back, crying, holding the unloaded gun against his chest, forcing himself not to look at the massive puddle of blood that now encircled Jason's body. He thought briefly of finding a way downstairs to retrieve Jason's gun but was paralyzed by the weight of the past week. The fear, the flight, and the fight...all of it was gone now. He remained there hunched over on his knees, face buried as his shoulders rose and fell with his sobs. The horror, the relief, and the fatigue all collided into waves of unbearable emotion that crashed over him again and again.

61

David Coldstone slammed the receiver down emphatically. He'd called five times in the past half-hour and still couldn't get through to Mark Richter. What was this guy's problem? Why wasn't he picking up?

He cursed and then ferociously threw the Scotty Cameron putter against the wall, creating a significant dent. His suit beyond wrinkled, his thick white hair disheveled, he paced the room, staring out the window. He'd had a mountain of bad news today already, and it was only ten o'clock.

The first bit of bad news was expected. One of the uniformed officers called him from Ogilvie Transportation Center a little after nine and confirmed that Richter was nowhere in sight. Units were stationed three blocks in every direction, and there was still no visual of the accountant. He didn't pick up the bug from the ticket office either, confirming that Richter had lied about the meeting point.

He knew Richter would be a no-show. Still, he'd deployed over 25 men to watch every exit and cover every angle of that train station. He didn't go personally, but he heard updates via satellite radio. The uniforms all went there that morning expecting action and getting nothing. Of course he acted surprised, and truthfully he was annoyed that Richter had lied to him, but suspected Richter's scheme long beforehand. His reaction to it now was all part of the plan.

The second piece of bad news, however, was not.

The call came at 9:20, a mere 40 minutes earlier. The FBI analyst sounded young and worried right from the start of the conversation. He knew immediately something was wrong.

"Mr. Coldstone?" the nervous woman asked.

"Yes."

"The bank account you told us to watch..."

"Yes?" he responded impatiently.

"Sir, it's been emptied."

"It's been *what?*"

"There is no longer any money in the account."

"What the hell is that supposed to mean? Where did it go?"

"I don't know, sir."

"You don't *know.* Who am I talking to?"

"Agent Ramirez, sir."

"Well Agent Rah-mirror-ezzz," he said with deliberate, insulting inflection, "why don't you tell me what happened from the start?"

"Well, sir," the flustered, terrified woman went on, "we were watching the account just like you instructed when all of the sudden, it went straight to zero. There's no money in it right now."

"When did it happen?"

"About 15 minutes ago, sir."

"Tell me you know where the money is. *Right now.*"

Silence gave him his answer.

"Let me ask you something. How do you lose five million dollars? I told you to watch that account like a hawk, to make certain you followed that money. You were not to let it out of your sight."

"I know, sir. But the money was transferred in a way we couldn't trace. There are privacy laws that—"

"Privacy laws, Rah-mirror-ezzz? We're the FBI!"

"Sir, it was a Swiss account, and they—"

"I don't want to hear about Swiss accounts. I want that money!"

Agent Ramirez didn't respond. He again cursed into the receiver, louder and with greater force.

"You find that money, Ramirez. Do you understand me? You find that money, or you'll be in a world of hurt. I don't want to hear about Swiss accounts or not having access or privacy laws or any other excuses. I want that money, and I want it now. Don't contact me again until you've found it, or just hand in your letter of resignation! Do you understand me?"

"But sir, there's something else—"

"*Do you understand me?*"

"Yes, sir."

He slammed the phone down for the fourth time that morning. He didn't want to hear about anything else. He wanted the money.

* * *

The bad news kept coming.

A quick call to Washington confirmed Agent Rah-mirror-ezzz's story. The computer geeks were working as hard as they could to explain how, but it appeared someone had figured out a way to transfer the funds from that specific account in an "untraceable" way, as if that word should even exist in their vocabulary. That prompted him to make repeated phone calls that led to nowhere but voicemail, which was the third piece of bad news.

At five past ten, he got the fourth piece, by far the worst.

It started with a knock on the door, despite his stringent request he not be interrupted.

"Go away!" he shouted.

"Sir," began Tim, the security officer from downstairs, "there's an urgent manner that requires your attention."

"I'm very busy."

"I'm sorry sir, it can't wait. I need to speak with you."

Infuriated, he stormed to the door and flung it open with rage.

He simply wasn't prepared for what was on the other side.

"I thought I said *no* interrup—"

His words were stopped short by the visual of four armed FBI agents standing next to Tim. Two of them pointed their guns at him, one held nothing, and the fourth, Terrance, carried a bright-green folder stuffed with papers and a clipboard.

All four reported to him directly, but none looked like they were there to report. His mouth fell open in surprise, and he looked at each man, then finally at Tim, before Terrance broke the awkward silence.

"Mr. Coldstone, we have orders to place you under arrest."

"You work for me, Terrance! Whose *orders* do you have?"

"We have orders from the Director of the FBI."

"What? Montgomery sent you? What are you talking about?"

Terrance ignored all his questions, proceeding instead with the standard textbook arrest, despite his objections. The two agents with guns closed in on him, the third approached from behind and withdrew handcuffs. Seconds later, he felt cold steel pressed against his wrists and failed to register what Terrance was saying, despite having spoken the same words hundreds of times himself.

"David Coldstone, you have the right to remain silent. Anything you do say can and will be used against you in a court of law..."

62

One thing was undeniably certain: 722 John Nolen Drive in Madison, Wisconsin, had never seen so much action.

Locals observed unmarked police cars and knew something was up but didn't know what. Tourists, walking past undercover cops on their outdoor strolls, commented on how many people were in the lobby that particular Saturday. Employees balked with noticeable surprise and concern at the vast number of security guards in and around the Comfort Inn. Parked cars surrounded the building's perimeter, their drivers holding pictures of the two subjects.

Police chief Andrew McDermott led the operation.

The relatively young, dark-haired, still-wet-behind-the-ears chief had been appointed to the position a mere six months earlier. The decision to choose him over at least two other, far more experienced candidates had been the source of much debate within the booming college town.

In McDermott's favor were his impeccable record and local boy status, allowing him to very uniquely communicate and identify with college students, those responsible for a majority of the disturbance calls in the first place. But several citizens had also questioned his qualifications and age; his own team at times seemed unsure of their stance. And although he had the commissioner's support, to survive in the long run he knew he needed their backing. He worked hard to earn the job every single day, but winning them over was much more difficult than he'd originally thought, and for the first time in his career he'd begun to doubt himself.

That made the task-at-hand even more important.

It was the first time in Madison's rich and storied police history that a direct order from such a high authority had been given. And he wanted to make sure nothing went wrong on his watch. He'd been told the two subjects would be unarmed and wouldn't resist arrest, but he'd pulled out every stop nonetheless.

Three-quarters of the Madison Police Department were at the hotel by 12:30, despite the fact that, at least in theory, only one was needed. Every officer was carrying the subjects' photos, even though it was explained to him that neither one would have any intention of escape. They'd be sitting in their room, alone and cooperative.

He preferred to plan for the worst and hope for the best.

He walked through the lobby confidently, wearing a brand new pair of dress pants, a short-sleeved, white-collared shirt, and a pair of black Kaenon sunglasses with yellow plastic rims. He approached the front desk slowly, reminding himself of the operation's importance. He cleared his throat and revealed his credentials first.

The surprised, college-aged blonde hotel desk clerk fidgeted as she checked her computer, acknowledging the same room number he'd been given over the phone. He asked for a key and politely nodded in thanks before pacing through the lobby towards Room 132 with anticipation and control.

The clerk watched him as he walked, whispering to her coworker in excitement. When he arrived, he didn't break down the door like they did in the movies, storming in with his gun, demanding they get facedown on the ground. Rather, he knocked gently before quietly sliding the magnetic card in the slot and walking in slowly when the light turned green.

* * *

Both subjects were on the bed, her head on his stomach, her arm wrapped around his waist. The room was quiet and dark, and they were watching TV without sound. Curled in the fetal position, Caroline Hubert jumped up and cowered behind Brad Tarnow's shoulder when she saw him, stunned and afraid. Her hair was matted, indicating she'd been lying there for some time. Her eyes had dark purple rings beneath them, belying an obvious lack of sleep. She looked disoriented, as though his entrance had awakened her. At first she was quiet, still registering his presence, orienting herself.

Then she screamed.

"Relax," he urged her, flipping on the light and showing her his badge.

She didn't relax.

She only yelled louder and more hysterically. He sighed, knowing he'd have to wait this one out. The volume was impressive. Her screams for help were surely causing his eardrums irreparable harm.

What was interesting, though, was that Tarnow didn't stir one iota. He didn't say anything at first, putting his arm around her and pulling her towards him, trying to comfort her. His jaw didn't drop and he didn't appear flustered. He was calm and in control.

This visit was no surprise to him.

"Caroline. Shh. Caroline, please calm down," he then said quietly, no excitement or fear whatsoever in his voice. "It's okay. He's one of the good guys."

Tarnow put his finger to her lip and nodded slowly, reassuring her. She stopped screaming but still looked full of fear. Her body shook and lips trembled. It didn't seem that either would change anytime soon. McDermott stood back by the dresser, five feet from the bed, watching silently.

"What's going on?" she finally asked Tarnow. Her eyes fixated on Tarnow's face, her hands tightly clutching his.

"It's okay. Mark asked them to come. It's okay. We're safe."

"Mark sent you?" she turned towards him.

Now it was his turn.

"I don't know anything about anyone named Mark, ma'am. I'm Chief McDermott with the Madison Police Department. I was asked by Milton Montgomery, the National Director of the FBI, to escort the two of you to our police headquarters this afternoon for your own protection. You're not under arrest, and I assure you I'm not here to cause you harm in any way."

He wasn't rude, but he made it clear this was not an optional escort. Caroline Hubert turned her head, alternating stares between the chief and Brad Tarnow. Then, against his will at that particular time, he added the information he'd been instructed to provide.

Knowing exactly what it would do...

"Ms. Hubert, I've also been instructed to inform you that both your son and niece are safe. The Mount Sterling Police Department picked them and Mrs. Howard up earlier today."

"*You have my son?*"

Her facial expression changed in microseconds, from concerned and afraid to angry and fearless as her protective instincts kicked in. That, he told himself, was just the beginning.

"No ma'am. As I said, the Mount Sterling Police Department has the children, for their own protection from what I understand. I don't know why, and I don't know what the children were doing in Mount Sterling to begin with. But I spoke with the police chief over there and do know they're safe, and that I've been instructed to bring you and Mr. Tarnow to our headquarters downtown. So, if you would be so kind, please get off the bed and come with me."

"*I want to see my son!*"

"Ma'am, I don't have him. You'll see them both as soon as the director gives clearance."

"I don't need any *clearance* to see my family!" she cried, springing from the bed and confronting him directly.

"Caroline, it's okay," Tarnow said gently. "He's just doing his job. Mark arranged this."

"*What?*" She paused, clearly surprised and angry. "You knew about this?" she demanded, turning away from him much to his relief.

Oh, boy, he sheriff thought to himself.

Tarnow didn't answer, and they all knew that meant yes. It also meant Tarnow was in deep, deep trouble, but he refrained from comment.

She suddenly turned her attention back to him.

"Is Mark okay?" she hoarsely whispered at him.

"Ma'am, I really don't know anything about any Mark. I'm just doing what the Director of the FBI told me to do. All your questions will be answered soon. But for now, you really do need to come with me."

She shrugged her shoulders and straightened her T-shirt, pulling it down at the bottom, revealing a lovely figure. He quickly looked away.

"Do I need my computer?" she asked, as if her computer was of significant interest to the FBI. That made him even more curious as to what was going on here.

"No ma'am, our team will take care of all your belongings. They'll bring them to the station after we leave."

"I'll just bring my computer myself."

"Whatever you'd like." Having no desire to reawaken her rage, he wasn't going to argue with her about something so insignificant.

The biggest escort in Madison's recent history went down without a glitch. Both the undercover and uniformed officers watched their chief silently strut down the hall a few feet behind the two subjects. He required no backup, needed no assistance, and called for no help. He'd done it all himself, adding another star to his credentials.

Mission accomplished.

There were no handcuffs, no guns, no big scenes. A casual stroll all the way to the car, parked in the hotel drop-off area. Both of the subjects squinted when the sun hit their faces, indicating they'd been indoors for some time. She still didn't look happy, but she wasn't as upset any more, either. Whatever Tarnow had whispered to her on the walk must've helped.

He noticed in the rear view mirror that as soon as they buckled up, they interlocked hands again.

63

Summer had arrived.

At only three o'clock the sweltering mid-June temperatures would only climb over the next two hours, but people were already using newspapers as fans, an ice cream shop line extended down the block, a bank thermometer read 97, and words like "sweltering," "melting," and "brutal" floated along on the nonexistent breeze.

Riding in the well air-conditioned FBI car hadn't prepared Milton Montgomery. He parked in the visitors' lot across from the two-story Arlington Heights Police Department and opened his door to a wall of humidity. Tendrils of dampness hung down like clothes on a line and seemed to stick to his cheeks and hips as he walked forward towards the station.

Sandwiched between the older, dark red brick village hall to the west and the block fire station to the east, the newly renovated white stone building looked like it belonged in a magazine. Five small, ornamental trees and several intentionally placed bushes only added to its modern feel. He walked across Sigwalt Avenue and through the freshly painted green door entrance into an "ahh" of air-conditioned goodness.

Once inside, he looked around. He'd been briefed beforehand on how little crime actually occurred in this town. Last year there were no murders and the crime index was .01148, less then half of the nation's average. Most of the police activity revolved around petty theft, speeding tickets and out-of-date car registrations. There were only seven reported robberies per 100,000 people in a town with fewer than 80,000 residents.

This wasn't exactly the south side of Chicago.

The station's modern inside mirrored its outside. The previous floor and overhead lighting had been replaced with glossy white tile and elegant chandeliers. This place looked like a banquet hall, not a police station.

The guard sitting behind a large, non-bulletproof oak desk wore a nametag that said Karl. An elevator bank to both the left and right, there was no visibility beyond two closed doors and fresh brick walls. Karl lowered his pencil and looked up, his horseshoe-shaped balding black hair and thick mustache matching his glasses.

"Hello. I'm—" Montgomery began.

"Yes, sir, I know who you are," Karl said. "We've been expecting you, sir. Let me get the captain." Karl then sprang out of his seat and scrambled through the door behind the desk.

Karl didn't give him the chance to say he didn't need to talk to the captain, and that he certainly didn't need any exaggerated excitement. He just wanted to see the prisoner, the only prisoner, in the police station. He sighed and remained silent, turning towards the wall that displayed pictures of Little League baseball teams and gymnastics groups that the department had sponsored for the summer.

Karl's reaction was typical. It came with the job and always would, he reminded himself. Formalities were inevitable. Whenever he needed to get something done, he had to fight things just like it, which was why in most cases he didn't come personally.

But he needed to be there. And he didn't want a driver or anyone else to come with him. This was for him and him alone.

"Mr. Montgomery, it's an honor," a confident, loud voice echoed from behind him. He turned and shook the hand of a man who stood 6′2″ and didn't appear to have a single ounce of fat.

His skin was tan, his muscles small. He wore the standard blue uniform and his thin, straight hair was perfectly combed to the side. It was clear this guy hadn't seen the inside of a Dunkin Donuts in a long, long time.

"I'm Captain Koziol. But you can call me Pete."

"Nice to meet you, Pete. We spoke on the phone."

"We surely did," Pete responded crisply.

"You picked him up at ten-thirty?"

"Yes sir, on the nose."

"And you haven't talked to him yet?"

"No sir. Per your instructions, no one has spoken to him."

"Excellent. You've done a nice job here, Pete."

"Thank you, sir," Pete answered, understandably beaming with pride. It's not every day that a suburban police captain gets a direct compliment from the Director of the FBI. Between Pete and the Madison Police Department captain, he was making all sorts of happy campers today.

"I'd like to see him now."

"Yes sir. Follow me," Pete replied, waving his arm.

They walked to the left of the desk, Karl still staring with an open jaw, neglecting the all-important paperwork. The elevator felt like it took forever. After they got in, a very awkward minute passed and they exited to the end of a short hallway before stopping at the last door on the right, labeled simply as "A."

"Want me to go in with you?" Pete asked.

"I appreciate the offer, but I'm sure you've got things you need to take care of."

"It's no bother, Mr. Montgomery. No bother at all."

Pete might've defied physical stereotypes, but he didn't make a case against them mentally. He tried once to let him down softly. He didn't have time to try again.

"I'd rather speak with him alone. I appreciate your help."

Pete nodded firmly, trying to save face, then walked away. Milton took a deep breath and forgot all about Pete before exhaling.

On the other side of the door was the man he wanted.

***

Mark Richter was cleaned up but still looked like hell.

The accountant leaned back in a green plastic chair, resting his leg on the seat in front of him. His hands were locked behind his head, supporting his neck. It wasn't a cocky position, it was an exhausted one.

The sawdust and blood had been washed off, but numerous cuts and bruises remained. The nurse had bandaged Richter up nicely and given him a pair of loose-fitting black athletic pants and a blue T-shirt sporting the Arlington Heights Police Department.

The guy looked like he could fall asleep on command.

Richter turned his head when he walked inside, then quickly snapped it back.

He couldn't help but smile at the irony. The one guy he wanted to talk to, and to respect him, didn't want to talk to him or laud his entrance.

He pulled one of the two remaining chairs from the four-person table, opposite Richter, and collapsed into it with a sigh.

"I'm getting too old for this." He rested his arms on the table next to his thick, black glasses. Richter kept a poker face.

The camera had been unplugged. There were no two-way mirrors, or any other mirrors for that matter. The only recording device in the room was an old-fashioned tape recorder sitting in the middle of the table, turned OFF. He stared at Richter, smiled again, and began.

"I was wondering if I could talk to you off the record a little bit."

Richter looked up, exposing large, dilated eyes. His face looked even more tired and worn than the rest of him.

"Mr. Montgomery, I'm sitting here, and you're sitting there. I don't think I have much choice."

He liked Richter immediately.

"May I call you Mark?"

"Sure."

"You can call me Milton. You've had quite a day, Mark. Are you okay?" he asked, pointing towards the large, stitched gash on the right side of Richter's forehead.

"I'll live."

"I've been to the St. Mark's woodshop. You're lucky to be alive."

"You don't need to tell me that."

He nodded in silent agreement. Richter did know he was lucky. He was too smart not to.

"First things first: we have your sister and Brad Tarnow, as well as your daughter and nephew. Everyone's safe in police custody."

"Thank you," Mark whispered, clearly relieved.

He loosened his red tie at the neck, instantly feeling relief. He wished he was the one in the T-shirt.

"It's been quite a day for the FBI too, Mark. Earlier this morning we arrested a man named Dan Kevil at the Candlewood Suites in Madison. Everything that you said would happen has happened. We caught him red-handed, and he submitted without a fight."

"Who hired him?"

"We don't know much about him yet, other than he served in the Army in Afghanistan. And that he's got a resume for destruction. He did the kinds of things the military doesn't necessarily want printed in the papers."

"I thought that might be the case."

"He had a .357 caliber revolver in his possession and already admitted that he came to the hotel searching for two people who fit the descriptions of your sister and Brad Tarnow."

"How did he know Jason?"

"We don't know that and probably never will. But whatever that connection is, it's strong. He'd follow Albers to the edge of the earth and won't break that loyalty, even when he finds out Albers is dead."

"Okay."

"But that loyalty is to Albers and Albers alone. He's already given us more than enough evidence to put Bilbrey away for the rest of his life and then some. He blames him for him getting caught in the first place, says it was poor planning. That's why he just came out and told us why he was at the hotel. He knows he's finished, but he wants to take Bilbrey down with him."

Almost as soon as he started talking, Richter's face turned to an obvious blank stare and remained that way throughout his answer. Rather than ask, he waited for the accountant to explain why.

"Who's Bilbrey?" Richer finally asked.

"The guy you kicked the crap out of in the woodshop."

Richter looked surprised.

"Something wrong?"

"No. I just thought his name was Tom."

"Tom?"

"Tom."

He shook his head. "We've got confirmation his name is Douglas M. Bilbrey, former member of the KKK. I guess he decided it wasn't violent enough and wanted in on some real action. We still don't know how he hooked up with Albers, but we'll find out."

"Strange that Edward didn't use a fake name. I was under the impression he was higher up than Tom...I mean Bilbrey."

"Edward Doran was higher up. Bilbrey was Albers's protégé, being groomed to take over when Albers left. Like a CEO in training. Doran was technically dotted lined to Albers, but he certainly had more authority than Bilbrey. And from the intelligence reports I've read, it makes perfect sense that Doran didn't use a pseudonym. He thought he could get away with anything, that he could outsmart anyone. And I'll tell you, I can see why. He got away with a lot and outsmarted some really bright people."

"It helps when you've got the Regional Director of the FBI in your pocket."

64

"It was probably Edward's cockiness that got him killed. Albers didn't like it much from what Kevil said."

Richter just nodded. He clearly didn't care.

"Mark, I've got to ask, how'd you figure this out? Coldstone kept his partnership with Albers under the radar for years without anyone finding out. And that's including Ron Mitchell, who might have had a temper issue but was pretty smart and certainly not a traitor."

"I didn't know that for sure. But after Ron Mitchell was murdered, I figured the FBI had a rat. He was getting too close, closer than he'd ever gotten before. He found out about Jason being the leader. And he knew which companies they wanted me to steal from. He knew they killed Doran and had a theory as to why. He was building too much of a case, getting too close. My guess is he got much further than Coldstone expected him to get."

"So you assumed that someone in the FBI was keeping the PEACHES posted all along. And that's what stopped Mitchell from cracking the case all these years?"

"It seemed to fit. It was a little too convenient that the PEACHES killed him right after he figured out Jason was involved. Plus, my friend Sam told me, before they killed him, to be on the lookout for a traitor."

"Why'd you suspect Coldstone? Just because he was Mitchell's boss? Or was it because he was the first person to get updates on the investigation?"

"I didn't even know who David Coldstone was. But the day after Mitchell died, he just handed over the five million and didn't really address the PEACHES. It seemed a little odd. Like he was playing the sympathy card but was far more concerned with keeping a lid on things than with catching Albers. It didn't add up. And I realized that Coldstone's involvement would shed some light on a few things."

"Such as?"

"Are we playing twenty questions here? This isn't my problem anymore. You figure it out."

"Mark, please don't be difficult. Just answer my questions, then I promise we'll get to you."

Montgomery again silently reflected on the heavy implausibility of this situation. Impressive as Richter was, it felt simply outrageous to him that a civilian, with limited resources and no surveillance training, on the run from both his own federal government and a secret terrorist organization, with a young daughter that could be held as leverage against him by either side, would be telling him, the FBI's National Director, how he'd ascertained that such massive treachery had occurred within the Bureau and actually be correct about it. And yet as crazy as it felt to think or say it out loud, that's exactly what was happening.

Richter sighed deeply, but then continued.

"I knew there was a rat, and I was pretty sure it was someone high up, but I didn't have any idea who it was until after Mitchell died."

"Go on, please."

"Mitchell told me he was very close to busting the PEACHES a number of times, but they always just barely got away. 'Always by a nose' was how he put it. It actually justified to me why he was always so pissed off in life. To be *that* close to getting your archenemy every time after so much effort, only to find they were just one step ahead of you, every time, no matter what you did. It would upset anyone, even an FBI Agent."

"But?"

"But nobody's that lucky. Sam said the same thing...he told me he had information on Edward right before they killed him. They had to have someone on the inside watching. How else would they know so soon that Sam was onto him and react so quickly?"

"And after Mitchell died..."

"I spoke with Coldstone. And that's when I developed a theory..."

"And you figured you'd test that theory with Brad Tarnow's call from the hotel in Madison," he finished.

Richter nodded. "I knew if I was right, if Coldstone was dirty, he wouldn't send the cops to get Brad and Caroline. He'd tell Jason. And then Jason would send someone to kill them. If I was wrong and he was clean after all, there'd just be a bunch of cops in an empty hotel room. No big deal."

"And you had video footage to tell you one way or the other," he added.

"It was the only way to know for sure."

"How'd you know Coldstone would trace Tarnow's call?"

"He's FBI."

"That was pretty slick, Mark. You even had Tarnow call from a payphone so Coldstone would think he was trying to be sly, just not sly enough. Well done."

"Thanks...I guess."

* * *

The logic was simple yet profound; it made perfect sense, but only after revealed. Milton stroked his chin and studied the worn-out civilian some more. Dark stubble popped up in patches across his face contrasting with the white bandage covering his upper forehead. His arms rested on the arms of the chair, scratched and bruised. His red, bloodshot eyes still looked like they could close any second.

"What's going to happen to Coldstone?" Richter asked.

"He's in police custody right now. And he'll be in a maximum security prison in a few days."

"No trial?"

"We have a special courts system for traitors. It's expedited compared to the normal legal process. With the tapes you provided and the testimony I've gotten from Kevil and will get from Bilbrey, it won't take long."

"Give Coldstone my best regards."

"That I will," he replied with a chuckle. "He actually asked to speak with you when we arrested him."

"I don't think so."

"It's a funny thing, Mark. Right around 8:30 this morning, a strange thing happened to five government bank accounts. Never happened before. Out of nowhere, money started being withdrawn electronically. The first transaction was $50,000 and the other four were a little bit more. Ironically enough, each of those five accounts had recently transferred $500,000 to your personal Swiss account."

"That is strange..."

"Yeah, quite a coincidence if you ask me. I also thought it was a bit odd that you requested five million dollars to be deposited from ten different FBI accounts. I'm sure Coldstone thought so too, but he was probably too focused on Mitchell's headway on the PEACHES to be curious enough about that. So was I, to be honest."

"Plus, you figured you'd get the money back anyway."

He couldn't conceal the chuckle. Richter remained straight-faced.

"That's right, Mark. I did assume we'd get the money back. Regardless, because we don't like giving people five million dollars, we kept a pretty close eye on those ten accounts after we made the transfers. In fact, I think we even mentioned to you on more than one occasion that we'd be watching them closely. So when money started disappearing from five of them this morning, we were able to trace the source and identify where all that money went."

"Oh, that's convenient..."

"Yeah, pretty good deal," he paused for a moment. "And since we now know that it was the PEACHES transferring the money, I suppose we owe you a debt of gratitude for indirectly leading us to their launderers. You wouldn't believe some of the places that house their dirty money."

But the truth was, he was quite certain that Richter *could* believe it. Charities, respectable businesses, non-profit organizations...the very last places you'd expect to launder terrorist money were doing just that. And something told him that Richter knew exactly what kinds of places these were, but didn't care to hear specific names.

"Congratulations on cracking the case," was all Richter said.

"Mark, another thing I have to know: how'd you get our account numbers after we transferred the five million to you?"

He hesitated for a moment, obviously considering whether to tell him or not.

"Off the record?"

"That's what I said."

"A friend of mine in Switzerland pulled some strings."

"I didn't think even a man like Trevor Malowski had those kinds of connections."

Richter smiled for the first time and tipped an imaginary cap.

"He's pretty high up the food chain. I think he cashed in on a favor or two to get the numbers. But listen...he didn't want to do any of this. I made him—"

"Don't worry, Mark. We're not going to pursue him. But do be sure to tell him that for his own benefit, he's never to even come within a stone's throw of those, or any other, FBI accounts again."

"He won't. He didn't want to this time..."

"But he knew how bad you needed it. For your daughter."

"Yeah."

"I understand."

"Thanks for not going after him."

"Let's get back to this five-million-dollar transfer. Once Malowski moved the money from the account we transferred it to, what were you planning to do? What was on your mind?"

"Costa Rica."

Another chuckle that couldn't be concealed.

"We've already been to the office building you rented down the street from Lafferty & Sons. That's where we found the tapes and folder on the desk, under a desk light. We see how you changed the account numbers. I understand why you got your sister involved. You needed her to replace the actual account numbers with the FBI account numbers you got from Malowski. Your plan with the fire alarm and copying the files, it all adds up, except for one final detail."

"What's that?"

"How'd you know there'd be enough money in the FBI accounts to make the transfers? Even if Malowski could get our account numbers, there's no chance he could see the amounts. And we both know that if the PEACHES did the transfer and something went wrong, you'd be a sitting duck."

Straight as an arrow, Richter looked into his eyes.

"I didn't know. I hoped that the FBI would put enough money in the account for a large transfer to go through, so that if I tried to steal more, you could trace the transaction. But really, I just got lucky."

He nodded his head silently. It was the final confirmation that Richter's story was true.

* * *

"Now I have a question for you," Richter said.

"By all means, Mark."

"Where do we go from here?"

He smacked his lips and leaned back in his own chair, mirroring Richter from across the table.

"Well, let's see. You've got eight million dollars you didn't have a few weeks ago. Five from us and three from a terrorist organization."

"I don't want a penny of their money."

"Regardless, we've started tracing previous transactions from the PEACHES' laundering accounts, and we should have all the money back to its rightful owners very soon, the FBI's included. Everyone in custody will go to jail for the rest of their lives. People will—"

"I meant what happens to me."

"Best I can tell, you're safe from the PEACHES. Edward Doran, Douglas Bilbrey and Jason Albers were the only ones who knew about you, according to Dan Kevil. And not even he knew your name. He just referred to you as 'the reckoner.'"

"What about other members?"

"Albers kept a pretty tight lid on member information, and the few remaining members we'll start getting one-by-one. I don't see any indication that anyone else knew about you. But I won't lie to you either, that's strictly an educated guess at this point. I can't tell you what you really want to hear."

Richter shut his eyes, contemplating the brutal truth.

"Like I said, it's our understanding that this was an extremely small group," he continued, "so it won't take long. If you start at the top, the rest of the pyramid crumbles pretty quickly."

Richter ignored the suggestion and didn't ask *the* question, the one that had to be on his mind. Instead, he waited.

Bravo, Mark.

"As for the money, you're right about the three million from the PEACHES. That's evidence you can't keep. You already spent the majority of the 30 grand they gave you upfront, between yourself, Brad Donavan and your sister, so we'll call that a wash. And as for the five million from the bureau, I have a proposition for you."

"I'm all ears."

"You know that with enough manpower and leverage, and I have plenty of both, I can find out where that money is and have both you and Mr. Malowski thrown in jail for the rest of your lives."

"Yes I do."

"But, that's a lot of work. And frankly, I'd rather spend my time putting away the PEACHES. Selfishly, I don't want you to arrange for someone to blog or post on social media to the world about how the FBI was connected to a terrorist organization, either. I'm sure you have copies of all the tapes and footage you gave me, so we both know we can do some damage to each other. And we both don't want that to happen."

Richter didn't say anything.

"So, I'd be willing to let that five million dollars go in exchange for all the tapes and any other evidence you have pertaining to the PEACHES and the FBI's involvement. That gets you off my radar unless I need you back on it. You disappear from this city and this situation, and no matter what the papers say or whether it's true or not, you stay away. You hand over all the evidence you've got and promise to keep your mouth shut for the rest of your natural life, the money's yours and the rest is history."

"How do I know you'll keep your end of the deal?"

"As a gesture of faith, I've made another deposit into the original Swiss bank account. You'll be able to live comfortably for the rest of your life. Consider it a token of my and the FBI's appreciation. But ultimately, like I told you when we first spoke on the phone, you have to choose to trust me or not. This is unfortunately another one of those situations where I can't give you the answer that you really want to hear."

Richter blew out a long breath.

"But if you choose to trust me, Mark, everything you know about these past two weeks is strictly confidential, or the deal's off."

"Mr. Milton Montgomery, are you, the honorable Director of the FBI, bribing me?"

"I think it's pretty obvious what I'm doing."

Richter got up from his seat and slowly walked around the table towards him, his right leg limping. When he got there, he extended a bandaged right hand.

"You'll never hear from or about me again. But I do have one more favor to ask."

Epilogue

The six-person booth sat the five of them rather comfortably.

They had to wait 15 minutes to sit together, since Sunday morning at eleven was a busy time for Butterfields Pancake House. It was busting with families and churchgoers, but it was well worth the wait. It was Katherine's favorite place with her favorite waitress, Erica. Years back, she and Mark went there every Saturday morning, but that felt like eons ago now.

Caroline sat between Brad and Will, gently gripping Brad's hand and rubbing Will's back. He and Katherine sat on the other, laughing at Will as he gulped down one small creamer after another from the small dish on the table.

With each new shot of Coffee mate Creamer, Katherine and Will laughed louder. Childhood innocence. It was perfect. Caroline didn't tell Will to stop. It wouldn't kill him, and the laughter it brought to the table was worth more than a health lesson. Luggage rested against the wall in front of them, a constant reminder of the excitement they all felt.

"Dad, do you think we'll see real palm trees, like in the pictures?" Katherine asked, pure jubilation in her face, smiling from ear-to-ear.

How he loved her smile.

"You bet, kiddo. Hawaii's nothing *but* palm trees and beaches."

"Woo hoo!" Will yelled. "I want to go in the ocean!"

"How long is the flight?" Katherine asked.

"A *really* long time," Brad answered from across the table, "but you get to ride in a fancy airplane! Cozy seats and a TV! *Finding Nemo* is first!"

"Neat-o!" Will yelled again, between shots seven and eight of Coffee mate. "*Star Wars* second!" he proudly proclaimed.

Caroline laughed and squeezed Brad's hand beneath the table. Their feelings were obvious to even Mark now, though he hadn't thought about it before. He was thrilled. They were a great match.

Erica approached the table with a smile and tray full of food, each plate steaming hot. They'd be cutting it close, he worried, until he remembered they were flying on Milton Montgomery's personal jet and didn't have to worry about departure time. Eleven o'clock was just a suggestion; the plane would leave when they got there.

When the food arrived, table conversation came to a screeching halt. The kids dove into their golden brown pancakes smothered in warm maple syrup; Brad and Mark enjoyed their ham-and-cheese omelets, his with cheddar and Jack. Caroline made quick work of the Sunday Morning Special: homemade waffles with strawberries and a dusting of powdered sugar. After ten minutes of delicious silence, all the plates were empty and he was paying the bill for the promised stop before their long flight to Maui.

The accommodations had been made well in advance, courtesy of Milton Montgomery and the FBI. They were staying at the five-star Four Seasons Resort until they felt like leaving, flying in style on Montgomery's jet, and didn't have a concern in the world. He didn't much care for the FBI knowing exactly where they were, but he also knew they could find him no matter where they went or how they got there.

He was excited to leave Erica a huge tip. She was a hard-working young mother with a good attitude who more than deserved it. And, he could afford it. Montgomery had informed him that Jason's daughter, Kristina, had been sent to live with her mother's cousin, and through the FBI director he'd created and seeded an anonymous trust in her name. But even with that, and after the hefty fee to Trevor for his assistance, the additional transfer Montgomery alluded to in their conversation was more money than he even knew what to do with, especially combined with the original five million.

Just then, as he started to stand up, it hit him again: he was lucky to be alive. He had a good plan that seemed realistic enough. But even he knew there was always something left to chance in life. The smartest people in the world still had to depend on luck, no matter how foolproof their plan was or how experienced or talented or clever they were.

He then silently promised God that he'd never forget how lucky he had been, nor fail to make the most of it for the rest of his life.

"You kids ready to go?" he asked after dropping a Benjamin on the table.

"Yes!" they shouted in earsplitting unison. Will rushed towards the door, leaving Brad to get the suitcases. Caroline followed her little boy, still smiling. As they approached the exit, Katherine pulled him aside and whispered into his ear.

"Dad, don't tell Erica, but I like your pancakes better."

He smiled wide, his heart fuller than his stomach, and whispered back:

"I'm glad, sweetheart."

Milton Keynes UK
Ingram Content Group UK Ltd.
UKHW040616131024
449535UK00013B/194